Pixel

First Printing: December 2018

ISBN- 978-1-9993599-0-4

Publisher and designer: Lexa Chara Meadows

Editor: Char Wells

Pixel

Lexa Chara Meadows

I couldn't have possibly written this book without the influence of my best friend. Even though you're not with us any more, you still have such a positive effect of my life. Thanks for always believing in me and showing me how to see the good in everything; even myself. I hope I've made you proud by writing a book, which is something I'd always dreamed of doing. I only wish you were here so I could share it with you.

Thanks for encouraging me to be the best me I can.

I miss you, always.

Chapter 1

It's strange, every sentiment that I'd ever heard from society told me that finding love would change my life. It had been at least a few weeks since she had basically moved herself into my apartment, and life was the same it had always been; working alone at night.

It took a loud noise from the next room to remind me, I wasn't actually alone; it was hard during the uncharacteristic silences to remember that Allie was home. I suppose it was more correct to say that not much had changed; with the biggest change being that I now had to share my personal space with another person.

Allie did have a tendency to come and go as she pleased, at times it felt more like owning a cat than living with a partner. She always wanted to go out at the weirdest of times and more often than not, silence was a sure sign that she was up to something.

The way I met her wasn't dissimilar to someone picking up a stray either, she followed me around and somehow ended up coming home with me; and hadn't really left for more than a couple of hours at a time since.

It was far too quiet. Quiet used to be comforting but now it filled me with a sense of dread. I didn't really want to, but I knew on some level that if I checked on her it would be far better than leaving her to her own devices. Out there I didn't really care what she got up to, in here though, was my space; anything she fucked around with in here would impact me.

I took a breath, finished the last bite of my protein bar and attempted to prepare myself mentally for whatever it was she was up to.

"Allie, what the hell are you doing?" I asked, as I pushed through the door of "her bedroom" which really was just my storage room with a bed now in one corner.

"Nothing." she replied, which might have been convincing had she not been stood next to a pile of which were once neatly sorted boxes.

I barely used any of these things any more anyway, I had long since grown out of the phase of needing various devices and hardware to do my job. It would have been a different story if she was touching my laptop but this was effectively junk.

"Whatever, just don't trash the place." I told her, I didn't care about the objects but I didn't want my place to be a mess. There was a reason I often lived, and pretty much existed alone up until this point; other people have a tendency to ruin everything.

"I won't. I'm going out soon anyway, wanna come?" she asked.

I really really didn't want to, dealing with her here was enough. It was quite a relief when she went out and became someone else's problem for a few hours, then it wasn't me that had to deal with her shit.

"I can't, I've got work that needs doing." I could work anytime but this was a great excuse.

Before I had even a chance to look away she began to undress right in front of me, pulling off a pink t-shirt and jeans, before pausing for what seemed like an eternity staring at me.

"Can you put on some clothes?" I asked.

After a while she began to pull a poofy white dress over her head and her long pink hair.

Don't get me wrong, she was probably attractive; but my concept of that wasn't exactly normal. That wasn't the problem here, the problem was her concept of boundaries.

"Anyway, I'm going now," she said, shoving me out of the way before slamming the front door on her way out.

With a sigh of relief, I took a moment to take a look at the mess she'd made. It wasn't actually that bad, just a few knocked over boxes; which I promptly picked up and put back into their proper place.

I shoved all the old parts back into their boxes. Old motherboards, old hard drives, nothing particularly interesting. Until I saw something that caught my attention, something I had forgotten about, an old WiFi jamming device. That thing sure brought back some memories, mostly things I had no interest in thinking about; so I quickly shoved it back into a box.

With Allie's mess cleared up, I could finally get back to some normalcy. My normal nightly activities; work.

This generally involved being on the phone to someone that wanted me to do something morally gray at best.

"I've given you all the information you asked me for. That's all there is, stop yelling at me. Please just fucking wire me the money. I've done everything you've said to do," I told whoever I was talking with.

Dealing with these idiots day after day was tiring, though the amount of money they were willing to pay made it worth it. It felt amazing to be this needed by so many people; which admittedly was a huge part of why I still bothered doing this.

In general people were angering to deal with, but the way they made me feel important made it worth every second. The best part was if someone made me feel any other way; then I got to shout at them. Safe in the knowledge that next time they screwed up, they'd come crawling back to me.

"Maybe you shouldn't have been so careless and got yourself caught? But you'll never learn will you? You know where to find me for next time," I yelled back at the man on the other end of the phone. Whether it came from a place of smugness or one of confidence didn't really matter. The only thing that mattered was how good it felt.

People placed such an importance on me, which made it impossible for me to ever scare them off. I knew too much, the risk they ran trying to screw me over was too high.

Not only was exuding my superiority over all of them fun, it happened to be incredibly cathartic too.

Tonight was a typical night for me; irresponsible people turning to me to cover their tracks when they fucked up online.

Pixel saving all the assholes of the world from the consequences of their fuck ups. It was frustrating; but the moment that five thousand dollars was in my account, it would all feel worth it.

With that irritating call out the way, it was time to move onto the next job. Whilst scanning the listing, my phone began to ring once again.

This time it wasn't work, it was Allie. Most nights she was off doing her own thing, so a call from her was a strange occurrence.

I had no idea what she did when she spent the night out by herself, and I wasn't quite sure I wanted to know either.

"Hey Allie-cat what's up?"

It was always nice to hear from her, even if it was always at the most random of times. Well not really random, not much is; but I couldn't find a pattern in the rare times she called me.

"Nothing," she replied, in a tone that I knew all too well.

Her tone was reminiscent of a child hiding their parents cell phone that they had just taken apart, being asked what they've done. That tone might have worked on everyone else, but I always saw through it.

"What have you done this time?" I asked, prepared to hear the absolute worst.

She wouldn't have called me, if she didn't want me to know; she either wanted my help or my attention.

Nothing with Allie was that easy though.

Asking her anything was the first step in a little game she liked to play every time we spoke. I had become all too familiar with the cycle, next came pretending not to know or being intentionally obtuse with me.

After going round and round for a while, she always got to the point. Which usually came when she had gotten enough attention, or perhaps when she'd become bored of her own game.

"Nothing that serious, come pick me up though 'kay?" Her tone remained the same. It was at this point that I realized something was wrong, she wasn't acting the way she normally would.

The unnatural emphasis she put on "that" was disconcerting. The nothing-games would have carried on for much longer; she got bored easily, but this was quick even for her.

There was something different here, which wasn't a good sign. She wasn't the type of person to act differently for no reason.

Well that wasn't the complete truth, she always acted differently; but within set patterns. The fact she was behaving outside of her normal reactions was unsettling.

"Alright I'll be there soon." I told her.

Going out wasn't something I enjoyed doing all that often, I tried to avoid it at all costs.

I wasn't sure whether it was a good thing that she made me go out more. There were benefits of getting fresh air and being away from my screen for a while, but the outside world was scary.

I hung up the call, switching to my tracking app in the process. Asking where she was was never worth the effort, she never had the slightest idea. It took the app mere seconds to tell me, what could have taken several minutes to get out of her. According to the app, she was in an alleyway next to a bar.

I could only assume she'd gotten into a fight again, something she was prone to do.

Heh, Allie-way.

I quickly discovered that putting on a leather jacket whilst going downstairs wasn't an easy task; especially when distracted by my own amazing wordplay.

The number of times I almost fell was ridiculous, but Allie needed me and there was no time to waste being careful.

My eyes caught a glimpse of my own reflection as I shoved the keys of my bike into the ignition. I looked pretty great, even if everyone mistook me for a girl. I never understood what about a leather jacket, leather pants, and a side cut made people think "girl". But whatever.

"Damn Pixel you're fucking hot." I whispered, as I took a few moments to admire my own reflection.

The streets were pretty much traffic free at this time of night. One of the benefits of going out at 3 am meant less cars to try weaving between; even though the city was supposedly named Circadia to encourage 24 hour activity.

The fact that my life enabled me to avoid most of the world, was one of the best perks. Human interaction was such a difficult thing, there were so many unwritten rules.

Online etiquette was much easier to understand, and if I struggled with that there were usually guidelines in text format. I wished real life came with guidelines or even a guidebook.

It took around ten minutes to reach where the app told me she was. She wasn't hard to spot, the long pink hair made her very distinctive. Which now thinking about it, might have been the point of that hair colour.

From the moment I saw her, I knew something wasn't right. Everything about this scene had an ominous feeling, if it wasn't Allie here I would have ran in an instant.

The look on her face was particularly unsettling. She was an excitable person in general, but she looked way more excited than usual.

As I got closer, everything started to look worse than I imagined. I had hoped she was just high or something, which wouldn't have been good; but it would have been better than what I saw.

Chapter 2

In front of me stood Allie, with a splattering of red all over her.

"What the fuck have you done?" I shouted.

"A lady was wearing a hat that didn't go with her shoes and we fought about it and now she's dead," she recounted very matter-of-factly, with an unnerving grin on her face.

I had no qualms about ruining someone's life for money when they deserved it, but this felt so much worse.

She was stood there covered in a stranger's blood, smirking as if she was proud of what she'd done. There wasn't a trace of unease or guilt, she seemed to be on a high from it.

This wasn't the time or place to psychoanalyse my partner though, we needed to get out of here. Fast.

The longer we stayed here, the more dangerous it would be for her. We had to run, and hope to hell that nobody saw anything.

I sat on my bike ready to leave, but she stopped next to me. Before I could tell her to hurry up, she had pulled me by the jaw into a heavy kiss.

Kissing her always felt good, but it was far from the time to be doing this. After enjoying it for a few moments, I shoved her towards the back of the bike in hopes she'd take the hint.

She did, however she struggled to get her leg over the seat; which made me feel better about the amount of times I'd nearly fell down the stairs.

"I love you Pix." she said, as her hands grabbed at me.

"I know you do." I replied, not thinking much of it as she was clearly drunk; at least I hoped it was just alcohol.

I hoped she did love me, but I could only feel anger toward her at the moment.

It astounded me that she could be this reckless. Something that confused me even more, was the fact that I was helping her. I couldn't understand why I'd put myself at such risk for her, it had to be out of love.

The ride back home to our penthouse apartment was quicker than the journey here; I didn't care any more.

Even getting into a car-wreck wouldn't have made this night any worse, in fact it would have been an improvement.

Nothing happened on the way back, no matter how fast I drove. Nothing other than her constantly groping me instead of holding onto my waist.

Sex wasn't something I wanted at the best of times, never mind right now. It was confusing that she'd want that after everything that had happened tonight.

When we arrived, I dragged her inside by the wrist. We needed to have a conversation.

From her expression, she knew how angry I was at her. The way she slammed the door behind her only further proved this.

I closed my eyes in a desperate attempt to calm down, taking a few deep breaths in the process. When I opened my eyes, there was Allie stood right in front of me; running her hands up and down my arms.

This had to be one of her hypersexual phases. I pushed her away, hoping to start the conversation we needed to have.

"We need to talk first Allie." I told her as sternly as possible, not wanting to yell at her again. Yelling would have made me feel better, but it wouldn't have been helpful; for some reason I cared about her feelings.

She said nothing. She just stood in front of me doe-eyed, which only made this more difficult. It might not have been her fault that she was this way, but she needed to hear this.

At least it was coming from me, rather than anyone else. This meant it came from a place of love and care, rather than one of anger.

Well anger too, as I was so furious at her; but a place of love and care.

"Allie, what the fuck is wrong with you? You can't do that because you didn't like someone's outfit. Worst of all I'm your fucking accomplice now. You've been nothing but trouble since I met you. I can't believe I ever thought it was a good idea to talk to someone who stalked me all day," I said, failing at not screaming at her after the first word.

I took a few moments to catch my breath, and attempted to compose myself a little. I looked over at her for a second, and despite the yelling, and tears in her eyes, she had that unsettling grin that I saw earlier.

There had to something wrong with her if she was enjoying this, which the grin seemed to indicate. The one benefit was that I could say whatever I wanted and she wouldn't care.

"I can't fucking deal with you, even if you love me I can't do this any more. The fights and stealing were bad enough, but this, fucking murder, Allie? I have too much to lose to be associated with someone like you. I'll give you some money and you can fuck off and be someone else's problem," I continued to yell.

It hurt to say all that, but she needed to hear it. I was trying to help her out, hoping she would see that what she did was wrong.

"Okay, money please." she said in her frustratingly nonchalant voice; after which she gazed up at me with the most angelic of expressions.

Part of me envied her; the amount I cared for most people was minimal, but she didn't seem to care about anyone. It was doubtful if she even cared about me, which was both hurtful and impressive.

I had helped her out of a bad situation only a few weeks ago, and she didn't seem to care about me one bit.

Sometimes I felt like nothing more than an object to her, which frustrated me. Though at the same time, it made me want her around even more.

"I said money please," she said, this time with her hand shoved towards my face almost expectantly.

I slapped her hand away from my face, when I had a realization; this was exactly what she wanted. The look on her face said it all.

The fire in her eyes told me that I had just played right into her hand. She had manipulated me, but I didn't care; this was exciting.

"I hate you," I whispered under my breath, shoving her away. On some level I knew this would escalate things even further.

I wasn't sure if she heard me, a second later however she had me pinned against the wall.

"You hate me do you? You really really hate me?" she mocked with her hand pressed hard against my throat.

"mm-hmm"

It was impossible to talk, but I wasn't about to be quiet.

"So if I do this-" she said as she released the grip on my throat for less than a second, only to slap me hard across the face.

"-It won't change how you feel at all?" she continued, with her hands back against my throat.

My entire body trembled, in a combination of both terror and excitement. She had literally killed someone tonight, and now those same hands were around my throat.

There was a chance she'd kill me too. I was sure that she wouldn't, I was too useful; but with her there was always a chance of impulses winning.

Even if she did I wouldn't complain, not that I could; being choked to death by her would have been one hell of a way to go.

Once again she released her grasp, which gave me a chance to gasp for air. This respite only lasted a few seconds, before she grabbed me by the skull and forcefully kissed me.

What made it even more exciting, was the fact such roughness came from someone with such a cute facade. It was rare that I ever felt this way.

Our tongues interacted for a while, before she shoved me to the floor.

"I hate you too bitch," she told me.

I envied the level of smugness, even on the phone to clients I couldn't muster that much.

The next hour or so, was the most pleasurable and painful I had ever experienced. My whole body was both drenched with sweat, and agonising pain; even just breathing was a struggle.

I took a moment to process what the hell had just happened, as I continued to gasp for my breath. It was impossible to piece everything together, it was all a blur.

I was pretty sure that I loved every moment of it, even if I couldn't remember any of the specifics.

The pain I felt was too much, I needed my bed. Tomorrow morning was another chance to process and sort things out; well more likely the afternoon, I was exhausted.

***

I had no idea what time it was when I woke up. The fact it was light out meant it was still daytime, but that was all I knew. As I adjusted to the waking world, I noticed Allie soundly asleep beside me; rather than sleeping in the bed she begged me to buy.

This room was supposed to be my space, but last night made it clear that boundaries were something she had no grasp of.

I couldn't let my entire life revolve around her, there were many more pressing things to focus on.

I winced in pain as I sat down at my computer, there was always work to be done. The distraction it would provide was something I needed right now.

None of the job listings posed much of a challenge, or were particularly well paying. But even the most simple tasks still paid a decent amount, and more importantly would take my mind off Allie.

Later on I would have to deal with the mess she'd caused, but first I needed to work. The idea of having a few unproductive hours was the worst feeling in the world.

Deleting some pictures from the internet in return for a couple of thousand dollars provided the distraction I needed; even if was incredibly boring.

Follow a few links, run a couple of programs and then all the evidence was gone. Jobs like these were so unengaging that it was often a struggle to stop myself from consuming way more protein bars and energy drinks that I should; which judging from the emptiness of the box, I had failed to control.

I had pretty much consumed a days worth of calories, which thankfully meant I could put off going shopping until tomorrow; unfortunately it was much cheaper to buy food in person than online, at least living here. It certainly was a benefit of living in a populous city that multiple stores seemed to be in direct competition with each other.

Even when I wasn't distracted by food there was some fun to be found, it always amazed me how often people lacked awareness; and how many incriminating pictures ended up online because of this.

People needed to be more careful, not that I was complaining; the more negligent people out there, the more easy money I made.

I sometimes had the urge to leave the photos up. The idea of ruining some asshole's life was amusing to me; but money was more important than fun.

The goal was to make enough money to allow me to never have to deal with people again; but until then this was my life. It wasn't all bad though, not having to fake caring about people was a huge positive.

I didn't care about them, and from a practical standpoint I couldn't; it was a business, feelings would only make it messy.

Between the sounds of my furious typing, I noticed noise emanating from the other room; it had to be her getting up.

A few seconds later she wandered into the room not wearing anything at all.

"Still hate me Pix?" she said in the most mocking tone imaginable.

It would have been an understatement to agree with her, I hated her more than anyone. Despite the hatred, I still admired her lack of care; as well as envied it a bit.

I wished I could have been more like her. Everything must have been so easy when you don't care about anyone, maybe not even yourself.

"A bit." I told her.

There was no way I was going to let her know I admired her, nothing good would have come from that. The way she acted was exciting, but fuelling her ego and encouraging her wasn't the best of ideas.

"Aww poor girl," she continued to mock me, this time with a crying gesture.

"Don't call me that," I snapped back, which was probably what she wanted from me.

I wasn't a girl, I was just Pixel.

My gender was vaguely female aligned, but anyone calling me a girl made my blood boil. Binaries were for computers; which having my life centred around them, I would fucking know.

"Oh okay, sorry." she replied, without a hint of emotion behind her words.

She didn't mean it. I had only known her a short time, but I had already learned to never trust a word she said. This wasn't her fault though, nobody ever understood my gender.

I had tried on multiple occasions to explain it to people, but nobody ever got it. The usual reaction was to double down and call me a girl even more.

I was so far beyond their concept of gender, and having it enforced on me was infuriating.

"Whatever Allie, I know nobody fucking gets it." I shouted, more angry at the world than I was at her.

She just happened to be almost the centre of my world in this moment, so made a good proxy.

In response to the yelling, she once again had that grin on her face; almost as if any negative attention fuelled her.

One thing I had figured out, was that the grin meant she was plotting something. That was as far as I got, the game of figuring her out was one I would never be able to win. After last night, I had even less idea of what to expect from her.

At least it wasn't boring.

I spent a few moments considering my next move; the idea of provoking her was exciting, but I was still in too much pain from last night.

There was also the fact that she for sure, wanted me to provoke her and give in to her need for drama. The smart choice here was to take some space, rest up a little and have enough energy for the next conflict.

Without a word, I headed to my room hoping she would take the hint that I needed time away. This was the only room that still felt relatively untouched by Allie, last night was the first time she had been in here.

Despite that intrusion, this place was still my sanctuary. She might not have much concept of boundaries, but she at least somewhat seemed to grasp the concept in this case; or maybe it was the fact I was mostly in the other room on my laptop that she didn't come in here.

With my head on the pillow, eyes closed I faced a common problem; my body was exhausted but my brain was still fired up. Emotionality always seemed to send my brain into overdrive for some reason, and I still didn't quite understand it even after all these years.

As thoughts of Allie and what the hell I'd gotten myself into swirled around, I attempted to counter them with more calming thoughts. Repeating pieces of code over in my brain served as a calming mechanism, something I had found out quite a while ago.

Whether it was my code, or just random garbage it was calming.... Not that I had code, I was a human; something which I admittedly seemed to forget from time to time.

41 6c 6c 69 65 20 79 6f 75 27 72 65 20 73 6f 20 61 6e 6e 6f 79 69 6e 67

41 6c 6c 69 65 20 79 6f 75 27 72 65 20 73 6f 20 61 6e 6e 6f 79 69 6e 67

41 6c 6c 69 65 20 79 6f 75 27 72 65 20 73 6f 20 61 6e 6e 6f 79 69 6e 67

41 6c 6c 69 65 20 79 6f 75 27 72 65 20 73 6f 20 61 6e 6e 6f 79 69 6e 67

I repeated over and over, until I felt calm and drifting off to sleep.

My peaceful and calm state didn't last long, apparently I was only allowed a few minutes alone. Sounds of the door brought me out of my sleep state. It wasn't quickly apparent what was going on, but it had to be Allie; who else would it be entering my room, without even the decency to knock.

"Allie change your folder location," I barely managed to say, without even really knowing what I was talking about.

She didn't listen to me, she only approached me even more and looked quite confused. Just then I realized that I hadn't quite said what I wanted, "Allie get out of my room." I told her this time.

"But why? I wanted to see you," she said, whilst at this point practically being in my bed.

This girl frustrated me so much, we had literally just had a fight but here she was trying to cozy up to me. With everything that had happened between us in just the past day, the fact she couldn't seem to comprehend that I might want space from her was astounding.

"I know we had a fight, but we still like each other right?" she asked.

Whether or not I liked her right now was a very complicated subject; There were parts that intrigued me and I parts I perhaps even envied, but at the same time there were things about her that I absolutely hated.

In particular her lack of respect for boundaries was particularly grating.

"I'm tired and I need some space." I told her.

"What have I done that's so bad?" she asked.

Not only had I just gone over all those things with her yesterday, but she was still doing them. I lacked the energy, and it was apparent that if I stayed here she would just become increasingly pushy and continue to not respect my boundaries.

It wasn't often that I thought this, but perhaps it was safer to be outside then it was in here. Staying here would only lead to a repeat of last night, which I was still emotionally drained from.

Relaxing in my own room was apparently not allowed, the only real choice was to go for a ride. At least it was relatively late, which meant most of the world would be in bed; which in turn meant less people to cause even more annoyance.

Chapter 3

I picked up a jacket and my keys from the chair in my room, as I headed past Allie. It was best to not engage with her, which was a struggle; especially with the antagonizing glare she was shooting me from across the room.

It took all of my strength to not yell at her, but I headed out of my room and then out of the apartment.

Even something as simple as being separated from her by a wall made me feel better, if it were anyone else I could have probably stayed in the lobby for a while; but I didn't trust Allie to actually give me any space, I had to get further away for a while.

Riding usually cleared my head, and right now my head was filled with Allie's bullshit.

It puzzled me how she could even be a real person; the fact an actual human could act the way she did was bizarre. Logically it didn't make much sense but, if someone had told me she was some kind of shapeshifting alien, or even a demon; I would have had to doubt everything I knew.

I could just imagine it; some internet show attempting to summon demons or some other nonsense, just for Allie to show up. Sure she wasn't goatman or anything, but I'd argue she could be just as scary.

As I delved deeper into my imagination, as was becoming even more and more common, I stumbled going down the stairs again. There had to be something about being around Allie that made my attention span even worse than usual.

It wasn't long before I had made it down the numerous flights of stairs.

Perhaps I could have taken the elevator considering we lived on the top floor, but this was just the way I had done things. I wasn't about to change the way I'd lived my entire life now, things were fine up until this point; change was what caused things to turn to chaos.

Outside was refreshingly brisk: perfect riding weather.

There was a spot I always liked to go to when I needed to be away from humanity for a while, which was quite a common occurrence; and since meeting Allie it had only became even more frequent.

It took about 15 minutes or so of drifting along first the main streets of Circadia, then the out of town forest lined roads, until I reached where I wanted to be. Everyone around here called it a mountain, but in all honestly it wasn't much more than a hill.

The view from here was always spectacular, especially at night. It was far enough out of town that the stars were visible to the naked eye, at least on a clear night. Tonight was unfortunately too cloudy for me to see much, but the dark sky and crescent moon still proved quite the sight.

The downside of being here, was the city being so small in the distance; which reminded me of my own insignificance and which I hated. Though somehow at the same time it was comforting, if I didn't matter in the grand scheme of things then nothing I did mattered. I suppose it helped to remember that whilst on a universal scale I didn't have much of an impact, I could affect other people's lives and my own.

I sat on the seat for a while, as my thoughts fixated on my own futile existence and the enormity of the universe; before they shifted back to Allie.

As I got off the bike to stretch my legs a little, I started to process everything that had happened the past few days.

She was the most frustrating person I'd ever met, but there had to be some reason I kept her around.

I would have liked to think it'd be pretty easy to get rid of her, she'd probably be long gone if I stopped giving her attention; but part of me enjoyed giving her what she needed.

There was the matter of her killing someone, but I wasn't really in the position to judge her for anything she did. I had probably ruined more people's lives than I could ever remember, for just some money. At least Allie enjoyed what she did, the only enjoyment I got was from problem solving and getting paid.

In all honesty, if I was given the choice of being someone killed by Allie and someone wrongfully sent to prison because of my hacking, I would have chosen being killed by Allie every time.

She might have taken a life, but I had ruined many and probably subjected people to torturous conditions at the hands of whichever government agencies.

On top of all that it was apparent that she'd accepted all my flaws, either that or didn't notice/care about them. Despite my frustrations I did care about her, so the least I could try for her to do the same.

We would need to have a conversation about her not murdering anyone in the future, or hell even just not doing it in such a conspicuous manner; because I certainly wasn't going to change what I did or my methods.

Allie and I were certainly extremely different people, but we had potential; there was certainly common ground that we could work together on. We were going to need to try talking to each other, but I had hope for a change.

I hopped back on my bike, preparing to have a potentially difficult and emotional conversation with Allie. There were even less people around on the way back, which meant I didn't even have to worry about my speed.

The journey back took even less time, as I didn't bother even stopping for red lights; it wasn't hard to make those tickets disappear when you knew the people that I did, as long as nobody was around to see.

After I'd rushed to park up and up the stairs to the apartment to see her, I began to wonder what would happen. The problem with Allie was that even if you had the best of intentions she had an amazing ability to turn it into something malicious.

Surprisingly when I entered the apartment, I found her asleep on the sofa. I had assumed she'd be waiting for me in my room when I got back, sometimes she was surprising in nice ways. I'd never knew if she actually felt bad being in my room without me, or she'd just gotten bored; but at least this time I was willing to try thinking the best of her, even if it might not have been the truth.

I was eager to talk to her, but I knew better than to wake her up. Most people would be angry at being woken up at this time, but Allie's reactions tended to be more explosive than most. The best way to handle this was to wait until the morning, after all I could also use some rest after the couple of days I'd had.

After slowly tiptoeing to my room as to not wake her, I pulled myself into bed and once again started my usual ritual of calming code; as even if I had some hope, there were things about Allie that still worried me.

74 68 69 6e 67 73 20 77 69 6c 6c 20 62 65 20 6f 6b 61 79
74 68 69 6e 67 73 20 77 69 6c 6c 20 62 65 20 6f 6b 61 79
74 68 69 6e 67 73 20 77 69 6c 6c 20 62 65 20 6f 6b 61 79

***

I woke up the next morning feeling renewed and refreshed, something I hadn't really been able to feel since, well since meeting Allie really.

After taking a few moments to stretch and adjust to the waking world, I decided it was finally time to at least attempt talking to Allie; who was still asleep on the sofa.

"Allie we need to talk." I told her, waiting for any signs of her being awake before continuing.

"What have I done this time? I was just sleeping," she replied, followed by a huge yawn.

"Just things from the other day." I told her, to which I got no reply.

"I know you can't help being you, just like I can't stop being me; but could you try to... I don't know, be a little less obvious when you do things. I want to try keeping us both safe, but you make that hard sometimes."

"Okay." she replied blandly, which made me unsure if she was paying attention or not.

"Allie I'm not angry with you this time. I just want things to be okay for us." I told her, as I attempted to approach her for a hug.

Before I could fully embrace her however, something unsettling popped up on my desktop; anonymously sent pictures. Anything from an anonymous source was never a good sign. At best it was usually a guys... well... you know, and at worst it could be something even more disturbing.

CHAPTER 4

With a deep breath, I apprehensively opened the attachment.

"Fuck." I yelled.

This couldn't be happening. I was supposed to be better than this, I shouldn't let things like this happen.

"Allie, we have a problem. Come look at this." I shouted over to her, which caused her to instantly run over to me, not unlike a puppy.

"Oh my god I look so hot covered in blood." she squealed excitedly.

It shouldn't have surprised me that she didn't see the seriousness of this, she never saw the serious side of anything. Expecting her to ever see consequences or feel regret for anything she did was unrealistic.

I couldn't help but sigh at her typical Allie-ness.

"You look good too,"she replied to my sigh. It was ridiculous how important physical appearance was to her, but knowing her I wasn't shocked.

It was obvious that I looked great, I always did. The way I looked wasn't the problem; the problem was the photographic evidence from last night.

"Allie, Don't you get it? Someone took pictures of what we, well mostly you... did last night." I yelled at her, frustrated by her constant obliviousness.

I couldn't comprehend how she could be this oblivious. She was always oblivious, but this was way more than I'd ever seen from her.

"We'll either be killed or taken to jail, you dense bitch listen to me," I continued to yell at her, in hopes she would begin to understand.

At times treating her this way was enjoyable, and her grin told me that I wasn't the only one enjoying it.

If she enjoyed that, she was going to enjoy the next part even more. Everything here had to be destroyed, I couldn't leave a trace of anything. We needed to wreck my entire apartment and everything in it.

"We need to destroy everything." I told her.

Most people would have probably needed some clarification, but she wasn't most people.

It took less than a few seconds for her to be stomping my laptop into at least a dozen pieces on the ground. There was something strangely heart-warming and attractive about the joy she found in destruction.

After watching her for a while, I decided to not let her have all the fun; as I went to get my hammer from the closet.

When I returned moments later, she had given up destroying the laptop and had moved onto the rest of my expensive equipment.

Shards of USB drives, monitors, and the Wi-Fi-jammer that I bought during an uncharacteristically optimistic phase, filled the floor of my apartment.

She had somehow found my childhood hockey stick, which made an efficient tool of destruction. The sight of Allie destroying everything with one of the last remnants of my childhood, was the fitting end to this place.

I had been here since I realized my parents were holding me back, and didn't deserve someone like me.

The way she swung it but also managed to keep a firm grip was mesmerizing. If she had better co-ordination she would have made a great hockey player, well enforcer.

Images of her pulling off her helmet and her pink hair cascading out of it, like in the movies, to fight someone filled my mind. I wasn't sure why I found that an attractive image, but I did.

My admiring gaze was soon broken, when it struck me that she wasn't wearing anything. We couldn't go anywhere if she had no clothes, and the ones from last night needed to be destroyed along with everything else.

Her walking around in a blood stained dress would have defeated the purpose of all this destruction.

Luckily, there were still some clothes in my laundry basket. I dug through, finding one of my oversized hoodies. I threw one over to her, I figured the height difference between us would make it dress length on her.

"Put it on." I told her.

"And then wait for me outside, this part is going to be dangerous." I continued.

I shouldn't have expected any other reaction from her; she clung to my side the moment I said the word dangerous.

Hidden at the very back of my closet was a bottle of kerosene, that I kept for this exact scenario. It was surreal that it had actually come to this, it was always a contingency plan that I hoped I would never need.

I poured the liquid over as much of the apartment as I could; using my hammer on the gas pipes for good measure as I did so.

As I poured the last remnants by the door, I had an idea.

"Allie, do you want to do the honours?" I asked, as I handed her the box of matches.

Her grin grew even wider, clearly she wanted to do this. The speed at which she took them from me only further proved it.

Clearly she'd done this before, with one smooth strike and a flick the entire place was in flames. Not one second later, she pulled me into a kiss.

There was quite a perverse sentimentality that came with being kissed inside a burning building. Not that I quite understood why.

As I took her hand and pulled her into the fresh air, it dawned on me... I had no idea whatsoever where we could go.

Somewhere there was a place we could go, though standing outside of a destroyed home wasn't the place to figure that out.

Holding her hand was comforting, it would have felt even better if I wasn't having to drag her away from admiring the fire.

There was literally an entire country out there, an entire world even. The safety of being a blur in a crowd was vital however.

CHAPTER 5

I looked back at the smoke billowing out of the place I spent most of the past 5 years, as a confusing mess of feelings came over me.

The old me, my old life, everything was in flames.

Losing everything upset me, but having no ties to anywhere and having the freedom to go anywhere did come with some excitement. Leaving Circadia forever was something I almost knew was inevitable, especially with the work I did; though I hoped it would be under much different circumstances.

There was one huge positive to leaving, I didn't have to be this version of myself any more. If I wanted her to, the old me could die here.

Starting over wasn't anything new, but this time was different. This time I wasn't alone; I had someone that for better or worse, I cared about. It wasn't just about me any more.

Having wasted enough time admiring the flames, we needed to flee before the authorities arrived.

"We need to go." Forcefully I took her by the wrist and I began leading her into the city. Without much of a plan, we walked into the city. it was at least easier to blend into a crowd there.

Though I towered over most people I saw in public, the only attention it would attract would be from assholes. Idiots who can't even grasp the concept of gender luckily weren't much danger, at least to me.

While their words did hurt, being around them was much safer than where we came from.

Our walk was quite uneventful, though it was amusing that Allie would get distracted by every little thing she saw.

Whether it be someone passing with a dog, or something shiny in a shop window there was a wondrous excitement to everything she experienced. An added bonus was that she was quiet for once.

We ended up just a short distance from a computer store I often visited. With everything I owned destroyed and probably burnt by now; a new computer was going to be vital. All the important parts of my life revolved around using a computer, work and.... Well mostly work.

A burner phone would be useful too, security was important right now. There was a high chance that somehow people recognized me from those pictures.

The sad thing about being in my world was, despite the amount of trust needed to carry out jobs people often ended up betraying that trust. It was for the best if none of the people who had my number could contact me.

As much as Allie wouldn't agree with me, it was better to be safe than sorry.

The brightness of the light in the store was the first thing that hit me, the sheer fluorescence was painful. Soon enough I was distracted, as Allie yelled.

"Pix why don't we just steal a computer."

From the stares and glances, it was obvious everyone heard her. Not that it was surprising, even though she was small she was capable of making a huge amount of noise.

Shopping was going to be even more awkward now, I could feel the hawk-like observation from the staff almost instantly.

Looking over at her, she seemed to be proud of the attention she was getting. It made no sense, if she was being good for attention it would be understandable. Any kind of attention was good enough for her, the fact she was getting it from someone else for a change did feel nice however.

She probably didn't know what anything here even was, not that it stopped her from picking up and touching everything. Her level of immaturity was astounding.

If it wasn't for the fact that I'd seen her records, I would have been worried I was actually dating a 16 year old. There were good parts to the immaturity though, her almost childlike wonder at everything was quite endearing.

On the top shelf, I noticed the computer I needed. This was one situation where my height wasn't a detriment. Without much effort I reached up and took it, much to the chagrin of the sales assistant that had been walking over to me.

Not needing help from anyone was the best feeling in the world, well anything that proved how much better I was than everyone else.

Sadly none of the phones in stock had the security features I needed, frustratingly that would have to wait. Waiting for anything wasn't the easiest thing, but it often came down to the fact I had no choice but wait.

The self admiration was soon cut short; whenever I looked at Allie she was causing some kind of trouble.

This time she was stuffing things into the pockets of my hoodie, literally grabbing random packets from shelves and filling her pockets.

After what I'd been through with her the past couple of days there wasn't much she could do to surprise me any more.

There was a real temptation to just leave her here, but there was the small matter of her knowing too much about me.

As much as I wanted to trust her, I knew she would sell me out in an instant if I ever left her. She was cold and calculating underneath the cute exterior, nothing mattered to her especially not other people. Not even me.

"Allie what the fuck are you doing, we need to pay now."

It was strange how she always responded to my voice, especially when it was yelling her name. Without question she followed me over to the queue, which was just one old lady.

She asked a million questions about the most basic of laptops she was buying when it was quite literally the easiest thing in the world to figure out. Dealing with people that didn't even want to try understanding things frustrated me to no end.

After what seemed like an eternity, it was finally our turn to pay.

"Would you like the insurance Sir-Mada, would you like the insurance?" the clearly confused man behind the counter asked.

This might have hurt most people, but there was a strange sense of joy I got from confusing gender binarists. Being confusing and unable to place was exactly what I wanted from my gender.

"No thanks," I responded, with no interest.

"Oh and the things I asked you to hold Allie."

The last thing we needed right now was more trouble, murder and arson were enough for now.

Ironically, stealing a few dollars worth of bad quality computer accessories was sure to get the police here quicker than anything that had happened the past day or so.

I was more intrigued than anything as she pulled various items from her pockets.

The things that caught her eye enough for her to try stealing, probably gave some insight into her personality.

Though, with her being as confusing and contradictory as she is; it could just as well have been completely random.

A few pink USB cables and cases for a phone neither of us owned any more were scanned through the checkout.

By now I was frustrated, swiping my card as quickly as possible I grabbed my things and headed for the door.

Allie was frustrating enough but there was something about the light and sound in there that made me so much more irritable than she ever could.

There was nothing I wanted more than to ask her "what the fuck was wrong with her", to which there was surely a multitude of answers.

Even if I were to ask, it was doubtful she'd give a straight answer. Nothing with her was ever straight.

There was still an admiration for how carefree she was able to be, underneath my annoyance with her. She clearly didn't care about anyone, not herself and not even me.

Maybe one day I could be as uncaring as she was, life would be so much easier that way.

"I hate you." I leaned over whispering in her ear.

"I hate you too," she yelled back, with that all too familiar grin on her face.

I wasn't quite sure why I provoked her so much, though the control it exerted over her did feel great.

The fun would have to wait, we needed to find somewhere to stay for the night. Even though I had lived here most of my adult life, I had spent the majority of it alone in my apartment.

I turned to Allie, to ask if she had any idea where we could go. There was no choice, as much as I might regret this decision I was stumped.

"There's a cheap hotel round the corner, they don't ask for anything except money. No questions asked, no matter how much you trash the room," she matter-of-factly stated.

I was curious but I probably didn't want to know how or why she knew these things.

But it looked like our only choice, she would no doubt spill details without being asked anyway.

Which was one of the main reasons it was hard trusting her, and why I needed to not leave her.

"I haven't been here for so long. It's been a while since I've needed a private place to sleep with strangers that wanted to buy me stuff or give me money. I don't need to do that any more because I have you now!" from her tone it was almost as if she thought this was a nice thing to tell me.

Being unable to tell whether it was supposed to be sweet, or was just for shock value I stayed quiet.

Every time she spoke to me I learned more and more about her, the more obvious it was that my first judgment was way off the mark.

There was nothing resembling the innocent girl I first took her for, this way was much more fun though.

Any other girl I met was scared off by my way of living, her excited grin every time something went wrong or we did something morally ambiguous was refreshing.

I was starting to like her a lot more than anyone who actually knew her should.

"Thanks for helping." She honestly deserved praise on the rare occasions she helped instead of causing more trouble.

Though she didn't react, other than a look of confusion. It was as if niceness was something she wasn't used to. Given her past, it wasn't surprising at all.

She hadn't told me all that much, but the few details she let slip were always the same; mistreatment, abuse and such.

It was a short walk before we reached the rundown hotel, which didn't look like somewhere we would get much rest. The vibe was oddly fitting for us; shady and potentially dangerous.

There was an unsettling feeling that we could die here, something that was impossible to shake.

Not having to think or be in control of everything for a while felt nice, she seemed confident enough so following her lead was easy.

Whether it was actual confidence or apathetic stubbornness, there was something about her like this that made it hard to not go along with anything.

The way she dragged me into the building by the back entrance, avoiding the front desk confused me.

"The room on the end doesn't have a lock on the door, so nobody ever wants to use it."

It fascinated me how she knew these things, as well as these things being normal to her. Her having no issues with stealing was strangely attractive, seeing her doing whatever she wanted without a care was incredible.

Chapter 6

Once we'd snuck into the room, it was obvious why nobody wanted to stay here. It was the most run down place I'd ever seen in my life.

Sure it was free but it was more disgusting than unedited back-end code, and similarly felt like it just existed to anger me.

Tonight there was no choice, tomorrow we would get our future sorted. I had to put up with this hellhole for one night.

After shutting the door I dropped onto the bed, I was completely drained and needed to rest for a while.

Today was a bad day, and tomorrow had the potential to be even more draining.

With my eyes closed, I was barely able to enjoy a few moments of rest. Before I was disturbed by a weight on top of me.

She had the weirdest timing, though the way she took control was enticing. What she wanted was obvious. I wasn't in the mood, but it was easier to let her do whatever she wanted.

Fighting back would have been fun, if I wasn't already exhausted.

Part of me hated it, though there was a perverse niceness in just giving in to her. Letting her do whatever she wanted wasn't the worst thing in the world.

Physically experiencing what she was doing to me, mentally though I was some place else. Somewhere empty and blank.

Calming void-like feelings filled my brain for what must have been at least half an hour. I was unable to feel anything other than physical sensations of whatever it was she was doing to me; and then those only felt faint compared to the emptiness.

Emotionally my entire body was disconnected from the rest of me, for once calmness and dark was all I could feel.

Sadly some time later, I began to feel like myself again. The few emotions that I felt quickly flooded back.

Next to me, she was falling asleep. Whatever she did must have tired her out.

When I looked at her, the contempt I felt was almost overwhelming. I hated her, but was it really her fault? She essentially forced herself on me, but I never told her to stop.

It was my own fucked up enjoyment of her taking control, that let this happen. Judging from the way she was calm and falling asleep, it was probably for the best.

Whether or not it was right, me taking one for the team and letting her have not wanted sex with me was probably the best option.

It was finally quiet and calm, there was now a chance for me to try fixing everything. After setting up the laptop, I got to work.

First of all I, or we rather needed somewhere new and safe to live. Thanks to Allie, staying here or anywhere close by wasn't a safe option any more.

The lengths I was willing to go to just to protect her didn't even make sense to me.

I justified it by telling myself that she'd sell me out in an instant. The attention she'd get from reporting me would be huge, though it was doubtful just how serious she would be taken.

Despite everything she'd put me through this far, I grew more and more attached to her all the time. Even just looking over at her sleeping made me smile.

Of course this trash heap of a hotel had no wireless security; for once it seemed that something was going my way. Not that any old WiFi would have been much trouble getting into.

With no idea at all of anywhere practical for us to go, deciding wasn't easy. It took time for me to weigh up all the options, making decisions wasn't something that came easy to me.

The whole of this godforsaken country was an option.

Crisis situations were particularly stressful, and that's what this was. I had to find the perfect solution.

I had prided myself on my ability to reach practical and logical solutions. The urgency on this choice, made it harder.

Anywhere had to be safer than staying here though.

As much as I loved being able to blur into the crowd of a city, her being around, probably forever, made me think differently.

The bigger the city was, the greater potential for her to cause trouble. On the contrary, she'd surely be even more noticeable in a smaller place.

It was a dilemma, both options had their merit. Maybe a smaller-sized city would be the perfect mix of both.

Almost out of nowhere, a place came to mind. A couple of times growing up, my family had visited a city out west by the sea. It was always full of tourists and for whatever reason I had always been drawn to it.

With nothing holding me back any more, it was a tempting idea.

It had been years since the last time I had visited Azura, luckily I had enough money to make this happen.

A crucial step was covering my tracks, unlike normal people my money wasn't in banks. Having impromptu deposits of large amounts of money, well thousands at a time, would have raised more questions than the security of banks was worth.

Mostly my currency was stored in various types of cryptocurrency, the majority of which was Nyancredits. It had the benefit of being essentially untraceable, with an added bonus that theoretically a company would purchase everything to protect my identity.

This all came with the risk that if I fucked over the wrong person, the company could put all of my info out there in an instant. It was a calculated risk, but there was still a need to be careful. Especially with her around, having contingency plans was a must.

Within a few minutes, I'd found the perfect place for us. At least in terms of it being available right away, a two bedroom beach-front apartment right in the centre of Azura.

Being around her constantly was starting to feel normal, but I still needed my own space. Spending 24 hours a day with Allie, was by far the most draining of things.

We needed this place more than anything, 250 thousand was almost of my money. I had no doubt that it was worth it; it would only take a few months of hard work to build up a decent amount of savings again.

After hastily completing the purchase through the Nyancredit company, it was now just a matter of waiting.

Though I couldn't shake the feeling that there was something I had forgotten to check; and after a while it came to me. I wasn't sure how we would even get the keys. I hoped the process would be the same as when I bought my last place.

Oh how I was going to miss it, it still hurt that I was soon going to have to leave Circadia entirely. There wasn't really any choice, this was what had to happen.

After my momentary distraction by sentimentality, I realized it was a good idea to check how I would actually obtain physical possession of the new place before actually committing to the purchase.

It seemed there was a benefit to being impulsive and spontaneous as Allie had showed me, but buying an apartment wasn't really the time for that.

After endless scrolling though fine print littered with legal rhetoric, I found what I needed. My hopes had been right, it was essentially the same as when I bought the last place; the keys would be in a secured lockbox near the door.

All I would have to do is input a code, luckily I was amazing with codes.

With that it was done. Tomorrow, I would wake up as the owner of an amazing new apartment.

I still had conflicting feeling towards her but even so, I curled up next to Allie. I hated her but being with her felt better than being alone.

It only took a few moments for the hate to once again overpower the love I felt for her.

Hating her this much gave me a real temptation to just leave. My life was peaceful and calm without her, so surely without her it could be that way again?

After the week of chaos I'd endured, all centred around her, any rational and logical person would leave her here.

Maybe I wasn't as logical as I thought, nothing made this more apparent than when I looked at her. Feelings I had never felt before filled my entire being, I hated her guts but there was also a warm adoration.

Tomorrow had the potential to be the most stressful of days. Which with Allie around was saying something, putting up with her made most days like that.

Before her, there was at least a semblance of normalcy, routines and patterns.

The past few weeks had thrown that completely out the window, blood soaked and on fire.

The worst part of all? They had been the most fun of my whole life.

Laid awake with my usual brain noise, I began processing things.

Maybe, just maybe the safety of my stable life was better.

In my normal life, I never felt anything. With Allie around I felt alive, though I was having doubts about this whole thing and just how sustainable it was.

Having fun was great, but it never lasted. Nothing ever lasted.

Not that I'd ever admit it to her, but the way she lived her life was intriguing. Part of me wanted to experience living her way, placing fun above everything else.

Fun was more important than morals, more important than me.

Oftentimes I felt nothing more than an object to her, something for her to use. And deep down? I loved it. For better or worse, I was far too exhausted to actually analyse why it was that I felt that way. I needed as much energy as I could get for tomorrow, or really any time I was around her.

I once again recited some code to calm myself to sleep.

74 68 69 73 20 69 73 20 6a 75 73 74 20 61 20 72 65 62 6f 6f 74 20 6e 6f 74 20 74 68 65 20 65 6e 64

74 68 69 73 20 69 73 20 6a 75 73 74 20 61 20 72 65 62 6f 6f 74 20 6e 6f 74 20 74 68 65 20 65 6e 64

74 68 69 73 20 69 73 20 6a 75 73 74 20 61 20 72 65 62 6f 6f 74 20 6e 6f 74 20 74 68 65 20 65 6e 64

74 68 69 73 20 69 73 20 6a 75 73 74 20 61 20 72 65 62 6f 6f 74 20 6e 6f 74 20 74 68 65 20 65 6e 64

***

Light flooding into the room woke me, the brightness of which was almost painful; the positive of my eyes burning, was that it was clear at some point I had managed to drift off. What wasn't as much of a positive was the fact my body still ached, which made pulling myself up from this awful bed even more difficult.

Whatever it was Allie did to me was almost enjoyable, but afterwards it hurt a hell of a lot; but now wasn't the time to question my enjoyment of how she treated me, we had to be out of here.

Unsurprisingly, she was still passed out next to me. The amount of energy she had while awake probably took some time to recharge.

There wasn't time to mess around, I couldn't wait around for her. Today was planned, and the sooner those plans got started the better.

Calling her name a few times did nothing, not even a stir or movement from her. I tried again, louder and louder each time; but still nothing.

Maybe this was a sign to just leave her here, I couldn't centre my entire life around her. I had existed on my own before, it would be simple to do so again.

She'd be fine too, the next person who fell for her innocent facade could take care of her. If even I fell for it, it was obvious everyone else would too.

If there was a chance to be away from her, this was it. As she slept, I made my way quietly over to the door, laptop in hand.

As I took a moment to take one last look at her, a rush of emotions filled me. I had to push them down, being overcome with irrational emotions wasn't going to be helpful right now.

CHAPTER 7

Stood outside the door, slowly shutting both it and this chapter of my life, more feelings came over me; despite everything she'd done, I still cared about her.

She'd easily be able to survive on her own, as little sense as it made she'd managed 25 years being like this.

Nobody would be able to support her like I could though. Even on the off chance that someone was willing to try, doing it as well as me was impossible.

Containing her wasn't appealing to me or her. As obnoxious and controlling as she was, at least with me she could be herself.

It made no sense and I hated it, but we were better off together.

Repeatedly I called her name, still to no avail. She could sleep through anything. As I got closer to her an idea came over me. She would probably be into this anyway, I took my hand I slapped her hard across the face.

Finally she stirred, I didn't know why but slapping her felt good. It working in waking her made it feel even better.

"Pixel what the fuck?", the amount of energy mere seconds after she woke was astounding. Not a moment later she was stood in front of me, fist swinging toward my face.

Instead of the usual stinging sensation, I felt something different; a forceful impact upon my jaw. Before I could process what just happened, a darkness came over me.

Some time later, in even more pain I awoke on the floor. Everything hurt, however the pain seemed to emanate from my jaw.

After piecing things together, it was clear she hit me harder than usual; apparently with enough force to knock me out, which was new.

The thing was, I slapped her first. I provoked this reaction, what did I expect to happen? Her reactions were always exciting, even if they often hurt.

It took a while to get my bearings and pull myself from the floor. With her sleeping again, it was apparent plans would have to wait. As frustrating as it was, things often had to be her way.

Sat on the edge of the bed waiting bored me. The concept of sitting around doing nothing bothered me more than anything. In every waking moment there was surely something productive I could be doing.

Just a few minutes later, she finally woke up. This was followed by another ten minutes to find her clothes, that she somehow lost. All these delays made waiting for her more and more regretful.

"We need to go now," I dragged her by the hand out of this awful room.

Uncharacteristically without even a word, she followed my lead. The worried look on her face as we headed toward the exit, concerned me slightly.

Doing whatever I told her? Being quiet while doing so? This was such a sudden change from the Allie that was here earlier.

When we reached the exit though, I saw why she had looked worried.

It was locked.

"Allie why is the fucking door locked?"

This was her fault, it was her idea to come to this terrible place.

Neither of us had the cash to pay, the only other way out was past the front desk. Even hitting the door did nothing, of course somehow even the fire exit in this place was broken. It was just my luck.

The only option left was to kick it down. With my foot raised ready to try, I felt her grab me.

Being dragged by my sleeve toward the front desk, I hoped to hell she had a plan. If there was one time it was logical to have faith in her, it was to manipulate her way out of trouble.

The exit was in sight, but there was still the problem of the front desk. Sat there was the most bored looking middle aged man.

He looked awful; now I wasn't into guys in the slightest, with one exception in the past, but ones without hair were somehow even worse. Granted I had a side-cut, which was essentially lack of hair on one side but I could pull it off.

Without a care in the world, she wandered over to him.

"We're going to make some money tonight, I'll pay later I promise." Her tone was the most innocent sounding that I'd heard, with her finger on her lips.

He had no response to this, other than turning more red with every second that passed. Seeing her do this was quite impressive, on the fly she had come up with a plan and flawlessly pulled it off.

Maybe she just played clueless to get people's guard down.

Being back on the daylit streets felt better, a change in scenery wasn't enough to improve my mood however.

We still had no way of actually getting to Azura, most transportation methods would be risky.

CCTV was increasingly common these days, which took trains and taxis firmly out of the equation.

Knowing that in a pinch, she could come up with something gave me hope. As much as I wanted to be the one to fix everything, having her as backup was comforting.

From the moment I met her, it was clear she had a certain charm. Seeing it in action, on someone other than myself was amazing.

She had solved the hotel problem sure, but that wasn't the least of our issues. People by now must have been looking for us, murder and arson weren't just swept under the rug.

Well at least not for us, we were on the wrong side of the law for that. Considering what we'd been through these past couple of days, I didn't want to think about just how many crimes we were wanted for combined.

We needed to get to Azura as soon as possible, but it was 300 miles away. With public transport out of the question and my bike likely being tracked, it wasn't going to be easy.

Nothing was impossible, well not something as simple as travelling across the country.

This was such a banal problem but for the life of me I couldn't figure it out.

I went back over all the options, even the ruled out ones.

Public transport? No.

My bike? No.

Hitchhiking was an option but would it really be safe? Two girls hitchhiking, well one girl and me who constantly got mistaken for one; seemed like a recipe for disaster.

As much as being with her was nice, I wasn't sure I was willing to die with her.

There had to be something obvious I was missing.

"What are we doing?" From her tone, she was clearly bored with me standing around figuring things out.

"We need to get to Azura, but I don't know how." It was impossible to even look at her, admitting that I couldn't figure something out was shameful.

Hearing this gave her a familiar look in her eyes, without even uttering a word she dragged me down the street. I could have easily stopped her, but at this point her impulsive ideas were all we had.

Not only was it hopefully a solution, but not having to be in control made everything that happened on her head; Which was strangely comforting.

After being dragged for a few blocks, we ended up at a rundown house. The crumbling bricks and trashed front yard instilled such a sense of unease in me.

I almost felt sorry for the bad opinion of the hotel, this place was so much worse than that.

Places like this reminded me too much of my past, I had only met the worst of people in places like this. Well until I had met Allie that was, though was she all that bad really?

I hoped she knew what she was doing. There was nothing I could do except watch her knock loudly on the door before a chance to get any reassurance from her.

Her attempts being ignored only caused her to knock louder. It took a few minutes of this, but eventually there was the sounds of the door unlocking.

The door opened slowly, behind it was a blonde haired woman. By the looks of it she was at least quite a few years older than me.

I didn't want to jump to conclusions, but the way she stumbled made it look like she had been drinking. Which only made this situation even more dangerous.

Even though I attempted to stay out of the way, she still shot me a scowl. Which was quite unsettling as she had no idea who I was, nor did I know her.

Chapter 8

"Why on earth are you here? Why would I want to see you?" she yelled at Allie, though it wasn't surprising she would be angry. Allie had suddenly turned up on whoever this was's doorstep, presumably to ask a favour.

"Hey Laura," she replied smugly. She had that grin on her face. I was starting to love it, but in the moment it could be so frustrating.

It was best for me to play the role of observer, ready to pull her out of here when it went badly. When it came to Allie, it was always best to have a backup plan.

Especially with her uncanny ability to turn anything in the world to chaos.

"Again, why the fuck are you here" Laura yelled at her again, this time with even more fury.

"I need a favour." It was if she didn't notice the yelling, her smugness and that grin were unwavering.

"You really are insane if you think I'd help you." This time she started to close the door.

This only made Allie's smirk grow even bigger, as if this was exactly what she wanted. The few seconds of silence were nice, even if it was probably just the calm before the storm.

Knowing her like I did, this was likely just a dramatic pause intended to make the next part more impactful. She would never let an opportunity to increase the drama pass her by.

"Well Laura," her tone this time was uncharacteristically calm.

"Remember that night I stayed over? I passed out on whatever I took that night, we shared a bed. You see where I'm going with this right?" It was almost impressive how calm she was recounting such sketchy details.

The way she seemed to detach herself from all emotion whilst recounting events was something I envied.

"You're not actually saying... you wouldn't."

By now Laura had changed from anger to sheer panic, which was obvious the way she stumbled over her words.

"Well I remember waking up with you draped all over me, with your hands in let's just say very interesting places."

She still had no emotion in her voice, and her grin was replaced with an intense blank stare.

"Allie fuck off, you come over to your ex's house and make baseless claims? What the fuck is wrong with you?" Laura was now yelling louder than before.

It was impossible to stop watching as drama unfolded right before my eyes. The way Allie played this, was almost as if she was acting. The emotional detachment, the blank looks; if she was acting she wasn't very good at it.

Though it still made it hard to know who was telling the truth. One thing I did know, was that Allie was a master manipulator.

They continued their back and forth, as Laura got more and more agitated. Allie on the other hand was almost giggling at this point.

Would someone making these accusations really be laughing right now?

I couldn't help but doubt whether she was telling the truth, but we needed to get to Azura. She clearly had a plan, and I wasn't about to ruin our only chance out of here.

"Deny it all you want, maybe I'll go to the police." she said nonchalantly and turned to leave the yard.

That was a complete bluff, her even contacting the police would have been a huge risk. From the look on Laura's face and how panicked she looked, she wasn't aware of it.

Not only would Allie going to the police put her in danger, more importantly it would do the same to me.

It was impossible to figure out who was telling the truth. Laura could have either been panicking because she had been found out, or because Allie had charmed her into believing her version of events.

Either way, any second now Laura was about to cave; Allie always got her way.

"What do you want from me Allie?" By now Laura was crying.

"I can't go to prison, don't do this to me." Her crying grew more and more intense.

"Give us your car." Allie's tone was different again, the shift between emotionless and innocent girl voice was seamless; clearly she knew she was winning.

"Please Allie, anything but that. I need the car to go visit my kid." she pleaded.

"Oh. I guess police it is, Pixel." Mere seconds and she was back at her emotionless tone.

Did she really have to say my name? Why did she have to bring me into her manipulative games?

Watching was fun, but I wasn't sure I wanted to be involved. Something told me with being around her, I'd better get used to being dragged into drama.
"Fine just take it." She threw the keys at Allie, slamming the door behind her seconds later.

I bent over to pick up the keys, when I felt a hand firmly slap me on the ass. This whole ordeal had turned her on hadn't it?

Seeing her like this was weirdly attractive, particularly the way she could get just about anyone to do what she wanted. The way she knew just which buttons to push, meant she was probably even better at manipulation than I was.

The smugness on her face was amazing and made me slightly envious, she didn't feel anything bad about what she'd just done. If she did, she was good at hiding it.

With a smirk, I waved the keys in her face.

"I'll drive." I said knowing just how much that would bother her. Provoking her was fun, especially when she was approaching her hypersexual moods.

The way she would instantly take control after me pushing her, was something I craved. There was something about being treated like I was nothing to her that I needed.

My bait didn't work; I was going to have to up the ante. Moving closer to her, I swung my hand and slapped her hard across the face.

I knew what was about to come, and it was exactly what I wanted. Stood there just staring at her, she didn't do anything for a few seconds.

She always kept me guessing, this time instead of a punch or slap she shoved me hard to the ground.

"You're a fucking bitch," she said, towering over me.

Crouched down, right near my face she gave me the hardest slap I had ever felt in my life. My breathing was already heavy, but she didn't care. Her forearm pressed against my throat showed just how little regard she had for me.

Wanting to see just how far I could push her, I threw a few more slaps. Predictably, she reacted by pressing down on my windpipe even harder.

It didn't make sense why it was this enjoyable. After the first time, there was a real sense of it being what I deserved.

I would happily accept whatever she did to me. Even when she forced things, that was probably what I deserved too.

As the world faded to static, the pressure on my throat suddenly eased. As I gasped for my breath, she pulled me up toward her. Then forced such a hard kiss on me that I had no choice but to go along with it.

After we were both back on our feet, I felt a weird sensation on my lip. From the blood on my hand, it was obvious what she had done. She must have bitten me so hard it bust my lip, what a bitch.

As I looked at the car, which was our ticket out of here it hit me; she had the keys didn't she?

"Can't drive if you're oxygen deprived Pix." Her tone was obnoxiously smug,

While she had a point, it didn't make it any less frustrating. To say I was angry at her would have been an understatement.

The amount of trust I had in her was almost non-existent at the best of times. Trusting her to drive was something I wasn't comfortable doing.

But was there really much choice? My body was in a distracting amount of pain, and being angry wasn't the best mindset for driving.

The risk of either of us driving was probably about equal, so I might as well take a rare opportunity to rest. I would still be getting to Azura, which was productive in itself.

CHAPTER 9

After looking around for a while, taking in what could be my last steps in Circadia maybe ever; I sat my bruised body down in the front seat of Laura's trashed red car. Travelling 300 miles with Allie driving was a terrifying concept, and it worried me to no end.

Knowing how reckless and impulsive she was, there was a real chance this could result in my death. It wouldn't be a long shot to assume my death was going to involve her anyway. But today was hopefully not that day.

I needed to calm down, so I closed my eyes for just a moment.

Her slamming the car door startled me. As did the way she forcefully stepped right on the gas, after shoving the key into the ignition.

These things were not a good sign, the possibility of me getting some rest seemed slim. Forceful was just the way she did things. This was not going to be a pleasant journey was it?

Before she set off, I made extra sure to tighten my seatbelt.

Unsurprisingly her driving style was erratic, she changed lane every few seconds and never kept a constant speed. It quickly became apparent that getting any kind of rest was going to be impossible.

The speed wasn't all bad, something about her fast pace in both driving and life calmed me. Every moment spent with her was nice, despite the constant chaos and drama.

It probably said way more about me than I was ready to explore, but being with her was quickly becoming enjoyable.

When we eventually reached the motorway, she somehow increased her speed. I wasn't sure which was more impressive; her being able to control the car going this fast or the car not disintegrating into base elements at this speed.

Her being a competently reckless driver, was the epitome of her entire personality. Somehow she was able to cause such chaos, but never for a moment did it seem like she wasn't in control of everything.

The way she was being quiet and almost smiling; not that grin, but an actual genuine smile made me feel warm inside. Seeing her almost calm and relaxed was rare, but I was glad there was something that helped her feel that way.

Thanks to it being early, the traffic was light and we made good time.

This whole situation wasn't how I pictured my life with Allie, but I wouldn't change it for the world. Running away from my old life, in her ex-girlfriend's car wasn't something I ever thought would happen but here we were.

The important thing was us being together, just being next to her filled me with a sense of caring. It didn't make much sense and it was doubtful if she cared back; but I really wanted to protect her from the world.

I was helping her escape a murder she committed, anything else seemed inconsequential at this point.

Something was still bothering me though... Laura.

It still confused me why she agreed to give us the car. How much of Allie's story was a lie?

She was adamant it was the truth, but I knew her. I especially knew how good of a liar and how charming she could be, I had first hand experience of it.

It made me fearful, would she throw me under the bus when she needed something? What if she stopped seeing me as useful? Would she threaten my livelihood too?

The way she manipulated everyone was exciting, but I had lived under the assumption she'd always be on my side. The way she treated a former partner cast doubt over that.

There just had to be a way of getting some answers or at the very least reassurance from her. It was going to be tricky, phrasing it wrongly would no doubt send her spiralling.

"So Allie... about Laura..." I trailed off.

She took her eyes off the road for just long enough to shoot me the most contemptuous glare. Asking might have been crossing a line, but I really needed to know.

Deep down I knew my trust in her was completely misplaced. As much as I would rather be blissfully ignorant, I wouldn't have been able to live with the doubt.

She refused to even look at me, instead going back to focusing entirely on driving. This was the most quiet she'd been since I'd met her, and her smile was replaced with that blank stare.

I knew this couldn't mean anything good.

With no idea what to say to her, I slumped down in my seat and stared out of the window.

About half an hour of awkward silence passed, which was just long enough to start falling asleep.

Just as I started to drift off she spoke right up, which startled me.

"You don't believe me do you?" she turned, yelling right into my ear.

Being still drowsy, it took a few seconds to process what she said. Without even giving me a second to reply, she continued ranting.

"Fucking hell Pixel, taking the side of someone you just met over mine, That's shitty y'know." Her screeching was painful.

If anyone else was saying this, they would have a point. This was Allie though, who had a history of not only murder but lying to people's faces.

There was something different, this wasn't her usual rage. Usually it would be explosive and impulsive, but she didn't take her eyes off the road at all.

It was as if she was avoiding even looking at me, even when she yelled. For someone who thrived on people's reactions to her, they way she avoided even a quick glance was troubling.

I got the impression that asking about this really upset her. Which wasn't what I wanted at all, maybe asking about such a sensitive thing so soon was selfish.

As important as it was for me to know, it shouldn't come at the cost of her feelings.

I felt guilty, which made it clear I needed to fix this. We had never actually talked about anything.

The extent of our conversations was us saying that we hated each other, or me yelling at her for being impulsive.

Every time we had an issue, I'd either provoke her hypersexuality or desire to hurt me. Which made it easy to avoid having to talk about anything.

But as fun as that was, it was becoming increasingly doubtful that it was a sustainable pattern.

"Allie-cat I'm sorry. I just know you're manipulative." I tried to use my softest voice, which didn't seem to be working.

"I wouldn't lie about that you fucking asshole," she yelled.

The tears streaming down her face meant something was really wrong. This wasn't her usual yelling, her smirk and giggle were missing.

If there was ever a sign to trust her, this was it.

"Pull over here, we should talk." I told her, pointing at the layby beside us.

We really needed to talk. The way she did what I said without question, only further proved something was going on with her.

"Sorry Allie, I should trust you more. I just know you, I figured lying to an ex wouldn't be something you wouldn't do." I stumbled all over my words, apologizing was so difficult; especially when I still wasn't sure if I trusted her or not.

"Is that supposed to be a fucking apology?" she shouted, without even looking at me.

Being gentle and communicating had never come naturally to me, maybe it wasn't even worth trying. Getting out of the car was such an easier solution.

If anything proved she was better off without me, me being unable to apologize for not trusting her was as good a reason as any.

With my hand clutching on the door handle ready to leave, I felt her tightly holding my other hand.

"No wonder you don't have anyone." She sounded almost disappointed in me.

Her words hit me harder than anything she had physically done to me. They were harsh and blunt, bordering on spiteful.

But the worst part of all? She was right, she was completely right.

For the majority of my life, I'd known just how inconvenient and unreliable other people were. Then at the first sign of trouble, I ran. We were both running from our problems, how could she judge me for that? It was just what I did.

"I don't want anyone!" I yelled back at her, as I struggled to pull my hand from her grasp.

Even though I didn't really believe that, it was best for both of us that I kept up that facade. Letting her know I wanted or needed her would have only given her more leverage over me.

The knowing expression on her face told me she wasn't buying it. She'd only known me, or known as much as I wanted her to, for a couple of weeks.

Maybe I was just that easy to read, or it was a sign of a deeper connection.

Nothing happened for a few moments, other than her staring at almost expectantly. Talking to her wasn't something I could do, opening up to anyone was uncomfortable.

The staring continued for a while, I tried pulling my hand away which only caused her to tighten her grip.

It was only a matter of time until I caved in and talked, and from the look on her face? She knew it too.

As much I wanted to avoid it, it started to feel like I had no choice. Begrudgingly I started to piece together what I wanted to say, despite running away still being the easier solution.

The deeper into my thoughts I got, more and more of the anger I had buried deep down boiled inside me. Inevitably it all exploded out.

"It's not fucking easy being me Allie. I'm not conventionally pretty, like hell I don't even like being called a girl. Nobody ever understands me and those that do? They all use it to screw me over at every opportunity. You're like everyone else, it's a matter of time before you screw up my life too.

I'm better off alone, I just don't trust you." I barely breathed between words, as the vitriol rushed out of my mouth.

Confusingly, after my outburst she let go of my hand. As if this alone wasn't confusing enough, she had that grin on her face again.

With me actually opening up to her, she must have realized I did somewhat trust her. Though whether her knowing this or not was a good thing, I had no idea.

A lifetime of being called and treated like the "weird girl" had taken its toll. The ability to trust anyone was all but shattered. While was good for my job, it all but prevented me from making any deeper connections.

It was lonely.

"First of all, I never said it was easy being you. Do you think it's easy being me? People can't deal with me because I'm "insane". Sure I'm fun and exciting for a while but it gets too chaotic and they just run. So go ahead, be like everyone else, run away from me." She sounded almost upset as she vented her frustrations at me.

It was hard enough for me to see things from other people's perspective, but I had never tried to see things from hers. It was easier to just assume she didn't care about anyone, which had the benefit of it not being personal when she acted uncaring towards me.

Everything being fleeting in her life wasn't exactly a revelation, though it never crossed my mind that it might not be all her own fault. She didn't exactly fit the mould of what most people would want in a partner.

Running away now would be unfair, I needed to prove I was better than everyone else. Plus, being with her could be somewhat fun.

Me and her, were completely different in all but one way. We didn't have anyone else; all we had was each other.

Most of the time I could deal with her, I might even go as far as saying that her chaotic nature was enjoyable.

"Allie, I'm sorry. I didn't think about how you felt, I just presumed everything was easy." Apologizing didn't come naturally to me at all but it needed to be done.

Another awkward silence passed between us, this time with her looking genuinely confused.

"I don't want to run away. I like... love your chaos, it's the most fun I've ever had." I continued.

"You're a jackass Pix." she said, slapping me hard across the face while doing so. It was nice seeing her getting back to her usual self.

"Laura drugged me when I was a teenager, and the rest was real," she nonchalantly mentioned.

It was weird how she could share all these things that would probably traumatise anyone else, just like recounting facts.

Maybe there was something to that, but not wanting to ruin our first conversation I let it go.

Without even chance to sit back into my seat, we were already speeding down the motorway toward Azura. It was nice seeing how comfortable driving made her; even with the constant fear of being in a car wreck.

After managing to have a conversation for once, I felt closer to her on an emotional level than ever. Which made it hard to not stare at her adoringly, as she concentrated on swerving to avoid hitting anything at the last second.

She applied the brakes just in time to avoid smashing into the back of a truck, when she noticed me staring at her.

"What?" she sounded defensive.

"I know you're trying to kill me" I said, attempting to come across teasingly.

"I need someone to shove around and be rough with, you can live for now,'" she replied, with her fist extended toward my face, with that all too familiar grin. If she wasn't driving I knew what she'd be doing, and oh how I craved it.

"Aw it's such a shame you're driving right now isn't it," I said, which I just knew would bother her.

A while passed without any reaction which was weird. Maybe she was saving it for later.

This complacency was quickly interrupted, by her taking one of her hands from the wheel and grabbing me by the throat. It was so quick that there was barely a chance to react, not that I wanted to stop her anyway.

Being treated like this was something I needed.

"You're such a bitch, do you want me to crash the car? I fucking would Pixel, I don't care." She screeched, as she let go of her grip on my throat.

Provoking this reaction from her was exciting, especially knowing what it would entail later. The feeling of her hitting me as hard as she could, when she was lost in that moment of not caring about me at all was something I craved.

Relinquishing all control and putting myself at her mercy was such a thrill, the unpredictability of it all only added to the fun.

After the excitement, soon enough she was once again focused on driving. Her being back to her normal and emotionally charged self, was somehow calming to me.

Her being emotional and open was strange, things being normal and routine helped me calm down immensely. Not that anything with Allie was normal. Staring at her focused face, I felt myself drifting off to sleep.

Chapter 10

The first thing I saw when my eyes opened was the darkness. It took a few moments but once the post nap haze faded, I noticed the car wasn't moving.

With the sound of waves crashing right beside the door, it was clear we had made it to Azura.

Allie was passed out on the steering wheel, which surprised me; I almost expected her to excitedly wake me up when we arrived, but she hadn't.

Her gently sleeping beside me was surreal, it was a stark contrast to when she was awake. The monstrous amounts of energy she usually had seemed to require hours of rest to recharge.

Even though it made complete sense, seeing her like this was strange. She was uncharacteristically vulnerable in this state, and no matter how many times I had seen her sleeping it was no less surreal.

Awake she was a creature who thrived on chaos. One that almost prided herself on being strong and not needing anyone, seeing her this soft and vulnerable was so far removed from all that; so far removed from her usual self, that if I didn't know her I would never believe such a soft girl was capable of everything she'd done.

She looked so peaceful, it was impossible for me to do anything but watch her sleep for a while. A warmness flooded over me as I gazed over at her cute face, listening to the tiny little noises she made as she breathed in and out.

Despite all of her flaws, there was something about her. Something that made me feel like I never had before.

Even after everything she'd done and the amount of trouble being around her usually was; it was impossible for me to not feel the way I did.

As much as I didn't want to acknowledge it, and honestly it would have made everything easier if i didn't; I loved her.

It made no sense at all, but that was how I felt. Not that admitting it to her would ever be a good idea, even just thinking it and admitting it to myself caused such discomfort.

I must have spent at least five minutes admiring her vulnerability, when I decided to reach over and gently pet her pink hair.

Despite the obvious dyeing, it was in amazingly soft condition. As I enjoyed the sensation of her soft hair on my fingertips, I caused her to stir and slowly wake up.

"Why are you staring at me like that?" she barely managed to say between yawns.

She seemed genuinely confused by this situation, which caused me to quickly pull my hand away from her as subtly as possible. Judging from her expression, I wasn't subtle enough.

We stared at each other awkwardly for several minutes, though with every passing moment I could feel the awkwardness begin to fade.

If it were anyone else in the world staring at each other like this; I would have been easily convinced they were in love. But this was us. This was me and Allie, we weren't like everyone else.

At least in my case, I didn't "do" love. All it was, was a pointless and inconvenient feeling. Maybe just maybe if I kept denying how I felt, logic would kick in and those feelings would go away.

If Allie had any sense at all, she'd agree with my reasoning.

Confusingly, she continued to stare at me for even longer than I could focus. The waves crashing outside my window instead grabbed my attention.

It was amazing that she managed to get us here safely, maybe I did need to trust her more. Sure she could be incredibly selfish and self-centred, but every so often there were glimmers of her caring about me.

Maybe driving me here and finding a place for us to stay last night were her ways of caring. Not everyone showed they cared in the same way that I did, though understanding what hers were seemed complicated.

"Thanks Allie-cat, you did great getting us here," I told her, as I gently petted her hair again.

"It's fine." she quickly snapped back at me, it seemed the calm and peacefully tired Allie was gone now.

With the tender sweet moment now being over, it was time to start heading toward our new place.

I didn't actually know Laura, and based on what Allie told me could I really trust her to not track the car?

With everything we'd been through, having a car that could so easily be claimed as stolen parked outside our new place would be a bad idea. Keeping it nearby just in case was the best option.

With the bag from the trunk in hand, I wandered slightly toward the sea. This was one of the few places that I had childhood memories from.

Not all of them were good, like everywhere I went for a second time it was tainted with bad memories.

Thankfully, my brain had a way of shutting them away from my consciousness; all I really remembered about the beach was my parents yelling at me for wandering off with a strange older boy.

Staring out at the ocean was a great distraction from bad memories, something about the chaotic nature of the waves always calmed me.

Even though I wanted everything in my life to be planned out meticulously, something about the chaotic and unpredictable always drew me in.

This was never more evident than when I thought about Allie, who had by this point joined me in leaning over the railings staring out at the ocean.

Perhaps she was all the proof I needed that on some level I loved chaos. She was the most fun person I had ever been around, she made everything enjoyable in her own screwed up insane ways.

The way she grabbed my hand and held it tight proved this. From any other person I'd interpret this as an affectionate gesture, but her motives were always confusing. Affectionate gestures weren't exactly what I expected from her.

We continued leaning over the railings, staring down at the beach below with our hands still interlocked. An urge came over me, if it was okay for her to show affection it had to be okay for me too.

I pulled her toward me. As her head rested on my shoulder, I leaned over and gently kissed her on the forehead.

Her reaction was confusing, especially as she had just initiated affection. She looked red in the face as she pulled away from me.

"What the fuck? Why would you..." she mumbled, clearly flustered by what I just did.

Maybe being affectionate like that crossed a line, but I was just following her lead. Why was a soft forehead kiss so much worse than her grasping my hand tightly?

Any attempts at understanding her would be in vain, an apology would be easier than that.

"Sorry," I told her, not exactly sure what I'd done wrong.

It would have been better if I had just left her alone. As I turned to start walking away from her, she started to talk.

"Oh for fuck's sake, abandoning me again? You give up on everything don't you? You're a selfish asshole Pixel you know that?" she yelled.

How could she call me selfish? Her; Allie the most self-centred person I had ever met, calling me selfish was the most audacious thing.

Either she completely lacked self awareness, or she knew the hypocrisy of it and how it would frustrate me. Knowing her, either option was just as likely as the other.

I glossed over the selfish comment for a second, she had a point about me giving up too quickly. There was a trend in my life that any sign of trouble caused me to flee from anyone or anything.

Though it wasn't my fault that people were confusing and hard to deal with. Especially her.

"You literally just pulled away from me," I shouted back at her.

Why was me walking away not allowed, but her recoiling away from my affection was perfectly fine?

The only difference seemed to be that me leaving her left her with a lack of attention. That or she had to always be the one in control, which was tiring at times.

"I didn't know what you were doing. Why the hell would you even do that?" she yelled, but by now she sounded more confused than angry.

She was making a forehead kiss seem like it was the worst thing in the world. Granted it sort of went against the type of relationship we'd had thus far, but so did her holding my hand and the emotional conversations we had.

What did she even want from me? All this drama that she seemed to conjure out of nowhere, coupled with her sheer trouble and unpredictability was a lot to handle.

I loved her, but at times like this I had to wonder if she was worth the effort.

"All I did was kiss you Allie. Are you that messed up that a kiss is the worst thing in the world, but you can have sex with me when I don't want it? Are you actually that fucked up Allie?" Yelling at her was never appealing, but I was too frustrated to hold back.

"Sex is meaningless, it's just fun." she stated, as if stating a commonly known fact.

Ignoring for a moment the fact that this probably meant she only wanted me for fun; The entire concept of having sex just because it was fun, was so bizarre.

To me, sex was something that only felt mildly comfortable with someone I connected with on a deeper level. The idea of sex with anyone other than a partner or potential partner felt really disgusting.

Unable to comprehend her point of view, I let it go.

Perhaps it wasn't the kiss itself that made her uncomfortable, it was the impression that it meant something.

It did mean something, we were together which also meant something. At least it meant something to me, as usual getting a read on her was impossible.

"It not feeling meaningless was the problem, wasn't it?"

"Yeah," she said, in an incredibly passive tone. She wouldn't even look at me, her gaze was firmly locked down at her feet.

"You held my hand first though" I asked, not buying into her cute innocent facade.

She wouldn't talk to me, and still refused to look at me. I might have been too harsh with her, even though it was just a kiss.

She'd done way worse to me, essentially manipulating me into everything.

Was it really that bad if I kissed her when she didn't want it? Or realistically if I did anything that she didn't want me to?

She set this precedent; doing whatever she found fun without regard for anyone else. If fun was the only thing that mattered; maybe I'd have to play her games.

A few minutes of quiet passed, when I noticed her crying. I didn't like her much right now, but I still cared about her. Her being upset at something felt like the perfect opportunity to start doing things her way.

Forcefully, I pulled her by the hair into a deep kiss. Not that it mattered, but from the way she kissed back it was clear she enjoyed it.

We enjoyed the sensation of passionately kissing for several minutes, which seemed to fade some of the anger and tension.

Soft gentle signs of affection didn't seem like our thing, we weren't like most other people in this world.

Maybe we just had our own messed up rough ways of showing love.

Maybe the manipulation and drama baiting was love. Maybe her hitting me and enjoying every second was love.

Maybe me threatening to leave her all the time was love. Maybe her having sex with me when I didn't want it was love.

I had no idea what love actually was, but whatever me and Allie had it was fun.

"I'm sorry okay? I had no idea what I'd actually done wrong," I apologized.

"It was just different, it felt like it meant something more than just fun. Holding your hand was comforting, but with the way you've been looking at me everything felt more than that." Thankfully by now, she had calmed down a bit and was talking almost normally.

There was a deeper meaning than just fun. Only the other day she told me that she loved me; which at least to me symbolized this was more than just fun.

It felt like the right time to say it back.

"It did mean something more than that, Allie I love..."

"Don't say what I think you're going to say," she interrupted.

Was I messing up again? It made no sense that telling her I loved her was so wrong.

Her being adamantly against me saying it only made me want to say it more, she clearly knew what I was about to say.

She was confusing, but like any new security protocol there was something enticing about figuring her out. The way her brain worked and all the games she played fascinated me.

From the way we were both shivering, it was clear we had been out here way too long.

Despite her best efforts to move away, I grabbed her by the hand.

We had to go check out our new place, the first space that was really ours. The last apartment was mine and she was just a guest. This though, this was for both of us. I was about to live with Allie.

It was confusing, moving in together was fine but affection was crossing some unspoken boundary. There was something she wasn't telling me, if it was all about meaning then surely moving in together meant more than a kiss?

She really was the most contradictory person.

Our new apartment was only a few blocks away, being this close to the ocean was nice even with the memories it stirred up.

Naturally we were going to be living on the top floor, as for whatever reason it gave me an air of superiority.

I stood frozen in place for a few seconds.

There had to be a reason I'd stayed away from here for the majority of my life, I desperately hoped coming back here wasn't a mistake.

We didn't have much choice though, there was nowhere else for us to go. This was it, the only place with any relative amount of safety. The only thing I could do was try to swallow down my apprehensions, being even more worried was only going to make things even worse.

The only thing I could do was climb the staircase and retrieve our keys from the lockbox that should be sitting outside the door. I was thankful that the code was easy to remember, it was something that everyone should know; 34 squared.

Without letting myself time to overthink, I rushed from the lobby over to the door where sure enough there was a tiny lockbox with a keypad. After entering the code, opening the box and retrieving the keys, the only thing left to do was and that was to open the door to our new place.

With the key in the slot, a flood of feelings overcame me. Once I opened that door and crossed into the apartment I was going to be living with her, it would be too late to turn back.

CHAPTER 11

Everything inside me screamed to turn around and run; the level of commitment this needed wasn't something I had considered until now.

Was I ready to live with Allie?

She was my partner, who admittedly didn't seem like she wanted to be treated like one. Even though I couldn't tell her I loved her, this all had to mean something to her right?

The living room beyond the door was enormous. Even if I wasn't ready for this, there seemed to be enough space for me to avoid having to be around her constantly. Whether or not she would actually leave me alone, was a different matter entirely.

Whilst I stood by the door in my trepidation, she was excitedly screaming being her usual self.

Saving her and giving her somewhere safe to stay made me feel important, no matter how she felt about me. Her excitement showed just how much good I was doing for her, and it felt great.

Caring for her and supporting her gave me a sense of having some power. She had her dramatic spontaneity and amoral edge, but deep down I knew she needed me.

The way she rejected my affection earlier still hurt, and I felt as if I needed to justify keeping her around.

As she ran around the various rooms exploring the apartment, I walked slowly toward the balcony.

The tumultuous ocean outside the window was the most fitting of scenes. There wasn't much that better summed up our entire relationship; She was the ocean, unpredictable and not really conscious about what her vicious waves destroyed.

All she was doing was being the only way she knew.

I was different, sure sometimes I was the beach that her waves crashed over. But there was too much passivity to that metaphor, every play I made even in passivity was calculated.

She was so easy to manipulate into doing what I wanted, instead of impulsivity I had logic.

If she was the ocean, then I was more like a polluting oil company. She caused the noticeable destruction, but I was behind the scenes fuelling the process.

Inevitably we were both damaging each other, but from the way things were going neither of us cared. She had her oblivious seeming lack of empathy and I had my calculated one, we were both sides of the same coin.

Me and her were a disaster waiting to happen. In this world though it's hurt or be hurt, and we each seemed to have a good balance of both. More importantly, our dynamic was exciting.

My introspection was quickly interrupted, when I felt something cold and plastic-like tighten around my neck. As I struggled slightly, it quickly became obvious what was happening.

"Don't think I forgot about how you were in the car," she whispered into my ear, as the tightness around my neck increased.

To any normal person this probably would have been terrifying, but I wasn't any normal person. Nothing made me feel more alive than Allie doing whatever she wanted to me.

Everything became a blur, as everything faded to static; something was different this time, she let go of her grip.

Usually she would have choked me to the point of passing out; this time though she stopped, dropping the USB cable to the floor.

"What's wrong?" I turned to look at her, tears were streaming down her face.

"Why would you try saying that earlier? How could you?" she cried.

This was about the love thing again wasn't it? The fact she bought it up again, only confused me even more.

All i wanted to do was tell her how I felt, but apparently that was the worst thing in the world. Especially when she had said the same thing to me just days ago.

Believing her may have been a mistake, but I genuinely thought she loved me back. It felt uncomfortable when she said it at first, but I'd come to accept it.

Right after we'd moved in together was the worst timing for deciding she was against this.

This wasn't fair to me at all, was she just using me like she probably used everyone else? Even Laura?

"What did I do wrong this time?" I asked, this time I was angry; I put myself out there for the first time in our relationship and she shot me down.

"You don't L- me, you couldn't. Nobody ever does. It's just a lie people tell me to manipulate me."

The amount she was projecting was ridiculous. It was a tender moment between two people that I thought cared about each other, it wasn't on impulse like when she said it.

I felt ridiculous for trusting her, she played me. She completely got the better of me, as if someone like her was even capable of loving anyone other than herself.

As well as the projection, she obviously didn't trust me. After everything I had done for her, it hurt.

Why would I help her escape from what she did if I didn't have her best interests, or at least what I thought was best for her, at heart.

"You don't trust me do you?" I questioned her, even though I doubted she would even answer.

As I figured, she wouldn't even look at me. Earlier today had told me this meant at least in her mind, that I'd done something wrong

The silent avoiding went on for several minutes, when eventually the empty air started to frustrate me.

"Allie please talk to me," I pleaded with her, hoping that she would say something and give some clue about what was going on.

She turned around to give me a glance, her look was one of pure contempt. This was a different kind of anger to the one I usually enjoyed, in this moment she hated me more than anything else; all because I loved her.

Shouting at her wasn't helping, she was more likely to open up if I was calm. With my eyes closed I caught my breath, ready to try again.

"Allie what's wrong?" I asked, in a calmer manner this time.

Her contemptuous look was replaced with her normal expression. As she wandered over to me, I had no idea what she was about to do.

Confusingly, she gently hugged me; as frustrated as I was at her being a complete contradiction, I hugged her back.

"I know you probably meant what you were going to say. But I don't think anyone can really love me." she told me quite sombrely.

That would have made sense, except our situation was different. Anyone might not have been able to love her, but I wasn't just anyone. Obviously she needed me to prove that to her.

"I bought a new place so we could be together, doesn't that show I care? I meant what I was going to say about you." I told her, if I didn't love her I wouldn't have gone through all this effort just to keep her safe.

Even just the implication of me loving her was enough to make her flinch and cower a little.

It was obvious now that someone must have either used love as a justification for abuse, or someone had betrayed her trust with love before. It was going to take a lot of work, but I knew I could make her accept it.

"I know you think you do, but it makes me uncomfortable."

At least she was admitting her actual feelings to me at this point, even if they still hurt.

"So many people in the past have said that, and they all ended up leaving me. Sometimes I doubt if L- it even exists at all."

Knowing that someone had hurt her like this, made me want to hug her even more tightly.

It wasn't really her fault she was like this, more than anything I wanted to hurt whoever hurt her.

"That stuff is so confusing too. I'm not even sure I'm able to love like everyone else can anyway." She was visibly disgusted by even the mention of the word.

In a weird sort of way, I could relate to how she was feeling. Her and love weren't dissimilar to the way me and sex were; they were seen as normal human experiences but something about the concept made us uncomfortable.

Especially the way she mentioned not experiencing it like everyone else, when it came to sex I couldn't really see what the big deal was. The way the whole world centred around it was something really confusing, and romance seemed to be framed in the same way.

Part of me envied her, it must be great to be free of the constraints of romantic love. Secretly I wanted to be more like her.

At this point she wandered away from me looking quite sad. I knew sharing personal things could be draining so I understood this response.

Even though I had slept most of the journey, I was still tired. Today had been an emotionally draining day, even with a lack of furniture sleeping wouldn't be an issue; I was just that tired.

The fireplace we had was quite substantial, sleeping in front of it seemed like the perfect idea. It was close by and would keep me warm, plus I didn't have the energy to move anywhere else.

As usual, when the lights were out and I was trying to sleep; my mind started wandering. Like always at the moment, my thoughts were centred around her.

We'd never fought like this before, what was happening to us?

Everything used to be chaotic fun, but at the moment it felt like anything but that.

For the past few weeks she'd been by my side almost constantly, now though she was somewhere else. She was still in our home, but her being this distant was worrying.

Then there was the confusing ordeal that was her not letting me show affection or tell her that I loved her.

It might have made her uncomfortable; but if I was willing to let her have sex with me, letting me be romantic with her was the least she could do.

Being awake and thinking about something other than work or myself was new, I couldn't stop thinking about her. The heating wasn't on, so presumably she was freezing cold somewhere in this empty apartment.

That's all it really was, as much as I tried to convince myself, it didn't feel like a home.

Making this place feel homelier could only help. I hoped having somewhere that felt like it was actually ours would help our relationship.

I wanted nothing more than to go back to normal, the fun and excitement of being with her. She seemed happiest then, and I was the closest to happy I'd ever been.

At this rate sleep was never going to happen, constantly worrying about her was going to keep me awake all night. I cared about her, nothing was going to change that. Wondering where she could be, I dragged my fatigued body across the living room.

She wasn't in the living room any more, but across the way I noticed a shadow in her bedroom. It wasn't usual for her to be by herself for this long and her silence was particularly unusual.

I could count on one hand the amount of times I'd experienced Allie being completely silent, and by the way the shadow in her room was sitting and almost rocking, it was clear that she wasn't sleeping.

Logic told me it was best to leave her alone in times like this, but I would be unable to calm my worries if I did so.

So despite my better judgement, I entered her bedroom; well room, I was almost certain that to be called a bedroom a room had to actually contain a bed.

"Allie? What's wrong?" I asked, as I slowly approached her.

There was something different about her, this silence was different; and as always different was almost always bad. None of the usual Allie traits were present; She was silent but there was no sign of angry expressions on her face, and instead of moving around erratically she was almost frozen in place with a slight swaying motion.

"Allie?" I called out to her once again, with once again no response.

This was a strange and somewhat distressing situation, one that I had no idea how to handle. On the one hand, I was worried about her; but at the same time I had to respect her right to personal space, even if she rarely appreciated my need for the same thing.

With that in mind, I headed back into the living room.

"I'm here if you need anything." I told her on my way out, even though I had no idea if she was hearing a word I said. She appeared to be weirdly out of it and not acknowledging anything going on around her.

Even though I was worried about her, I knew deep down that it was probably better for me to at least try getting some rest; at least then I could be better prepared for whatever curveball she was going to throw at me tomorrow.

***

Thankfully it seemed that I was so physically exhausted that not even my worries could keep me awake last night. I didn't feel very rested, despite the fact judging from the sun already setting outside my window it was already late evening.

After getting up and wandering around our apartment for a while, I figured it was time that I want to check on Allie again; she couldn't have possibly been awake all night, or even sat in the same position for that long. If I knew anything about Allie it's that despite her stubbornness, she was still incredibly susceptible to giving up on whatever game she was playing due to boredom.

To my surprise, I found her still sitting there with the same blank stare on her face that she had last night.

I wasn't really sure what she was doing or what she was hoping to accomplish, but I had to give her credit for being committed to it. If it was anything like last night, I knew she wouldn't even respond to me talking to her; though it was possible that if I upped the ante or provoked her, she'd have no choice but react.

After yesterday I knew just the thing that would get her dander up,

"Allie I I..." I began to say, but there was no reaction. Usually there would be some sign of discomfort, but not this time; just the same blank stare she had for however long it had been at this point. Provoking her wasn't as much fun when she refused to even acknowledge it; she might have carried on in the same situation, but I was starting to worry about her.

After all, it might be nice to have some silence with her around for once. There were a few things that I needed to sort out, things that would be infinitely easier without her noisy distractions going on around me. Even with my worry, a huge part of me was still convinced she was playing some sort of game; I was sure she'd come interrupt me as soon as I started to actually do something.

First on my list of tasks was to find an easy WiFi connection to use, as we didn't actually have our own right now. It wasn't going to be ideal, as I wouldn't have access to configuration settings of someone else's router without attracting suspicion but the important thing would be having the internet.

So much of my life revolved around the internet, that when I couldn't access it I actually felt ashamed sometimes; but it was what it was.

Rather unsurprisingly it was relatively easy to find an open WiFi connection, which was quite saddening; there was no challenge in using a connection that people refused to secure.

I had an idea though, instead of leaving this connection unsecured I would enable the encryption remotely; because it was best for everyone.

They probably had their reasons for leaving it unsecured; convenience, compatibility or just plain ignorance but I needed a secured network for work, so I enabled the passkey system, which was simple but better than nothing.

It wasn't a long term solution, but it would probably buy me at least a couple of days on a secure connection with no links to myself.

After spending about 15 minutes on fixing the internet connection, I was once again out of things to do. Usually I would work to distract myself, but today I was too emotionally charged which made the usual social interaction involved with working so much harder.

I never thought it was something I'd want, but I was hoping for Allie to burst out of her room and cause some sort of drama; but there was still nothing.

There was something different with me too, I found myself once again considering going out just to escape the atmosphere in our apartment. Something weird was going on and staying here was just going to frustrate me even more, which would probably just make whatever was going on with Allie even worse too.

It was probably best for both of us that I went out for a while, even if I had apprehensions about being out in Azura by myself; but I lived here now it was something I was going to have to get used to.

Once I had my jacket and the keys, I headed out of the apartment door and rushed out of the building. It was once again nice to be away from Allie, being around her constantly wasn't something that was easy to deal with; and I was sure she'd appreciate some time away from me as well.

Finding myself once again on the streets of Azura filled me with quite a strange feeling, I still wasn't quite used to the fact that I was here again.

I couldn't quite muster the courage to head much deeper into the city than me and Allie had been the previous day, there were still many hazy and unsettling memories associated with this place; as well as the slight bit of childish joy that I remembered.

Something had kept me away from even visiting here for so long, but for whatever reason I was drawn back. As I wandered back towards where we had left Laura's car, I turned to gaze out at the sea; the same sea backdrop that was the site of our latest argument.

I still wasn't quite sure what was going on with Allie lately, but I still clung onto the hope that it would all explode out of her and our place would once again be flooded with her emotional drama.

I spent what must have been at least half an hour staring out at the sun setting over the horizon, before I found myself once again in the twilight. Azura with glimmers of sunlight remaining was one thing, but I was in no way ready to yet face it in the darkness of night.

Night time whilst comforting did have a tendency to bring out the more sinister sides of places, and admittedly myself too; after all I did usually work at night, though that was almost always in the safety of my own place.

Feeling the chill in the air, and the impending darkness I decided to head back to our place in hopes of Allie actually talking to me now.

After almost jogging for the majority of the way back, and surprisingly not tripping whilst going up the stairs I was once again at the door to our place. The one barrier that was separating the outside would which was currently Allie-less to the one in there which at a moment's notice could become a chaotic mess.

As I headed in, I noticed light from the bathroom escaping under the closed door. This filled me with a slight relief, it had to have been Allie; and that meant she had actually moved from where she was sat all night. It was surely only a matter of time before she told me what was wrong.

Minutes passed and passed and there was no sign of her coming out from the bathroom. It was possible she was just using the bathroom, though must have been in there an awful long time.

Either way, it was probably best that I went to check on her.

"Allie are you in there?" I called out, even though it couldn't have realistically been anyone else. Her lack of reply only added to my concern, even if she was just still ignoring me; it was a bad sign.

When I opened the door, the scene was worse than I could have ever imagined.

CHAPTER 12

"Allie what the fuck? What the hell have you done?" I screamed in panic.

In front of me she was sitting on the floor in a pool of her own blood.

You better not be dead, Allie don't you dare be dead.

When I got closer to her, thankfully I could see her chest moving. The fact she was still breathing was a relief; I'd never admit it to her, but I needed her.

In a short amount of time she had changed my whole life; So much so that living without her didn't really seem worth it any more.

"Allie? Allie?" I repeatedly called her name, this time in a calmer voice. She had to be okay, I needed her to be. I'd literally have done anything to make sure she was okay.

"Pix..." she trailed off with slurred speech.

This worried me and I had no idea what she'd done to herself. All I knew was I wasn't supposed to move her, at risk of making her injuries worse.

Calling an ambulance could have put us in even more danger. Not only were there often police around hospitals, I probably couldn't trust her not to tell people what she did just for the attention.

Logic was failing me, spontaneous crisis decisions weren't logic based and it was difficult to figure out what to do.

She was the spontaneous one, she always had the quick fix ideas. This couldn't be happening, I needed her to be okay.

In my panic, worries started to creep in. Was this my fault? Had she done this because of my insistence on saying that I loved her?

I didn't usually care about how anyone else felt, but this whole situation was unusual.

It was almost as if I could feel her pain, both physical and emotional. This wasn't guilt I was feeling, it was almost as if her pain was mine. As much as this confused me I decided to ignore it for the moment, Allie's health was more important.

Even if it wasn't my fault, I felt a sense of disappointment; not in Allie but in myself. I was Pixel, almost the entirety of my value in this world came from being able to pick up patterns and fix things.

But when faced with evidence of something being wrong, which in this case was my own partner bordering on catatonia or some sort of trance like state, I had failed to use logic. I was unsure what was happening to me, it did feel like me to be this careless.

I turned her towards me, which let me see where the blood was coming from. Above her left eyebrow there was a wound. On the wall she'd been slumped against, there was a blood stain.

There was no time to question her about why she'd been hitting her head against the wall. Especially hitting it hard enough to cut herself open. Something needed to be done, though I hoped it was just a superficial wound.

"Do you know who I am?" I asked, hoping for proof she wasn't seriously hurt.

"You're Pixel," she slurred in reply.

To say I was relieved would have been an understatement, she was alive and replying. If there was any sign that she was going to be fine, this was what I needed.

With nothing else to clean her wound, my sleeve would have to do for now.

I helped her back to her feet and attempted to lead her back into the warmth of the living room.

A few steps later, it was clear this wasn't going to happen. With every couple of steps she almost collapsed back onto the floor. Using the last of my energy, I picked her up.

As quickly as I possibly could, I carried her and placed her down beside the fire.

As she was safe now, I could finally rest. Curled up next to her I started to drift off, hoping she was doing the same.

I managed about an hour of sleep, before I awoke to something feeling very wrong. Allie was turned onto her side, this wasn't what had me worried. It was the pool of vomit she was lying in, luckily the remnants of it made it easy to see that she was still breathing.

Though if I didn't do something, she might not have been breathing for much longer. What the hell was I supposed to do?

This was a serious situation, if I didn't figure something out quickly she could very likely be dead soon.

Why had I brought her with me? Her chaos was usually fun, but this wasn't at all.

My usual solutions, running away, logic and planning weren't helping. I needed to come up with something, it was literally life and death.

What the hell was she thinking doing something like this?

The answer was that she probably wasn't thinking at all. Something was going on with her, the distance and the hurting herself; this wasn't the usual Allie.

She'd make everyone else's life hell, she would hurt whoever she felt like; but she always cared or seemed to care about herself.

Moments of her being open were so few and far between, it was likely she'd never tell me what was going on.

Was she really worth all this trouble? If I ran away now, there'd be no consequences for me.

She'd probably die, and I could just run off some place else and start over. No connections, no attachments, just Pixel going back to her stable usual life.

I tried to convince myself I'd be fine, but deep down I knew I wouldn't. As illogical as it was, losing her wouldn't be good for me.

She was hell to be around at times, but there was something about her that I needed.

If I left her, I'd lose one of the only people I'd ever loved. I desperately wanted to believe I'd be fine on my own, but it was a lie. If I left her to die here, I'd have nothing. As nonsensical and dysfunctional as it was being with her, being alone was worse.

Even if she didn't want me to love her, I was going to anyway. She would have to accept it eventually, whether she wanted to or not. Saving her life was a way in, it almost guaranteed that I deserved to love her.

Now that I'd made my choice to save her, it was just a matter of figuring out how. Even though I still had no idea why she'd done this.

She probably wouldn't even appreciate it anyway, at the very least it would give me some leverage over her. With her being as manipulative as she was, that was always useful.

The hospital was the only solution, even with the risk that came with going there. Someone had photos of us, and her hair was distinctive; not many people had hair that pink.

There was a real possibility that whoever sent me the pictures, had also sent them to the police. Though, with what I knew about those types of people, it was just as likely they would use them to blackmail me instead.

I had to trust my logic, whatever situation arose at least I'd be saving her.

What other choice did I have? My partner was lying in an increasing pool of her own blood and vomit.

I had to take the risk. Judging from how panicked I was earlier, her death wouldn't be something I'd be able to handle.

With my phone in hand about to call the ambulance, I felt a slight trepidation. There was a real chance that my phone was being tracked. Was I sure she was worth risking my entire life and livelihood for?

The door was right there, it would have been so easy for me to just run. My life would be the same as it was in the past, admittedly boring but also safer than this. Would anyone other than me really miss Allie? I'd miss her forever but was she worth all this?

Her broken body was lying there on the floor blood and vomit soaked. She had nobody else in this world, and neither did I.

All we had was each other, leaving her here would leave me lonely again. Maybe all we could have in this life was each other. Being together was all either of us had, and we needed to cling onto that as long as we could.

After deciding to make the call, I lied my way through until the point where I had to describe what was wrong. Lying was easy, describing her state and what she'd done to herself wasn't at all.

"My partner had a breakdown and I found her passed out from hitting her head against the wall. She's still bleeding and vomiting in the living room."

Apparently, the situation was serious enough to warrant an ambulance being sent out right away. As grateful as I was that she was getting help, the urgency didn't do much to help my nerves.

Seeing her like this was awful. It really made me wonder, what awful things she could have gone through in her life to make her like this. It really wasn't her fault she was this way.

CHAPTER 13

A few minutes passed with me sitting next to her stroking her hair. She wasn't aware enough to be comforted by this, it was purely for my own sake; being near her and feeling the softness of her hair comforted me.

The tender moment was interrupted with a knock on the door.

After answering it, I wandered over to the window. I couldn't watch whatever they did to her, it was best to just leave them to help.

"Can you hear me?" they asked her, trying to gauge her responsiveness. I shouldn't have let her sleep, it made it harder to tell how bad her injuries were.

Anything bad that happened would be all my fault.

This whole ordeal was caused by me saying that I loved her. It was obvious I needed to stop trying to force it, at least until I'd worn her down a little more.

Several minutes must have passed with me lost in my thoughts. As the next thing I knew, they had her strapped to a board and started carrying her out the door.

"Coming Miss?" one of them yelled from outside.

Being gendered like that frustrated me, I wasn't a Miss; but right now Allie was more important than whatever my gender was. I would have plenty more opportunities to complain at people for gendering me.

As I followed I slammed the door behind me.

It was almost impossible to keep calm as I climbed into the back.

Focusing was difficult, the only thing on my mind was whether or not she'd be okay. The discomfort of the ambulance seat was the only grasp on reality that I had.

In front of me, she still wasn't awake; which threw me deep into thought again.

Why would she even do this? It was probably my fault, or it probably was to her.

Was making someone accept my love such a bad thing to do? Love was supposed to be good, so why did she do this?

Was it even worth caring about someone who so clearly didn't want me to love her?

As was usual at the moment, I considered if she was actually worth all this.

Before she was around, my life was calm and stable. Nothing ever really bothered me, I could do whatever I wanted without much care.

Feeling happy wasn't common either, but even that was much better than how I felt now. Panic was way worse than a lack of happiness. I didn't want to care about her but I needed her to be stay alive.

Nothing would have felt better than her waking up to call me a bitch or slap me. I didn't know if these were signs she hated me or just how she showed affection, either way I missed them.

Her being lifeless and not moving was surreal, the lack of response when I touched her hand made it worse.

This wasn't the Allie I knew, I missed my Allie. As much as it pained me to need anyone, I needed her. She just had to be okay.

The ambulance jolted to a stop, snapping me back to reality at least momentarily. We'd obviously arrived at the hospital. This was the place where she would get help.

Any other time a hopeless almost defeatist attitude would be my response, but I had to fight it. For once I wanted to be wrong about other people, I had to hope and trust that someone could help her.

There had to be at least one other person in this world who could help her. Unfortunately I wasn't a doctor so it had to be someone else, which was a terrifying concept.

Trusting didn't come easy, but more than ever I was willing to try.

"We'll take her inside and you should go to the waiting room." A voice from the front seat told me.

The doors were loudly opened, and Allie was wheeled away. With her being taken away from me, it was impossible to not get lost in my thoughts again.

Perhaps her being taken away from me was a sign.

I loved her, but was love all that important? My entire life it had only caused problems for me. Love was the reason I was in this whole mess, and what had I gotten out of it? A warm feeling.

Did being with Allie and the nonsensical comfort it bought make all of her flaws worth it? Was it worth risking my freedom, my money and even my life to keep her safe and protected?

As much as I wanted to remain stubborn, the answers to these questions were clear. I wouldn't have come this far if she wasn't worth it, something was keeping me around.

If I didn't think she was worth it I would have ran away days ago, me and her were in this together until the end.

As I headed into the hospital, I knew what I had to do. There wasn't anyone else in the world that could or would take care of her, so it had to be me.

White walls and pale blue accents were everywhere, it was way too bright. The overload of light at least changed my panic to a more familiar annoyance and irritability.

The waiting room at the end of the corridor wasn't much better. The rough and scratchy couch, the buzzing and flickering light bulb, and worst of all the other people here made it unbearable.

Staying in this room was impossible, I needed to be out of here.

Every second spent in this room, made every sensation more excruciating. I covered my eyes as I fled down the bright corridors looking for an exit.

This whole hospital was the worst for all my senses, being irritable made me more frustrated and mistrusting of doctors that were taking care of Allie. Air, less light and less noise was what I needed; somewhere to calm down.

Soon enough I found an exit, with just the sensation of cool air I began calming down. Atop a small wall by the exit, I caught my breath.

I hated it, but the people here were the only ones who could help. I could take care of her in every way but physically, which made me feel worthless.

I needed to be the one who fixed everything, even if that was impractical. Somehow I needed to accept that I'd done all I could for now, later I could take care of her more; If she was even herself or even alive.

In any other circumstance some time away from Allie would have been ideal, but not being with her right now only made me worry more.

With me and her nothing was ever ideal. Her past abuse and my own screwed up life, were presumably why we were drawn to each other.

Broken "girls" who understood how awful the world was, who clung to anything or anyone that made each day even slightly more bearable than it would be trying to survive alone; that's what we were.

I couldn't help but imagine how we would have been in an alternate reality; if both our lives hadn't been such wrecks from the start, everything could have been so different.

We might not have ever met, but things would have been better.

As I continued to imagine, I fell deep into a daydream.

If only I'd used my skills to get a safer job, I'd have been able to do everything so much better for Allie. The idea of having a house and a normal boring job to help take care of her, seemed like my dream world. She really had changed everything.

If I hadn't been so avoidant and closed off, maybe we could have met years ago. By now we could have owned a house, maybe even a dog, maybe we'd even be married.

Sadly it was nothing more than a fantasy at this point, we were both too far gone; Allie was a murderer and I was her accomplice.

My job essentially forced me to stay in it, with the risk of being killed or thrown into prison if I tried to stop. Some of the people I'd dealt with made me shudder to even think about now.

Even without those obstacles, the world had broken us both. Our mental states were in tatters, the cruelty of existence and other people was just too much.

Nothing we did was really our fault, the world and other people had made us this way and this was all we knew.

We'd never be able to adapt to a normal healthy life at this stage. We were too broken for normalcy.

There was still something I could do for us though, take our huge blood stained apartment and turn it into a home. We both deserved that much, I'd never really had a home and I got the impression she hadn't either.

Creating a home would hopefully make her feel more comfortable in our relationship and more willing to accept my love. I wasn't giving up on loving her, not by a long shot.

Sat here, nothing was going on around me. Inside chaos, outside an almost serene calmness, was quite the juxtaposition.

There was nothing more I could do to help her, the lack of control I had in this situation felt awful. I needed to control everything, and when I couldn't it left me feeling helpless.

As things were starting to feel bleak, someone walked over to me.

"Pixel?" she asked, from the uniform I could tell she was a nurse.

"Yeah?"

"Allie is asking for you," she told me, as she walked over to another part of the wall. Almost ironically, she lit up a cigarette, though if she'd been around Allie I couldn't blame her.

I was so relieved to hear that Allie was asking for me, I needed to see her. With my head down in an attempt to avoid most of the disorientating light, I rushed towards where I was before.

The confusing maze of corridors eventually lead me to the waiting room, opposite which was the reception desk. Social interaction with anyone else wasn't something I could handle at the moment, figuring I could find her by myself I avoided the desk.

Wandering through the department eventually lead me to her room, her voice should have been more help than it was. The amount of background noise here made interpreting sounds even harder than usual.

The first thing I saw was her lying on the bed. It was such a relief to see that she was awake, last time I saw her she seemed barely alive.

There were a few moments of awkward silence as I sat in the chair next to her bed. Just seeing her awake and staring at me, filled me with emotion.

"Allie I L" I started to say.

"No." she cut me off.

What was her problem? She could have died if it wasn't for me. Was saving her life not enough for her to accept my love?

My insistence on forcing it may have caused this whole situation, but I saved her fucking life. The least she could have done was accept my love, though this wasn't the most opportune time; her health was slightly more important than her inevitably accepting it.

After all I did have forever to get what I wanted. It was hard for me to show I cared, but she made me really want to try.

"I'm so glad you're awake." After the terrifying state she was in earlier, just seeing her responsive calmed me immensely.

"Well I'm not." she told me, in that emotionless tone of hers, which was never a good sign.

Did she really just tell me she wished she had died? Because that's what it sounded like.

She was in the hospital and there were people trained to deal with these things, but it still concerned me. Was what I did that bad that it made her want to die?

That was impossible, I wasn't that bad of a person; even if she didn't seem to appreciate me at all.

"But you wouldn't have gotten to see me again, you need me. I mean we need each other." If I was going to support and care for her, I sure as hell was going to make sure she knew it.

At this point in the conversation, I was dragged aside by one of the nurses. From the look on her face she wasn't happy with me, the way she brushed her auburn hair from her face only further proved it.

I hadn't done anything, but presumably being angry at a patient was bad practice; so lucky me, I got to be the target of her frustration.

"Miss, we're slightly worried about your-" she paused awkwardly, seemingly looking for the right word.

"-friend." she continued, looking clearly uncomfortable.

Nurses being concerned didn't surprise me, considering Allie had just openly admitted to me that she wanted to die. It was their job to take care of sick people, but was Allie really sick?

"As you probably know she injured herself, and has been openly talking about suicide. The most concerning thing is her obvious violent tendencies, multiple times she tried taking medical equipment and using it as a weapon. With your permission we'll transfer her to the care of our head psychiatrist with the recommendation of a long term stay. She's clearly suffering from severe mental health issues."

Her voice was monotonous and dull, which made it hard to keep track of. The parts that I could understand, I didn't like the sound of one bit.

Nobody was taking Allie away from me and she wasn't just my friend. I loved her, as much as she or anyone else didn't like it.

Staying calm was impossible, this whole situation had been awful but this was the last straw.

"First of all she's not just my friend, she's my partner and yes in a gay way. Secondly there is no fucking way you're getting my permission to take her away from me and admit her to some ward forever," I yelled.

I had to catch my breath but I wasn't done, there was so much more I needed to say. Since meeting her I'd been looking into her behaviours and the conclusion I reached wouldn't have even been helped with inpatient treatment.

Not that it mattered, I loved Allie the way she was and nothing was going to change that.

"Sure she's the most fucked up person I know, but no amount of treatment is going to fix that. She's a violent wreck but that's just who she is, she'd be like this even if she was the most sane person in the world. So treat her wound and probable concussion and let us get out of here." I continued.

The bewildered look on the nurse's face was priceless, she had nothing to say to me. Just a blank stare. And as she turned to leave I had one more thing to say.

"You can't treat a probable case of histrionic personality disorder with long term inpatient care, maybe you should give up being a nurse you clearly suck at it."

By now Allie was staring at me, clearly she noticed the drama going on. She wouldn't pass up an opportunity to enjoy it, especially when it centred around her.

This stare was different, it wasn't the contemptuous one; if I didn't know better I'd have presumed she admired me, or at least what I just did.

A few moments later, that stare turned into a smile.

My reaction was what I presumed she'd do in that situation, it felt good going with my instinct and not thinking about the consequences. The way she lived sure did have its perks.

I went even further with this feeling,

"Want to get out of here?" I asked, which seemed to improve her mood instantly. She may have been impressed with me yelling at a nurse, but I could tell being here was making her feel terrible.

With her hand in mine, I pulled her up from the bed. Together we headed for the door, luckily she was still in her clothes.

My hand in hers felt more right than anything in the world at any time; But holding her hand as we confidently strolled out of the hospital against protocol felt amazing.

As we strolled through the corridors, I lead the way as if I knew where I was going.

After about fifteen minutes or so, we reached the main entrance. The amount of people here was overwhelming. How was it possible for people who were supposed to be sick to be this loud?

More than anything, I needed to be out of here. With the door in sight, I increased my pace.

Freedom was right within my grasp; when a man about my height blocked our path. Obviously he was security, which I would have known even without the large print "security" on his jacket.

The problem for him was that I hadn't done anything wrong. It was well within my rights to decline treatment for my partner, but there he was blocking my way.

"You're going to have to take her back to her room Miss." he said, putting his hand on me to stop me from leaving.

Blocking my path was one thing, but touching me without permission was too far. Why did men feel like they had the right to touch me? I was already in a mood and this pushed me into anger.

"Actually I don't," I yelled at him,

"She's dangerous and the doctors suggest not letting her leave." He said, raising his voice to match my volume.

"Look, I'm her partner we've been living together for years. I have the legal right to decline treatment on her behalf."

Lying felt good, especially when there was no way I could be proved wrong. Allie was still out of it, or awake and semi aware at best. Whether or not she knew what was happening was a mystery, but I knew she'd be proud of me for lying to someone's face.

The most important thing was having her with me, no ridiculous bald guy was going to stop us leaving together.

"At least sign this, waiving all legal rights if anything goes wrong," he yelled whilst shoving a form in my face.

I was so far past the point of anger and was verging on full blown rage; the lights were painfully bright and everything seemed to be getting louder.

On top of all this, an obnoxiously loud man was yelling at me to sign a piece of paper.

After having it shoved in my face for several moments, I did what he wanted.

On the form I signed "fuck you".

"No need to be a bitch, silly girl," he yelled at me even more, clearly I had gotten on his nerves.

I didn't care about anything except getting Allie out of here. On an impulse and before I could stop myself, I was mid-way through swinging my fist at his jaw.

Nobody around was paying us any attention, so he ran away; presumably to get help.

With her hand still firmly in mine, I heard her giggle. This was hopefully a sign she was getting back to her old self, unsurprisingly all it took was some violence.

I couldn't believe what i was about to ask, but it was needed.

"Allie, punch me in the face." I told her, already bracing myself for it. Even in this state, she couldn't resist hitting me.

If there was anything guaranteed in this world, it was men being pathetic assholes, nothing ever going my way, and Allie being unable to resist violence.

As I predicted, her fist hit my cheek right below my eye. I wasn't sure what I'd done to deserve it; but from the way it felt, she hit me as hard as she could.

I enjoyed it in a messed up kind of way. More importantly, we had proof of the lie we would use to get out of here if anyone stopped us again.

If anyone asked, he punched me first. Even though I wasn't actually a girl, frustratingly I looked like one. Using the way I looked for something useful, was better than the usual feeling of apathy I had towards my body.

Nobody seemed to want to approach us; N#normally I would understand people not wanting to be around me or Allie, but after I just punched a security guard I expected a swarm of people. This was where me and Allie differed, she would have loved the attention whereas I was thankful nobody confronted me.

If nobody was going to stop us, I sure as hell wasn't going to wait for them to make their move. Perhaps they wanted us to leave, most people seem to avoid conflict whenever possible.

I was glad not everyone was like Allie, the world was enough of a mess with just one.

CHAPTER 14

I lead her by the hand into the openness of outside. Without the intense brightness and unbearably loud people in echoing corridors, freedom was mine.

Well, as much freedom as possible essentially being on the run. If only I could have been more like her, then I might have been able to feel more free, but sadly I did care about some things.

It was only a short distance to our place from here, but in this state I didn't know how far she would even be able to walk; she seemed about as steady on her feet as a newborn fawn.

Nothing about her was the usual Allie; despite laughing at my mindless violence, she had barely uttered more than a few sentences since we'd been reunited.

It may have been reckless and selfish of me, but having her around with post concussion symptoms was better than not having her around at all. Taking care of her would be easy, last night was just a blip. The rest of the time I had done an amazing job at caring for her.

Even with all her issues, I was doing better than anyone else could.

Nobody else in the world was able to help her. Nurses couldn't, and I'm sure the psychiatrist couldn't have either.

At least not the type of help she would have wanted, they only cared about breaking people and making them socially acceptable.

She obviously enjoyed the way she was, and her life being this way; more importantly I liked it this way too.

Her suicidality could be a bit much at times, but being around her was mostly fun.

Mostly...

It was disheartening being around her like this, she was almost lifeless. I might as well have been leading a corpse around by the hand. She had none of her usual energy.

I'd never known her to be anything but energetic, she'd be bouncing, playing with something or just trying to provoke me constantly.

This was so far from her usual state. I wasn't even sure how much awareness she had.

The next few days were going to be difficult; I often hated the way she could be, but I also missed it. Nobody had ever made my life this exciting, being around her felt like being on a roller-coaster with a time bomb attached.

Even in her higher moods, it was only a matter of time before something set her off.

I needed her back, I needed the old Allie; my Allie. I wanted the girl that had changed my entire world, I wanted her back to her old self again. Well maybe with one change, letting me love her.

"You okay, Allie?" I asked checking on her. More than ever I had to be attentive to how she was doing, in this state even a slight change could have meant something serious.

She still wouldn't look at me, maybe the silence wasn't just a symptom of her injury. This was my fault wasn't it?

The only thing I had done wrong was trying to force my love on her, but she shouldn't have been so stubborn and just accepted it.

"Have I done something wrong?" I asked her. I knew full well I had done something; but I wasn't about to admit it.

If I admitted what I did was wrong, it would make me obligated to stop. Fake ignorance is fake bliss; being ignored by her however, certainly wasn't bliss.

Eventually, she was going to want something from me; I knew her enough to know that. I also knew that waiting until she decided she wanted to talk to me would be difficult.

Being patient with her might have been good advice, but I didn't have time for that. Waiting around for anything was a waste of time, I was curious how other people could just sit around.

There were always things I could be doing, being productive was the most important thing.

"Please talk to me," I almost begged her at this point.

Her silent treatment continued for several minutes, and with every passing second it became more and more frustrating.

Without even noticing, we'd reached where we left the car last night.

Any other time being by the sea would have calmed me, but the sound of the crashing waves just added more unnecessary noise to my already overwhelmed brain.

My emotions were too much to handle, sadness, slight guilt, and intense frustration were all throwing my brain into overload.

"Please just talk to me Allie." This time I yelled, it was a sure-fire way to get a reaction from her.

Her reaction wasn't the one I expected; she let go of my hand.

She still wouldn't look at me, her gaze was directly at the floor. If the Laura situation was anything to go by, this few seconds of silence meant I was about to be yelled at. I braced myself for the screaming that was surely coming.

I waited, and I waited.

Seconds turned into minutes, but there was nothing. No shouting, no slapping, nothing. Her gaze hadn't once been on me, it was on either the floor or the ocean but never me.

A slight way down the coast, a bench overlooked the beach. Clearly she didn't want me around right now, so I wandered over and sat there. To my surprise she followed me and sat down; as far away from me as possible, but she was still here.

Yelling at her probably hadn't been the right move. As much as I struggled to see things from other people's perspective, I knew how bad it felt to be shouted at.

If I was going to get anywhere with her in this state, I had to apologize. Nothing was harder than admitting I was wrong, this was going to be tough; but it needed to be done.

"I'm sorry for yelling at you." I told her begrudgingly,

"You don't even mean that," she said, still refusing to look at me. At least she was talking to me now.

Granted I was just trying to diffuse the situation, but part of me meant it. I could relate to the position of being shouted at, and it didn't feel good.

"It wasn't useful. I shouldn't have done it." I continued with my apology.

"Useful? You're an awful person you know Pix?" she told me.

She had a point, but what had I done to her that was so awful? There was no way she had moral high ground over me, especially considering she made me black out and then had sex with me.

Didn't she know you can't consent if you're in a weird mental state? Or did she just not care? We were both manipulative, but apparently I was so much worse than her.
"And you aren't?"

If she was going there, I sure as hell was too.

"Or let me guess. It's fine when it's you, but if anyone dare manipulate pure sweet Allie suddenly it's not okay. You're a fucking hypocrite," I yelled, perhaps I was a little too harsh but she started it.

She confused me, I thought she was my partner. I had even told people that, and yet I wasn't allowed to love her.

It was fine when I took care of her and fixed her messes, but being in love with her crossed some arbitrary ever changing boundary? We lived together for fucks sake.

"I never fucking said that. Why do you always presume you can use logic and basically mind read? You might not have empathy, but fucking hell Pixel have some awareness. I wanted to die. I hate myself. I know I'm awful too," she cried.

How could it not have crossed my mind that she hated herself, especially after last night.

Like everyone else I had fallen for her facade, below that uncaring exterior there was something more. Her confidence and uncaring seemed to be a front, for someone who hated themselves so much that they wanted to die.

"Maybe we're both awful." I admitted to her.

As much as it hurt to admit, it was true. Both of us were beyond messed up mentally. I wasn't particularly fond of myself either. She hid behind uncaring chaos, and I hid behind a veil of superiority and logic to make myself feel valuable.

"Probably," she reluctantly agreed.

It was freeing to admit to each other that we were flawed. I had always needed to be perfect, but Allie wasn't. Maybe I didn't have to be perfect; or at least not when I was around her.

"I know we're not perfect Allie, but I really do care about you." I said as I put my arm around her.

It still made little sense, but I cared about her more than almost anything else. Even just sitting on a bench with her, almost cuddling by this point; made the world feel slightly less terrible than I knew it was.

"I care about you too, even if I can't really show it like a normal person. I can try to change if you want."

Her changing might have made things easier for everyone, but I loved her for who she was. She could be frustrating, but being with her was the most fun I'd ever had. The love I felt for her usually outweighed the hate.

"I Lov-." I started to say, but stopped myself a syllable too late; which caused her to tense up.

"I like you the way you are. The hospital wanted to take you away from me, and try to change you, but Allie..."

Placing a hand on her face, I turned her to look at me before I continued.

"You've changed everything, you're a lot to handle. But I still wouldn't change you for the world."

After a few seconds of staring into each other's eyes, she gently planted a soft kiss on my lips. The feeling of the kiss was amazing, but what was better was the fact it gave me hope for the future on the love front.

The fact she showed me affection, surely meant eventually she would be open to me reciprocating or initiating it.

"I'm sorry for hurting myself," she said sounding almost embarrassed, which wasn't a common emotion for her.

"The idea of being ...." she paused, making a hand gesture.

It was confusing how she couldn't even say the word love most of the time, despite having said it to me days ago. There had to be something going on with her, I just had no idea what it was.

Maybe love had traumatized her, maybe she just didn't love me, or maybe she was just aromantic. Whatever it was, If I figured her out it would make everything a whole lot easier.

"It's just so much pressure. I hate myself and I know everyone else hates me too, the pressure of keeping someone liking me is too much," she continued.

"I don't hate you," I interjected.

"I know everyone does, I'm a fuck up, I ruin everything. That's why I have nobody, I'm too intense. I give into my reckless impulses too much. I'm just waiting for the day you run off because you can't deal with me, just like everyone else."

Lying to her might not have been right, but how would telling her that I've been tempted to run away have been helpful?

"I've never wanted to run away from you. We need each other, I'm not going anywhere."

She didn't need to know about the countless times I'd almost abandoned her.

This made her move even closer to me, almost sitting in my lap at this point. Being beside the ocean with her wasn't the worst thing in the world, especially now I had calmed down and could once again enjoy the sound of the waves.

Being with her despite our many flaws, felt so right. Neither of us had anyone else in this world, we were so lucky to have found each other.

Usually I kept distance from everyone, but here I was holding Allie and watching the waves crash against the shore; knowing that I never wanted to let her go.

With everything she'd been through, staying out in the cold any longer wouldn't have been good for her.

"Come on Allie-cat, maybe we should go home," I told her, though calling her that was slightly forced.

Somewhere over these past few days it had hit me, we needed some niceness sometimes. God knows both of us haven't had enough of it in our lives, forced niceness was better than being selfish all the time.

With her by the hand more gently this time, we eventually reached our apartment.

CHAPTER 15

As I entered our apartment, it hit me just how much this place didn't feel like a home. We had no comfort items. All we had was a laptop by the fireplace, and the living room was now soiled with a pool of her vomit. I needed to do something about this.

It might have been too late for the dreams of puppies, children, and getting married but I knew I could at least give us both a home for the first time.

My old place had never really felt like a home either, it was just a building where I lived. We both deserved a safe place, and the idea of sharing a home with her comforted me.

I told her to relax and sit by the fire, as I started to clean up the floor. It was her mess, but making her clean it up would have been incredibly selfish; she was still hurt after all. Attempting to clean up day old vomit with just toilet paper wasn't enjoyable in the slightest, oh the things I do for love.

It took about five trips and as many rolls of toilet paper, but it was finally done. Who knew that cleaning up could be so exhausting, the bathroom would have to wait. After the day I'd had, I desperately needed to rest.

The lack of beds or even furniture for that matter, made even thinking about sleep difficult; there was a distinct lack of comfort in here. I hoped I was exhausted enough that it wouldn't matter.

The carpet was surprisingly fluffy, beside the fire was the only place remotely comfortable enough to try sleeping. This only further proved that tomorrow I had to start turning this into our home.

Within moments of lying on the floor, I could already feel myself drifting off to sleep; I guess I was exhausted enough. In the moment between sleep and being awake, I felt her arm slip under my head.

The way she still showed me affection and care after so harshly shooting down my attempts confused me. Though at the same time it did help me to relax, as long as I didn't think about it for more than a second.

Unsurprisingly, it was already afternoon by the time I woke up. Waking up to find the only person I had in the world next to me was wonderful. The ways she expressed it were contradictory, but I knew she cared.

There must have been hundreds of people she could have manipulated her way into living with, there had to be a reason she was still here. We'd been through so much together, the only logical conclusion was that she liked being with me.

I wasn't the richest person by any means, and I wasn't anywhere close to her level of excitement. The only explanation for her staying was that she loved me, and I had to make her realize it; then she'd surely accept my love.

Even being here together didn't make this place feel any more. like a home.

It took me a moment but after the post sleep haziness faded, I remembered the plan for today: shopping.

I needed to change my clothes. Wearing the exact same outfit for four days made me almost hate myself. It stopped me wasting time deciding what to wear, but was some saved time really worth feeling like this?

Allie with her pink hair and stereotypically cutesy look could pull off looking trashy, but on me it looked like literal trash. It was a toss up whether I would like how I looked anyway, but being this messy only exacerbated my dysphoria.

I gently prodded Allie, as I pulled myself up from the floor.

"We need to go out." I gently told her, which unsurprisingly didn't have an effect. I was envious of how much rest she got and how easily it came to her.

Sleep was, and always had been a struggle; unless I was on the verge of passing out before I got into bed... or on the floor.

I poked her a couple more times, which seemed to work. At least the jumbled speech that spewed from her mouth suggested as much.

"Huh What- Pix?"

"Our new place feels a bit empty, I figured we could go shopping to make it feel homelier. After everything we've been through I think we deserve it." I told her.

Whether it was just sleepiness or her reacting to what I just said; I wasn't sure.

What I was sure of was that she looked more confused than usual. Whether it was anger or silently avoiding me she always reacted, but this was completely different.

"I just want this to be our home." I explained, which made her start crying.

"I've never had a home really." she told me, at this point it was obvious she was still half asleep.

She would have never let herself be this vulnerable and open with me, it felt wrong to exploit her current state; but when would I get another chance to interact with her without her being closed off emotionally?

Hearing that she'd never had a home either made me sad, even though I completely understood how she felt. Nowhere had been more than a place I happened to live.

My entire life I had never really felt at home, even with my parents. Since running away all I ever wanted was to find a place I could feel a sense of belonging.

There was one distinct difference between the two of us, I had almost by choice ran away from everyone who made me uncomfortable; whereas from what she'd told me, everyone had abandoned her.

Even though it was hypocritical of me, I hated the people who left her. I could see why people might have, she was a lot to handle; though part of me doubted if I could leave her even if I wanted to. Clearly nobody had loved her like I did.

I wasn't allowed to tell her that I loved her, but giving her the first home she's ever had was a great way to show it.

It took her several minutes of confusion and stretching, but she was finally ready to go. As usual the waiting made me incredibly impatient.

Waiting frustrated me like nothing else, it was such a waste of time.

With her by the hand, we finally headed out.

Everything stressed me out much more than usual, and I had no idea why. Noises that before I could have just ignored, were now the most irritating thing in the whole world.

Sure I was emotionally drained, but blocking out sounds should have been easy. But it wasn't. When we reached the street I could hear the sounds of traffic all around me.

The noise was almost painful.

I had to ignore it, I couldn't let anything be wrong with me. Nobody else would take care of Allie, she was my responsibility. Even when she wasn't suffering from a concussion, she wasn't the best at taking care of herself.

Neither of us were capable of living normal adult lives, but I was slightly better at it.

"What's wrong?" She asked, sounding unusually concerned.

How could I explain to her that everything, even the sound of her voice, was painfully irritating?

I had to enjoy the niceness while it lasted. Things would inevitably go back to normal, but I didn't want to prematurely shove it back to being fully screwed up. I had to try whatever I could to keep things this way.

"Just a headache," I said, sparing her feelings.

The risk of upsetting her just wasn't worth it, especially as I'd have to deal with the aftermath. Her feelings were more important than telling the truth.

From the look on her face, she clearly didn't believe me. She glared at me, but didn't let go of my hand.

If I had done something bad, she would have avoided me. I knew lying was the right thing to do, and her reaction just further proved it.

My thoughts were a mess, so many worries swirled around my head. Thinking about work, money, and the little matter of the photos was overwhelming.

Anything could go wrong at a second's notice and make both of our lives hell again.

Focusing on anything was impossible, lights, sounds, and people were everywhere.

Moving to a tourist-filled beach city might have been a mistake. Every tire screech, every cough, every flashing light on a sign, all put me on the verge of rage.

If I stayed here any longer, it was all going to explode out of me.

My instincts told me to run, even paying attention to Allie was impossible. I needed to either get back home or at least somewhere quieter. I dragged her down the nearest side street.

"What the hell is going on?" she yelled.

"I'm fine, just give me a second." I snapped at her.

"You're so stubborn."

Did she really have any ground to call me stubborn? She wouldn't even let me love her, even though she said it first.

"Whatever." I said, not even looking at her.

Talking to her might have been a good idea, but I just couldn't focus enough. Even on this seemingly abandoned street, there was an immense amount of noise from the surrounding buildings. Everything was just too much, I wanted to hit something out of sheer frustration.

There was one thing I hadn't tried, I usually only tried it in the safety of my own room when I would be trying to sleep. Code. Code was always comforting, patterns were comforting and what I needed more than anything right now was comfort.

63 61 6e 20 6d 79 20 62 72 61 69 6e 20 70 6c 65 61 73 65 20 6a 75 73 74 20 73 74 6f 70

I repeated in my mind over and over.

I tried and tried, but something that in the past was a sure-fire way to calm myself wasn't working; and this was only making me more and more frustrated.

Something in her expression changed, as I balled up my fist ready to hit the wall.

"Pix, close your eyes and focus on my voice." she told me, in an uncharacteristically calm voice.

That wouldn't help, all she ever had was ridiculous suggestions.

"No."

"Please just trust me."

Just to avoid any of her screeching, I was willing to do whatever she wanted. With my eyes closed, I focused as much as I could on her voice.

"I know what's happening, everything is overwhelming right? The noise, the lights, just everything?"

How could she have known? It was as if she was inside my mind, though if she had this much of an insight; maybe listening to her for once wasn't such a bad idea.

"Keep doing what I tell you, like I know you enjoy bitch. Take a deep breath and hold it down for a few seconds. Keep doing that for a while."

This was entirely unlike the Allie I knew, except for calling me her bitch. She had never been this caring before, maybe it was the concussion?

I hoped it wasn't because of her injury, and that she was being nice because she wanted to. Her usual self was fun, but it was nice being cared for sometimes.

Following her instructions calmed me. The sound of her voice being the focus and not everything else around me, helped noticeably.

"How did you know all that?" I asked.

It shocked me that she seemed to understand what was happening more than I did; as well as how to deal with it.

"It's just something I picked up from years of therapy, from people who ended up doing things to me but that's not important." she told me, in her usual nonchalant manner.

The idea that she'd had therapy surprised me, the Allie I knew often refused help from anyone. From the last part of her sentence, it was easy to see why she would have adopted that attitude.

It seemed to be a common theme in her life that everyone mistreated her, I didn't even want to think about it.

it terrified me to even consider what could have happened to her with that power dynamic, I hated whoever did these awful things to her.

"I deal with it by focusing on my strongest impulse at the time." she continued.

To prove her point, she grabbed and kissed me.

"Just like that." she told me, as she pushed me away from her slightly.

Focusing on whatever my brain was telling me, rather than outside distractions could work. It wasn't going to be easy by any means, but I was willing to try anything.

It probably prevented me from being just like her, just with a broken hand instead than a concussion.

Anything that stopped me from being exactly like her was probably a good thing. I envied her and wanted to be more like her, but two Allie's would be overkill. I needed to take the traits I envied and not the ones that frustrated me.

"I'm surprised you didn't know what a sensory overload was. Didn't they tell you about them when you got diagnosed with autism?" she said, seeming confused.

What was she talking about? My parents never took me anywhere, especially not anywhere involving doctors or that kind of thing. They wouldn't have ignored something like that.

They eventually took me the hospital after I broke my wrist, when I punched through their TV.

Which I only did because it was frustratingly loud, and because my dad had sold my first computer to buy alcohol.

The sound sensitivity part of that memory made me realize that Allie had a point. If I was actually autistic it would explain so many things in my life.

Admitting it to myself was going to be hard, but admitting it to her would be even harder.

"That never happened, why would it. I'm not..." I trailed off, as I attempted to lie to both her and myself.

"You clearly are fucking autistic Pixel," she said with an eye roll, sounding almost insulted that I had tried to deny it.

Some things that had been going on recently did fit, but she couldn't be right. My parents would have done something about it, they were always so nice to me.

I had very few memories from childhood, but after the gaps in my memory there was always niceness; usually involving dad buying me expensive gifts, for reasons I couldn't remember.

She had to be wrong.

"But I'm not. Nobody ever." Words came less easily than usual, she had some points but I didn't want to accept it. I couldn't accept it.

My parents were never the most supportive of my gender or sexuality, but they weren't neglectful. At least I didn't think they were, but Allie made me doubt whether that was true.

"Everyone thought you were just a moody bratty child didn't they Pix?" she asked.

How could she have known? I wasn't anything like her, we were complete opposites. She didn't care about anything, especially not rules and I obsessively followed at least my own.

"Yeah, all the fucking time Allie. How did you know?"

By now the tears were threatening to come, though part of me still clung to the hope that she was wrong.

"Everyone said the same about me, except I got punished for it." she said.

That was the proof I needed; I never got punished, just yelled at and insulted. Which was nowhere near as bad as getting punished for things I couldn't help, like she did.

It was unfair that her own parents would treat her that way, no child deserved to be treated that way; with the exception of maybe me.

Without really knowing why, I burst into tears. Which prompted a knowing look from her. My parents weren't the best but they couldn't have been bad, could they?

How did she know that our upbringings were so similar?

I hated her for making me realize it, but she was probably the only person who ever really cared about me.

As my tears continued to fall, I clung to her in a tight hug. All this time I thought everything was my own fault, that I was just too different and weird for anyone to treat decently.

If my own parents were like that, how could I trust my assumption that everything bad that happened was my own fault?

Everything I'd ever done, or that had happened to me, was probably linked back to how I was treated by my parents. Which I was only just now accepting was probably not normal or healthy.

I cried on her shoulder for a few minutes, after which she stepped back a little. Most of the crying was out of my system, letting it all out left me calmer than I had felt in a while.

Allie had an angry look on her face which confused me, I hadn't done anything wrong this time.

"Pixel look at me, your parents were bad and so were mine. We're each other's family now, all we need is each other. Okay?" she yelled at me.

Even now her yelling was terrifying, but her being angry at someone who probably hurt me was comforting; maybe she did care after all.

Together we got out of a mess, we'd treated each other awfully and we still cared, and in my case I still loved her; if that wasn't family then I had no idea what was.

We were making our place into a home, and she had just said we were family. I would have done anything to be able to grab her and tell her how much I loved her.

I just couldn't do it. Something stopped me, ruining the nicest moment in both of our lives so far wasn't worth it. There would be many more opportunities to tell her.

I pulled her into another tight hug and cried on her shoulder again. My emotions confused me, this weird feeling felt like happiness.

Being with her was the most important thing now, we had to keep each other as safe and happy as possible.

"Can we be family forever?" I whispered.

"Sure." she answered in her usual tone.

Allie holding me felt so right, being with her felt more right than anything else. Despite her obvious and numerous flaws, we seemed to care about each other on a deeper level.

She was violent and unpredictable, but she got angry at someone who hurt me; which proved she was on my side.

Having her on my side, at least when it conflicted with her own wants and needs was nice. If this didn't prove that she loved me, I wasn't sure what would.

After loosening the hug, our eyes met.

In a slow tender moment that seemed to last an eternity, we slowly moved towards each other again.

Eventually, our lips met in what must have been the gentlest kiss we had ever shared. This only lasted a few seconds, as our usual instincts took over.

Before I knew it, the gentle kiss had morphed into our usual passionate ones.

It felt different; the physical sensation was the same as ever but on an emotional level it was more intense. The slowness of it, and the emotional talk before made it feel amazing. For the first time it felt like kissing someone i loved rather than just someone who I was attracted to.

Several minutes of this left us both breathless.

"Thanks for helping." I managed to tell her between breaths.

Feeling calmer and more relaxed, would hopefully make shopping easier.

CHAPTER 16

Everything on the busy streets was just as loud as before, but now it wasn't quite as angering. With her hand still firmly in mine, we headed toward the city centre.

The high street was different from the way I remembered it, the tacky but atmospheric local stores were all but gone. Every couple of meters it was a chain store or a coffee shop, the aura was completely different than I expected.

Having lived in a city for most of my life, the familiarity of generic city vibes calmed me.

We passed an endless amount of stores selling who knows what. A short distance away I noticed a furniture shop; being this close made everything more real. We were actually going to have a home for the first time in our lives.

Once inside, I started to regret coming here; there was an impossible amount of furniture. I didn't like too many choices.

I could do nothing except stare in amazement at the huge variety that I had to choose from.

Allie had instantly decided what she wanted, and was already lying on it.

It was the most princess-like bed I had ever seen. The fact these existed in real life, in adult double size, was more surprising than anything.

The frame was intricately designed, and admittedly quite stunning on an aesthetic level. The main focus however, was the huge canopy above it. Everything about this bed was exactly what I expected from Allie, she always had to be as dramatic and clichéd as possible.

"Pixel can we have this one?" she asked, as innocently as possible.

We? If she thought we would be sharing a bed, she was wrong.

Having my own space to get away from her sometimes, was the only way I would be able to handle living with her. As awful as it sounded, being in a room with her constantly wasn't something I, or anyone else would have been able to deal with.

If the cost of personal space was buying her a ridiculously expensive bed, then what choice did I have?

"You can have it. I'm getting my own," I told her. She didn't need to know the reason why, it would have only upset her.

In her current state, I had to be careful to avoid upsetting her. Not that upsetting Allie was ever really a good idea anyway.

Nothing in this whole store appealed to me, I realized as I wandered around the same sections of beds for the third time.

Why couldn't I decide on something as simple as a bed? Every sound distracted me, which made deciding even harder; which frustrated me, which distracted me even more.

It was a horrible cycle, and with every moment it got worse.

In a moment of clarity, I remembered what Allie said. An impulse decision would take the pressure off needing to find the perfect bed.

In front of me was an admittedly boring bed, but there were sockets built into it somehow. I liked the idea of being able to work in the comfort of my bed; while Allie was in hers playing out childhood princess fantasies.

I wanted the process of choosing to be over, so I settled on this bed. It wasn't worth putting more time and effort into a decision that didn't really matter.

The shop was strangely quiet, considering I'd left Allie by herself. This would usually have been an opportune time for her to be causing trouble, but she wasn't.

Technically she was still doing something wrong, but sleeping on a display bed wasn't her usual brand of rule breaking.

Bringing her out this soon may have been a mistake, even if it did fit the way she'd go about the world; recklessly doing whatever she wanted without thinking of the consequences. One of us needed to be more responsible, and as usual it looked like it was down to me.

Knowing this was going to be my role in the relationship didn't always boost my ego as much as I hoped. Sometimes having to be the responsible one was frustrating, everything had to be centred around her.

Was she really worth all this? Was this the way I wanted the rest of my life to be?

Taking care of a sleeping girl that had purposely given herself a concussion wasn't something I ever pictured doing. There were good reasons that I ran away from everyone, it was easier when I only had to think about myself.

I often thought about leaving her, but something always stopped me. Her laid on a display bed without a care in the world frustrated me, but I knew why I wasn't running. It went against everything I always wanted and how I tried to design my life, but I tried ignore those thoughts.

Being with her was the most exciting thing I had ever experienced. Loving someone like her wasn't exactly in line with the way I planned my life, but the most important thing was that I enjoyed it.

She had made me realise just how impossible perfection was. Being better than everyone was easy, that came naturally to me. But being perfect in a screwed up world, which was only amplified by Allie existing? Almost impossible.

I didn't want to give up on being perfect, but with her around it was going to be more difficult. Perfection could be ruined in a second, by other people; probably her.

Fixating on a goal that probably wasn't even achievable seemed like a waste; for the time being I had to remain focused on being better than everyone else.

I got the feeling that Allie knew she wasn't perfect, and didn't care either. She never seemed to care what anybody thought of her. There was probably more to me wanting to be more like her than I had realized.

My idea of perfection was probably imperfect to other people, it was more reasonable to strive toward my own version of perfection rather than society's.

We had both admitted to not being good people, but I couldn't shake the idea that had been drilled into me since childhood; that I was only valuable if I was perfect.

My parents' idea of perfect was living how they deemed acceptable, living how they wanted me to. Even things that didn't make sense or seemed wrong, which then needed to be kept a secret.

Allie bringing up my childhood brought back years of memories that I had blocked out. I had so many questions, but no way to get any answers without talking to my parents again.

I had closed that chapter of my life when I ran away, and it wasn't worth reopening. The answers had to be buried somewhere deep within my memories. If I really wanted to be conscious of them, all it would take was some exploring.

They never accepted me anyway, my not quite perfect life would have only disappointed them. All I ever was to them was a disappointment.

Dating a girl I wasn't allowed to love, was probably the furthest thing from perfection to everyone else; but I had started to believe that being with Allie was as perfect as I was going to get.

From the way she was still passed out on the bed, clearly she needed to rest more. Throwing perfection out the window and being impulsive like her was a very enticing prospect, if nothing else it had helped her rest in the middle of a busy store.

Stressing about my image and what people thought of me seemed like a huge waste of time.

Worries about what other people might think would also ruin any goodness between me and Allie; we didn't exactly fit socially acceptable standards.

"Allie let's pay," I yelled across the store.

By now I just wanted to be out of here, everything was stressful and the urge to isolate myself had come back.

The fluorescence of the lights, and being surrounded by people I didn't know, put me on the verge of another overload. Which was the last thing I needed, I needed to take care of Allie.

I just wanted to make our place feel better, but my brain was making that increasingly difficult.

By the time I had reached the checkout, she still wasn't here.

"Allie, hurry the fuck up," I yelled at her again, by now I had lost my patience with everything. I was barely hanging onto the idea of having a home, giving up was incredibly tempting.

She managed to stumble her way over to me, knocking over every display she passed. She shouldn't have been out like this, I was supposed to be taking care of her but I was failing.

It took a painfully long time to pay, for whatever reason the cashier was less attentive than me and Allie combined.

It took minutes to explain that I was willing to pay for delivery that night.

When they finished explaining the delivery protocol, I shoved my card forcefully into the card reader. If I wasn't completely done with being here before, the monotonous voice from the cashier would have pushed me into complete anger. It wasn't necessary to ask that many questions about furniture.

In my frustration my mind went blank. I must have used my pin a thousand times, but for the life of me I couldn't remember it at all. I knew that I knew it, which only frustrated me further.

I breathed deeply in concentration for a few seconds, which actually helped. It did slightly anger me that Allie's advice helped, I always needed to be smarter than she was.

Intelligence and logic were all I had, it hurt admitting even to myself that I needed her help.

Being outside hurt just as much, all it did was trade one set of painful sensations for another. The excruciating brightness of the sun, the loudness of the traffic, and even the distant crashing of waves was irritating.

"Why the fuck is this happening to me?" I yelled, directed at nobody in particular.

Thankfully Allie didn't react, I didn't need her making even more of a scene.

She frustrated me too, but taking it out on her would have been unfair. After all she had been useful, and she still wasn't her usual self.

She often was an easy target to unload on, and the fact she thrived on any kind of attention made it somewhat beneficial; but there were too many people around for that.

Whether it was a darker quieter place I needed, or somewhere to vent my frustrations; here wasn't that place. Home was where we needed to be, as soon as possible.

Neither of us were in an ideal state for being in public. She needed taking care of, and the longer I was out the harder that became. Not that I'd ever admit it, but I could have used some care too; which she had shown earlier that she was capable of.

Finding our way back wasn't going to be easy. I felt more and more dazed with every minute that passed, unable to focus on anything. By the look on her face, she was almost out of it too. I lead her away from the store and down the street, with her almost lifeless body by the hand.

One thing I did notice was the sound of the sea getting louder and louder.

Chapter 17

It took a while but eventually I realized that the beach was in the opposite direction to our place.

Apparently I was distracted enough that I'd taken us in the complete wrong direction. Annoyance at the mistake I made only added to my growing headache, which was going to make getting back even more difficult.

I knew we would need to rest soon, despite what my instincts told me. Resting was often a waste of time, but I could justify it as being for Allie's sake.

For most people a headache might have been a good enough reason to rest, but to me it felt like giving up. The unfocused look on her face was the perfect excuse to rest; which honestly I needed too, not that I wanted to admit it.

With us now being practically beside the seaside, an urge overcame me. It had been years since I'd felt sand, the last time being when I was a child.

One thing that drew me back to Azura was the beach. It might have been a cliché but resting there was comforting.

Less than a few minutes later we were on the beach. The moment my feet hit the sand, I dropped down to sit. I had no idea being sensorily overwhelmed could be this exhausting.

Allie sat down beside me, still looking dazed. The part of the beach right by the road didn't tend to be very popular with tourists. Everyone wanted to be down by the water, even though it wasn't the warmest of days.

Being in the sea had never appealed to me, watching it was enjoyable.

The idea of being in water, freezing cold, and worrying that I'd touch something disgusting; made me question why anyone would voluntarily go into the ocean.

It didn't help that I was never comfortable in any beachwear. I hated my chest, as it meant anything I could wear would only cause me to be misgendered even more.

Thinking about gender got me worked up again, which didn't help the headache. I took a few moments to calm down, using the breathing exercise Allie had mentioned earlier.

For something I was so ready to dismiss, it made a huge difference. I knew remembering it in the height of an overload episode would be difficult, but I hoped with more practice I could get there.

It took minutes of forcing myself to relax, but eventually I was back to my normal logical self.

Being on the beach with Allie was nice, we didn't get enough moments like these. The furniture delivery still wasn't due for hours, so I was going to cling to these sweet moments for as long as I could.

Being able to relax with Allie by my side was rare, I wasn't sure when I'd get another chance to do this. I hoped that even while she was recovering the beach could still be relaxing to her.

Allie had been silent for a while which concerned me. Either I'd screwed up again, or more likely she was still completely out of it.

Maybe I was being too reckless bringing her out, but there was no way I could know how a concussion would affect her.

All I knew about concussions was that some people recommended three days of rest, before doing essentially anything. Some places even warned against strenuous mental activities, but that wouldn't be an issue for her; when did she ever think about anything anyway?

We both needed rest, but this was a no-win situation. Neither of us could really rest without a bed, and I couldn't even take a break from being around her; leaving her alone after what she did to herself wasn't a realistic idea.

"Pixel?" she said, sounding half asleep.

"Yeah?" I replied.

"Why are we at the beach?" she asked.

"You weren't looking so good, so I thought you could use a rest." I told her, which admittedly was only half true. She didn't need to know that I also needed to relax for a while.

"Oh." she said, sounding disappointed.

Knowing her, she wanted me to say that we were here to have fun. Fun seemed like the biggest motivator for her to do anything.

"We can come here for fun when you're in a better state." I told her.

My choice of words may not have been the best, but her physical state wasn't the safest for having fun at the beach.

The last thing I needed was her drowning on me or getting hurt even more in some other way. My protectiveness may have been a bit over the top; but the last thing i ever wanted was to lose her, like I almost had at the hospital.

"I'm fine Pix, they wouldn't have let me go if I needed to rest still." she tried to convince me.

It was almost nice seeing her back to her usual self; stubborn as hell and trying to manipulate me into doing what she wanted. It wasn't going to be that easy to convince me, especially when it came to her physical well-being.

There was the little fact that I literally had to sign a waiver to even get her released from the hospital.

"That's not how it works, Allie." I told her.

"But," she interjected.

"You need to rest for at least three days after an injury like that, but I'll take care of you." I cut her off, I had to avoid being sucked into her whining and truth-bending.

Taking care of her for three days wasn't going to be easy. We were barely into the first day and she was already trying to pull away from me, presumably to go down into the water.

If it wasn't for me she'd have been drowning in the ocean, or at the very least angering everyone else here. She needed me more than she realized, She didn't seem to see just how much I protected her from the world.

After struggling to get away from me, she finally gave up.

"Fine." she said in the most begrudging tone imaginable.

"Three fucking days and that's it," she yelled at me. It surprised me that she even agreed to it. Accepting anything she wasn't happy with was so unlike her.

If I could manage to take care of her and control her impulses for three days, it would mean I was way better of a person than I ever imagined. It would surely get through to her that I cared about her and that being safe was as important as being impulsive.

All I wanted was a nice life with Allie, it was something neither of us had before. This was our chance, maybe our only chance.

The important thing was keeping her safe, I hoped that holding her tight would make it clear to her. She struggled trying to pull away, but after a few moments she stopped.

This surely meant she would accept me caring for her. Often I needed to push her into even the smallest amount of self care, if nothing else it made me feel useful.

Who else would put up with, and help someone that didn't want to help themselves?

Just thinking about taking care of her was tiring, how would I survive these next few days? Rest was going to be so much more important, so I closed my eyes for just a few seconds.

Next thing I knew, the beach was empty and the sky was much darker.

At some point, we had fallen asleep next to each other. Which meant it was time to head back, sleeping on the beach wasn't the safest of ideas.

Even though there weren't too many people around, one of the downsides of being around Allie was that she made it even harder to trust people. If I knew her and she was still unpredictable, how could I ever know what a stranger was going to do.

We needed to go, so she could rest; but also to avoid anything bad happening.

"Allie." I nudged her gently, in hopes of waking her up. Even though I knew it wouldn't be enough, gentleness was sometimes worth a try. With her being such a heavy sleeper, it was almost inevitable that more forceful measures would be needed.

I yelled at her again, and nudged her significantly harder this time.

"We need to start heading back."

By this point she seemed to at least be aware of me.

I pulled myself up from the sand, extending a hand to help her up at the same time. As usual, she didn't want my help instead choosing to struggle to her feet. The next couple of days were going to be a challenge, whether it was purely ego or my own stubbornness; I knew I would get through to her.

Thankfully she wasn't as smart as me, I still had a few tricks. An Allie as intelligent as me, now that was a scary thought.

The only way I had any control over this situation was with logic. If she ever managed to figure out the way I did things, that would be the day all hope was lost.

The sun setting over the beach made this place stunningly beautiful. By no means were the circumstances that lead us here ideal, but that didn't mean we couldn't enjoy it.

As I took in the sunset, I took her by the hand and turned her towards me. The way our eyes met, made it obvious what this was. We continued staring at each other for a while, before I noticed a slight eye roll.

Out of what must have been impatience, she pulled me down into a kiss. For any normal people, kissing on the beach would have been a perfect place to share proclamations of love.

The last few days had taught me that we were far from normal, and that doing such a thing would not go down well. I loved her, and being unable to express it was killing me.

As we strolled off the beach and back onto the street, I felt my mood drop. The magic of kissing her at sunset was replaced by a feeling of distance.

We walked apart, no longer holding hands, as far apart as people that were walking together could be.

Silence could be nice, but the quickness of it after affection was unsettling. She kissed me, but now was confusingly silent and walking a few steps behind me.

If she hadn't constantly crossed my boundaries, I might have taken the time to figure out what I had done wrong. I knew her though, as long as I didn't cross the "saying I love you" boundary everything else was fair; or at least there was nothing else she explicitly told me I couldn't do.

Nothing of note happened on the walk back, other than having to check on occasion that she was still following me. I wouldn't have been lucky enough to lose her that way, not that I really wanted to; though sometimes the awkwardness made me wish she'd vanish for a few hours.

I couldn't wait for when she had recovered, and would be able to cause trouble for other people; not just me 24 hours a day.

Though in her current state, she didn't seem to have the energy to cause much trouble. The calmness and silence worried me, she only ever did this when emotional trouble was brewing inside her.

As relaxing as the quiet walk was, I feared that any second she would explode. She always found something to be angry at me for, admittedly it was usually justified. Whether her reactions were justified or not, I had to always be braced for drama.

More than anything I needed this place to feel like a home, the feeling I got upon walking through the door was far from relaxing. With what was left of the light outside fading, it couldn't be much longer before the beds were delivered.

Taking care of Allie meant I needed as much energy as possible, sleeping on the floor for another night wouldn't help with that. I was already exhausted from whatever was going on with me mentally, for my own sake and hers I needed some rest.

Minutes passed as I gazed out the window waiting. The world outside got darker, and with it I became more impatient.. I had paid for express delivery, where the hell were they?

Just as I was about to reach rage levels of frustration, a truck pulled up outside. If this wasn't them, I was going to completely lose it.

CHAPTER 18

It didn't even take five seconds before the buzzer rang. It had to be them, so I buzzed them up instantly. I had no interest in hearing what they had to say, all that mattered was getting the furniture I paid for brought up here.

I opened the door before I was forced to interact with people even more, at the best of times I hated this; but being this tired made it even more angering. Me saying as little as possible was going to be best for everyone involved.

Seconds later, the most generic looking man with the worst beard was at the door asking where to put the beds.

"Miss, where do you want the beds putting?" he asked again.

Oh how I hated being called that, it was a reminder that everyone else was constrained by the rules of the gender binary or at least thought they had to be.

I wasn't a woman, at least not entirely but this wasn't a fight I was going to win. It wasn't people's fault they couldn't comprehend the complexity of gender, I almost felt sorry for them. Almost.

The worst part of it all, was that nobody would ever see me for what I actually was. I had no idea if Allie even understood my gender, though she seemed to be trying lately to not refer to me using overly feminine coded words.

Which admittedly was more than anyone else had ever tried. So I appreciated it.

"Miss?" he interrupted my thoughts looking frustrated with me, which snapped me back to reality.

"Just put the girlier one in that room." I told him in the most monotone voice I could muster, pointing towards Allie's room. Changing my voice might not have made a difference, but at least to me talking like that eliminated any feeling of gender when I spoke. It felt nice, not that anyone else would understand what I was doing.

"Then the other one in there," I continued.

"Thanks. You might want to stay out of the way whilst we bring them in, wouldn't want ya getting hurt now would we?" he said in the most condescending tone I'd ever heard, clearly changing my voice didn't have any effect.

It was obvious that he read me as female, but did he really think that talking to me like that would make me feel good?

What would anyone have found nice about being treated lesser, just because he perceived me as female. Why did men always think casual sexism was attractive?

Barely a few minutes ago, I had no idea he even existed but I hated him more than anyone. His job was to deliver beds, not to be a condescending asshole to me.

I was so tempted to respond the same way back, which he wouldn't expect because I'm "just a girl".

Just because he perceived me as weak, it didn't mean I couldn't take him out. Allie looked even more feminine than me and she'd be able to hurt him; probably permanently, in about five seconds.

I needed to calm down, was he really worth getting this angry over? Sure he was condescending as hell, but soon he'd be gone back to his normal boring life.

Maybe I'd be a complete asshole too if my life sucked that much, and I had such a boring useless job. If my life was anything like his, I would have ended it long ago.

Gazing at the stars outside the window calmed me. It wasn't quite enough to distract from the loudness coming from the other rooms, but it helped slightly. Everything was starting to come together, we had beds now; which made this one step closer to being an actual home.

Through all this, she managed to remain asleep by the fire. Yet another thing I envied about her was her ability to sleep through anything, I'd give anything to be able to sleep like she did.

To be able to close my eyes, and shut out the world around me drifting off to sleep; sounded like a dream. The way she slept was always adorable, being curled up next to the fire in our new place only made her even more so.

"Miss? We need you to sign this." The obnoxious man was back, waving a form in my face.

"Um we don't seem to have a surname on file, could I get it from you now?" he asked.

"Don't have one." I replied, which was technically a lie.

I wasn't about to give him my full name, all it did was serve as a reminder of being attached to a family that never accepted me. My refusal to ever use my surname was as much about safety as it was symbolic, the less identifiable I was in my work the better; and my family didn't deserve to have someone as amazing as me associated with their name.

"Uh, well can you please just sign this?" he said, from this voice I knew he was getting angry.

Provoking him further might have been fun, but if I had learned anything from childhood; it was that men were even more terrifying than Allie when they got angry.

At this point I was completely done with this whole situation, I glanced over at Allie for just a second. Something I always envied was how she could just do things on a whim.

I decided to channel my inner Allie a little, as I wrote "I hate you and your beard looks terrible" in the signature box; then folded over the paper and quickly handed it back.

"Oh here's your free bedding," he said, handing me a sealed package.

For once a pleasant surprise, this gave me one less problem; at least I wouldn't freeze sleeping in my new bed.

A few seconds after I closed the door, there was a loud yelling from the street. It was slightly muffled, but I could make out the words.

"What the hell is wrong with her?"

This had been an ordeal, which had only made me even more tired. Later I had to get some work done, but for now I needed rest. Lying down beside Allie, I closed my eyes.

I woke up in a much darker and quieter world, clearly I was more exhausted than I realized.

Rarely did I ever just fall straight to sleep, letting out a bit of my frustration had helped somewhat. Even if looking back it was incredibly childish of me, dealing with frustrations wasn't the worst of ideas when it came to relaxing.

The serenity of night-time flowed through our still admittedly empty home, silence was everywhere; the traffic outside had stopped, the sounds of other people doing things had stopped. For once in my life things seemed peaceful, the only sound was Allie gently snoring still curled up asleep by the fire.

We had beds now though, she'd get more rest and feel better if she slept in hers. Honestly right now what I wanted was a little space from her. I loved her, but being around her could be very tiring.

Before I went to relax and have some Pixel time, she needed my help getting to her room.

"You should sleep in your bed Allie," I told her waking her up. She refused my hand helping her to get up. These stubborn games she played were ridiculous and I didn't have the patience to play them right now.

Even though I was still exhausted, with the last of my energy I lifted her to her feet.

The slowness she walked with was almost frustrating, if it wasn't for the fact she was half asleep and recovering from a concussion I would have dragged her to her bed.

Maybe I had every right to be frustrated at her; but yelling at an injured girl would make me the bad person in this situation.

After I'd lead her to her bed, I ripped open the package of bedding. I was too tired to make her bed properly right now, I threw a sheet, a couple of pillows and blanket onto her bed.

Even like this, surely she'd be able to figure out how to at least not freeze overnight.

When she'd finally gotten into bed, I left the room switching out the lights on the way.

I loved her but being with her all day was a lot to handle. It was important that I took some time to myself, which I hadn't had the chance to do much recently. Having my own room and bed, which I could use to get away from her for a while was almost too perfect right now.

It would give me a chance to get some work done, having something productive to do would surely improve my mood. For most people, work might have been just something they do to be able to live.

To me though, it was more than that it was almost fun. Solving puzzles using logic and getting paid for it too, I loved my line of work even if it did come with obvious risks.

Enjoyment was one reason to get some work done, the other was decidedly less fun to think about.

With the amount of money I'd had to spend to keep Allie safe. I couldn't bare to look at my accounts, buying a new place wasn't cheap.

I hoped to hell that she actually appreciated everything that I was doing for her; as well as the fact I'd have to continue working hard to support her, probably forever at this point.

With my laptop and one of the blankets in hand I headed to my bed. The quiet was nice, the perfect environment for me to get some work done.

CHAPTER 19

For the first time in days, it felt like my normal life; on my laptop after midnight hoping to get some work done, whilst Allie is doing her own thing. Granted her own thing usually wasn't sleeping in her own room, this was too normal to actually be our normal.

At least on my end things had a hint of normalcy that had been lost these past few days. With Allie around I had learnt to cherish the little moments where I slip back into my routines, even if for just a few hours.

It had been days since I'd gotten a chance to check my emails. Scanning through my inbox, I noticed a few easy jobs. They wouldn't be exactly the greatest of pay, but it would help me get back into the swing of things.

I read through the emails, seeing what sort of mess I was going to have to fix for someone this time...

Something was different about one of the requests, which drew me in. I didn't often care for helping people out, it was all about the money. There was just something about this one email, which was asking to pay way less than my usual fee, which I just couldn't shake.

Mrs. V, which was presumably a vague name to avoid any consequences or revealing her identity; was looking for someone to hack into her husband's records and find something incriminating.

So far, there was nothing out of the ordinary; it was surprisingly common for spouses to request my services to screw each other over, from revenge for cheating to wanting them out of the picture so they could have control of all the money. I'd seen it all, this was different.

Usually the messages were vague, no questions asked was usual protocol in communities I frequented. Hell they were less communities and essentially marketplaces, nobody was friends there. It was too risky to have friends in that world.

Her request was filled with details, which made it unsurprising anyone was willing to help her out. She mentioned her husband being physically abusive towards her, which knowing the guys who frequent these places, wouldn't have gotten her any sympathy at all.

The problem was that she had no proof, according to her the only chance she had was getting him arrested or taken away.

It made no sense why I cared, but something about helping someone in a hopeless situation attracted me to this job. I wasn't sure why, but I almost sympathized with her.

On some level, I knew what it was like to be hopeless; thankfully I wasn't that way any more, I had Allie now. I fired a response back.

"Hi there, I'm willing to help you. How desperate are you? I have some ideas, but they are quite drastic and would essentially ruin his life forever. I do want to help though."

I was incredibly confused as to why I was so willing to help this woman out. It wouldn't be that long of a job, maybe she'd even reward me extra for helping her out.

There was a possibility she wouldn't even respond though, it had been posted hours ago. Someone else surely would have gotten to her first, their help wouldn't have been anywhere near as good as mine, but at least she'd be getting the help she wanted.

The reward she offered was way less than the usual, and knowing the type of people around here; there was a chance I would be able to help after all. Which, for some reason I needed to do more than anything.

After wasting a few minutes browsing more of my emails, I began to get impatient. Not everyone checked their email constantly, even I hadn't checked mine for days; and I was usually the most obsessive, which honestly only added to my impatience.

It would so much better if everyone was as productive as me.

Just when I was starting to give up hope, a reply came to my inbox. With an unusual anxious feeling coming over me, I opened it.

"Thank you so much, everyone else was insisting I raise the price. You're the first person who seems to actually care, I'm sorry I can't give any more. He controls the money and if he found out I spent anything, he'd get so angry. My life could literally be in danger from doing this, so do whatever you can" it read.

Being called caring surprised me, nobody had ever called me caring. Technically she said that I cared, but wasn't that essentially the same thing?

Somehow I knew what it was like to be mistreated by people, my parents were a bit uncaring towards me but nothing ever this bad. I certainly hadn't been subject to the levels of violence or life endangerment that she mentioned in her reply.

I emailed back telling her to give me a couple of hours and to send me his details. Now came the fun part, from her wording she had essentially given me free reign to do anything in order to save her.

I enjoyed this part the most, Allie had her reckless impulses and I had this; ruining people's lives, usually for the greater good, in whatever creative and fun way I felt fit. For a price of course.

Realistically, I couldn't go full Allie on this. There were sadly some things I had to consider, doing anything that could put his assets in jeopardy wouldn't be much help to her.

Her urgency suggested that her life and safety were more important than money, which did give me a little leeway in what to do.

It felt weird realizing that not everyone was like me, not everyone would do anything for money. Apparently some people had moral codes that they stuck to, well so did I; but mine didn't fall in line with the ones society expected from me.

All I could do was extrapolate from her posts and emails, though I wasn't really in a position to judge anyone else's motivations to do anything.

A way that would cause the least amount of stress for her, maybe even one that would garner sympathy was the best idea. I'd taken people's money and screwed them over in the past, but it never went down well.

Usually it was naivé men who wanted me to hack into their suspected cheating partners that I did that to, something about men who treated women as their property angered me.

In most situations though it was best for both sides to act professionally, there was a huge amount of trust on both sides in these kind of dealings.

Screwing over the wrong people could quite literally cost me my livelihood or even my life.

I still wasn't sure just why I cared so much, but I did and I could have fun doing my job at the same time. I decided to go along with whatever I wanted to do, like I usually did.

Before Allie, I was able to control everything. Nowadays though, every little decision devolved into a struggle for power. Both of us being complete control freaks made everything into an ordeal. She wanted her chaos and I wanted my stability and routines.

These next couple of days were a chance to do things my way and I had to savour every single moment of it.

Who knew when I was going to get a chance to live like this again, especially when she was back to her usual self.

As I might not have a chance to have this much fun for a while, I decided to concoct the most ridiculous plan I could think of. Various websites were monitored by intelligence agencies all over the world, being linked to some of the more nefarious ones could almost guarantee at least a trip to their offices.

Maybe even disappearing permanently if enough "evidence" was there.

There were quite a few sites I could choose from, though I knew of one which was had been recently taken over and turned into a honey pot. It was the site for a group which supplied chemicals which would only be needed to be ordered this way if someone had some very sketchy plans they wanted to carry out.

In short it was a chemical supply company; I had only frequented it to remove people's records from their site, but from what I saw anything you wanted they could get for you.

Anyone with world domination plans or murderous intents would have a field day on here. It was a good job Allie had no idea about this site, or that she wouldn't be smart enough to navigate it.

Though being on the run for poisoning someone or murder that left less evidence than whatever blood filled fun she had seemed more exciting, and easier to run away from.

With my security programmes running nobody would be able to know it was me adding Mrs. V's husband's records to this site. Within seconds, having hacked into the admittance area I created false order histories in his name.

I wasn't a chemist by any stretch of the imagination but the things I placed on the orders seemed like they were sure to land him in a lot of trouble.

Things I'd only heard about as theories in the news when spies would get poisoned or something, things no well meaning person was ever going to need.

When I updated their database, my work was essentially done. He was in for a fun time, whether it be days or a week he was going to be investigated heavily for sure. It served him right, karma's a bitch; but Pixel's an even bigger bitch.

Something about saving people and ruining bad people's lives in the process made me feel incredibly important, as if I was a hero. What would that woman have done without me? She'd be suffering a terrible life for the rest of her days, but thanks to me it was soon going to be over.

The only thing left to do was email her back, telling her the job was done.

When I did so, I warned her to act like she didn't know anything if anyone asked her any questions. The usual advice I gave to women I helped was to cry that they had no idea.

Gender stereotypes might have been awful in general, but they were good at being used for manipulation. Nobody was going to suspect the crying wife who knew nothing about her husband's terrible hidden life.

It wasn't just for her own sake I was telling her this though, any repercussions she got from this could easily and quickly be dropped on my head. The site might not be able to trace it back to me, but she could easily turn on me if things get complicated on her end.

Both our necks were on the line here, I needed to trust her. Weirdly, it was easier to trust a stranger that I had a professional secrecy agreement with than it was to trust Allie.

I suppose it had something to do with the fact I assumed these people had things to lose, and would do anything to keep themselves safe and throwing me in the shit wouldn't be a good way to do that.

Allie on the other hand, had a spiteful streak and incredibly low self preservation. Her lack of care for her own life made trusting her a lot harder.

I'd only made about $500 dollars in the past couple of hours or so, but my concentration and focus levels were hitting rock bottom.

Usually I'd be able to rush through numerous jobs and work all through the night. As I wondered what could be wrong with me, I noticed an intense pain in my stomach.

When was the last time I'd eaten anything? It must have been days ago, these past few days with Allie had been so hectic I'd seemingly forgotten to eat. I envied my computer, for only needing electricity to function.

Oh how I wished I too could be electronically powered, a logical machine without these human functions or emotions.

After going off on a tangent and fantasizing about being a robot for a while, I remembered that I needed food.

If I was hungry, it for sure meant that Allie would be too. Usually I would grab something overly caffeinated and power through the rest of the night, things were different now. I had Allie, and if I didn't make the effort to eat then I was sure she wouldn't either.

Taking care of her was a pretty great excuse to waste time taking my own needs into account too. I couldn't expect her to be better if I was going to be the same old mess of a person.

Granted before this whole mess, she'd be out having fun almost every night; but I'd only ever seen her eat once. And even that wasn't the most normal of things.

One night a couple of weeks ago she got back while I was still up working, she sat in front of me and she ate an entire package of cupcakes.

It still didn't make sense why she needed to do it in front of me, especially as she didn't even offer me one. My guess would be for attention, everything she ever did seemed to revolve around getting attention from people.

I couldn't judge her too harshly, or I shouldn't at least. Eating wasn't something I was great at, for years I had basically survived on protein bars and caffeine.

I had an urge to help her with her weird eating habits. Despite the fact that I'd not even tried to eat better for myself.

Back in her room, it was surreal how peaceful a room with her in could be. She was fast asleep under the covers, snoring gently but in a cute sort of way. In this moment, she was the most serene creature in the universe; which was a stark contrast to how she was in the waking world.

Awake she was the embodiment of chaos, and fun. In her world, the world that I'd been thrown into; the concepts of chaos and fun were inseparable.

From what I could gather, nothing could be fun if it weren't dangerous and spontaneous. Living in this world with her could be draining, but it sure kept me on my toes.

The way she lived her life was equally intriguing as it was frustrating; she lived almost like she was a fictional character in some kind of weird chaotic drama. Which showed in the way she never saw consequences in anything she did, giving the impression she always thought things would turn out well in the end.

That's why she needed me, the real world wasn't like this. Problems didn't just go away if you distance yourself from them. She couldn't get away with doing whatever she wanted just because she depersonalized herself.

My knowledge of this type of thing wasn't the greatest but her ego, her quirkiness and the way she treated herself; I got the feeling that she viewed herself as some type of clichéd trope instead of an actual person.

Even though she looked deceptively cute when she was sleeping, I needed to wake her up. Letting her do whatever she wanted, even if it was to her detriment was the logical answer to how she got away with doing all the shit she did.

If I was going to help her, ignoring her cuteness and charms was something I was going to have to get used to.

Though, sometimes she was too adorable for me to manage that. I leant over and gently kissed her on the forehead as she slept, before trying to wake her up. Tender moments like that were rare, it wasn't often I'd be able to give her affection like that.

"Allie?" I nudged her slightly, which made her stir a little.

"I'm sleepy just do whatever you want." she yawned, moving over in her bed seemingly to make room for me.

That being her first response wasn't surprising, I could only imagine why she would have thought that way…

She did say anything though, did that technically mean I could tell her how I felt about her? As tempting as it was something stopped me, this was a nice moment; no drama, just peaceful sleepy Allie and me trying to take care of her.

Surely, there would be more moments I could tell her that I loved her? Ruining a rare nice moment didn't seem like it would be of benefit to any of us.

I tried again to wake her up, gently moving her. It worked, but she gave me a look which I could only interpret as a mix of confusion and hurt.

The confusion I could just about understand, after all I had just woken her up. The hurt part of her expression, I couldn't comprehend; was she upset because I wasn't doing anything to her?

"I said you could do-" she said, which helped me understand what she could be feeling.

This small interaction gave me such an insight into her mind, it was almost like she wanted to be used; or at least thought that she deserved it.

I cut her off. "Allie I'm not here to do anything. I just wanted to know what you wanted to eat."

The confused expression on her face was almost as amusing as it was saddening; someone doing things to her whilst she was asleep was fine. Someone taking care of her, judging from her reaction must have been the strangest thing to her.

It wasn't hard to extrapolate things about her past from this. There was clearly so many terrible experiences and people she hadn't told me about.

Asking her wasn't something that would be good for either of us, it would just cause me to get angry; dealing with the emotions I had was already enough, without adding even more.

She probably wouldn't enjoy opening up to me about her past anyway, some things were best kept in or pushed down.

"I don't need to eat," she said, covering her face with the blanket.

Surprisingly she was awake enough to be her usual stubborn self, she wasn't going to win this time though. Neither of us had eaten anything for days, we'd both feel even worse if we didn't eat.

"We need to eat something. You'll feel even worse if you don't." I tried to appeal to the logical part of her that I knew existed. She helped me earlier, as much as I didn't want to acknowledge it; she wasn't as naïve as she wanted people to think.

Despite my pleading, she continued to avoid me. Not responding to me at all, luckily I was getting used to her games.

"I'll let you buy some cute things tomorrow if you eat something," I told her.

Just as I thought, this piqued her interest. As confusing as she could be, there were core things that were easy to figure out. When she was enamoured with pink cables in the store a few days ago, it triggered a realization; offering her something cute or pink and she'd essentially do whatever you wanted of her.

Luckily, I was only using manipulation to make her take proper care of herself. Intent matters, which made it completely acceptable. If I did this for selfish reasons it would be wrong, but this was for her own good.

"I guess pizza is good," she sleepily managed to get out.

Her answer was better I expected. I had no idea if the place still existed, but when I remembered a good place right by the beach. The place was one of the only good memories that I had growing up, a chance to experience it again under different circumstances was almost exciting.

Sharing food from somewhere special to me, with someone equally special to me made this idea seem an even better one. There wasn't many things I even remembered from childhood, let alone ones I could share; I had to take this rare opportunity.

Chapter 20

On the way out of her room, I grabbed my jacket from the middle of the living room floor. Leaving my stuff laying around probably didn't make this place feel any more like a home, but it was convenient and to be fair we didn't have anywhere to store things.

Living in a city, particularly a tourist heavy one like this had its benefits; even though it was late, there tended to be at least a few places open. It might have been easier to order food for delivery, but I still needed more space. A walk was the perfect chance to be away from her and clear my head.

Working in a separate room was nice, but she was still right there. At times I needed to be completely away from her, even if it was for a short time whilst going to get food.

The entire neighbourhood had a very different feel at night, or at least when it was this late. There was no traffic and nobody around at all. It didn't even cross my mind to check the time before I left, but it had to be way past midnight.

How great would it be if I could sleep all day and only go out at this time? The world seemed way more bearable, I felt alone in my own little world.

There was nothing except me and my thoughts, and Allie waiting for me to come back of course. How could I forget about her.

For once, it felt like everything was going well in my life. Not that getting complacent was a good idea. Sure, she was mostly the reason why my life felt better, but I knew in an instant everything could be turned on its head.

Even knowing her unpredictable nature, it was hard to not get wrapped up in feeling like we were starting to make real progress as a couple.

I had a home with someone I could actually handle being with, and it made me want to be different. I had to be a better and more reliable person. Shutting down and isolating myself wasn't an option any more., I had someone that needed and depended on me.

The way she needed me as much as she did was enjoyable, it gave me value. The most important thing in this world is having value, the day I stopped being valuable was the day I'd give up and die.

There was another benefit of taking care of her, it gave me an outlet for the love I wasn't allowed to show explicitly.

Eventually however she was going to have to let me win, especially if I kept being perfect and doing everything for her. At this point it felt like a game; when someone told me I couldn't do something it only made me want it more.

Everyone had always told me what I couldn't do, and I always proved them wrong. This was just another case of that.

Oh Pixel, you're a girl you can't cut your hair short.

Oh Pixel, you can't get a job that's just online.

Oh you can't do this, you can't do that.

Oh Pixel, you can't love me.

My entire life was people telling me I couldn't do things, and then me proving them wrong. It was just the way things had always been, and probably would be forever.

As frustrating as Allie's stubbornness could be at times, I had my own variety. Though it was better for me to think we were completely different, we were different; we had to be.

I had to be perfect and able to take care of her, being imperfect or vulnerable would make that impossible. Letting her see the overload incident and help me was a mistake, I was supposed to be the one that took care of her. I wasn't supposed to be the other way around.

Thankfully awareness wasn't as important as it was during the day, as I kept getting lost in thought. The most dangerous thing would be tripping, there wasn't any traffic around I needed to pay attention to. In the distance, I saw the place I was headed towards.

Being stood outside somewhere I hadn't been for about 15 years was strange. Anything that brought up memories had a tendency to make me feel uneasy. Which thanks to Allie, I now knew probably came from the fact my parents were awful.

My entire life I had tried to avoid anywhere I had memories of, which made me even more confused why I wanted to come here; or to Azura at all for that matter. Aesthetically and practically being here made sense, but so many of the places added fuel to the realization that nobody ever really cared about me.

The fact of the matter was that me and Allie lived here now, I was going to have to get over whatever my issues were.

Going inside the pizza shop, which I was almost certain had changed its name, was a good start. Bay Pizza wasn't the most original of names, but considering it was by the beach it at least made sense.

It wasn't called that any more, they had to have changed it recently. Bae pizza. It was a cute pun but was clearly just trying to take advantage of younger people and make it sound cooler.

Now that I was inside, I had the task of deciding what I wanted to eat. Even more daunting than that, was having any idea what I should get for her. She hadn't eaten anything more than cupcakes around me the entire time I'd known her, and I had no idea what she actually liked.

Logic was going to be my best bet here, what did I know about her? She was intense and always liked excitement; it wouldn't be improbable that philosophy also applied to the food she liked too. Something hot was going to be my best chance of getting it right.

With that figured out, it was time to decide what I wanted. There was always an awkwardness that came with eating, I tried to avoid it until really necessary. Especially eating things that weren't protein bars which at times I essentially lived on. Everything looked good in theory, but in practicality there were only a few things I would eat. Knowing what I know now, it was probably another sensory issue.

With my face buried in the menu, I ordered Allie the biggest hottest pizza they had. After going back and forth for a while, I eventually decided on just a cheese pizza. Probably a boring choice, but a safe and easy one. I swiped my card on the machine, all I had to do now was wait.

"It'll be about 5 mins okay babe?" the person behind the counter told me. In confusion at being called babe, I looked up at them.

The person stood there looking at me, looking quite cute, flashed me an adorable smile. Nothing like Allie's terrifying grin, this one had an almost shy quality to it.

As much as flirting with her would have helped me to feel better, Allie was waiting back at home for me. Guilt was the only feeling that would come with going along with my impulses.

Before I had more chance to think about it, I took myself outside to calm down. I tried, but my mind wouldn't shift from the girl who just called me a babe. Her dyed black hair, the lip piercings, that adorable smile, none of them would leave my thoughts.

Was Allie really worth everything? From the looks of things, I was capable of forming attachments with other people.

Other nicer, easier people existed in this world; maybe my time would have been better spent focusing on them.

There was one flaw in this line of thinking though; I loved Allie. The fact we'd essentially been through hell together gave us a bond that would have been impossible to have with anyone else.

Being with other people made sense logically, but it was becoming increasingly apparent that love wasn't logical.

The crashing of the waves helped calm me down, finding someone cute panicked me. I had no real reason to panic though; nothing was going to happen and soon enough I'd be back in my apartment.

The one place where I felt the most comfortable, that's where I craved to be right now. In small doses being outside was comforting, but I was starting to reach my limit.

Behind me, the shop's chime rang. As it caught my attention i turned around and saw the girl from the counter standing there with my order.

"Thought I'd bring these out to you. Nice night out isn't it?" she said, sounding shy.

"It is." I replied, having no idea what to do in this situation; as she placed the boxes on the ground and leaned on the wall beside me. A few seconds later she was almost leaning on me. At this moment the attention outweighed the feeling of guilt by a huge margin.

As I looked over at her, I noticed her staring back at me. Before I had a chance to say anything, she spoke.

"You're really cute y'know. I'm loving the whole confusingly androgynous look by the way, it looks super good on you," she let me know, without breaking her gaze for even a moment.

I was enjoying this way too much.

I couldn't help but think of all the times Allie had seemed disinterested in me. She'd hurt me so many times, it was doubtful if she even appreciated me. Even though she was trying right now, was it really enough?

My thoughts of Allie and justifying everything going on had distracted me. Without even paying attention to it, me and the girl who's name I didn't even know hadn't stopped.

By this point our mouths had ended up just centimetres from each other's. I knew what was about to happen, and I wanted it more than anything. Lying to Allie would be easy, she never had to know about this.

Moving forwards, my lips pressed against hers. I couldn't believe this was happening, but I was already past the point of no return. Nothing I did now could make it any worse surely? Even if I wanted to stop, she was already pulling me towards her and kissing me back.

When did I ever get the chance to do something like this? As her tongue touched mine, all my thoughts and worries faded. Nothing mattered in this moment, other than my own enjoyment.

This continued for several minutes, in which I somehow ended up right against her; as she'd backed herself up against the wall.

After a while we both pulled away breathless.

"I'm Clair by the way," she said, with a distinct lack of shyness this time.

"Pixel."

"Well Pixel, it was really fun meeting you." She said, pulling out a pen and scrap of paper from her uniform. With a smile, she scribbled something down.

"We should do this again sometime, maybe when I'm not supposed to be working?" She continued, somewhat playfully as she handed me the scrap of paper; which had her number and lots of hearts on it.

"I'd better get back before the food gets cold." I told her, even though the chances of it being warm by the time I got back were zero already.

The truth was, I needed to get away from here; I had completely messed up. I was back in reality and the guilt from this was already heavy.

"I should get back to work." she told me, as she headed back inside; not before she kissed my cheek however.

Before the shop was even out of sight, the gravity of what I'd done hit me. I could have potentially ruined everything I had worked so hard towards.

How could I have let myself be so reckless? The right thing to do was to tell Allie what happened, but I had no way of knowing how she'd react.

A few meters further along the path home, I completely froze. What the hell had I just let happen. Everything was going great and now, for a couple of minutes of fun I could have thrown it all away.

I hated myself so much right now, so much that even my calming methods were betraying me.

The only code my brain could conjure was 49 27 76 65 20 72 75 69 6e 65 64 20 65 76 65 72 79 74 68 69 6e 67; which was not helpful in the slightest. Even breathing was quickly turning to hyperventilation.

She needed me; she caused issues and I fixed them. I wasn't supposed to be the one who screwed up, at least not like this.

Where had my logic and need to always do the right thing gone? Where was my admittedly abnormal moral code? In one moment I had thrown them completely out of the window, for a stranger's attention. When had I become Allie?

Thankfully I wasn't her, but this seemed like something she'd do.

I just couldn't shake the feeling that I'd betrayed her trust. She was at home recovering, and I was here kissing strangers. It felt incredibly unfair to her, this was one societal rule I knew was bad to break.

All of these emotions overwhelmed me, finding the nearest bench I sat down.

I was all she had, and I screwed her over completely. The thought that she might leave me for this was terrifying, not for my own sake but for hers. As much as I tried to block out the past, I just couldn't any more.

Sat staring out at the ocean, memories I had tried to ignore were coming back.

I loved the narrative of myself as the lonely agender person who never had anyone, but it just wasn't true. Allie wasn't even the first person I'd loved, there was someone before her. Who now thinking back had an uncanny amount of similarities with her, maybe I had a type? A reckless impulsive but admittedly fun type.

Granted I didn't know Clair, but she had just kissed me; a complete stranger. So she seemed to fit into that category.

But Allie...

I knew how things would go if I wasn't there for her whenever she needed it; the last thing I needed was another person I loved dying, because I didn't pay enough attention.

I still blamed myself for everything that happened; Allie wasn't only a chance for me to be happier, she was a way to almost absolve myself of guilt over the past.

Without me, who knew what sort of dangerous shit she'd be doing.

She wasn't exactly going to hack into government files, for secrets on various political cover ups but she had her own version of dangerous.

How could I have ever let them do that anyway? I'm smarter and have more sense than most people, I should have known it was a bad idea; even if I was only 18 at the time. It was just a case of me choosing to play things off as harmless or inconsequential, something I'd even began to do with Allie.

It would start with something like jamming the signal at government offices, and then slid down the slippery slope into even more risky hacking. If I didn't keep constant watch over her I was going to lose her, just like I lost Cameron.

Lying to her about what happened was probably the safest option, but part of me knew that I needed to let her make her own choices.

Even if she took every opportunity to have a big reaction, at least this time it would be justified. It was her silence and avoiding that I couldn't deal with.

I had to make a decision, tell her the truth and potentially lose her or lie and live in guilt filled blissful ignorance forever. The important thing was keeping Allie safe and with me wasn't it?

Logically the best way to prevent hurting her was to never mention it, all that sharing would do is make her angry with me. As guilt-ridden as I would be, it was probably for the best. Feeling bad about something I did wrong was what I deserved.

Now that I had figured out my plan of action, it was time to head back.

CHAPTER 21

The rest of the walk back was a complete blur. If it wasn't for the fact I was standing at the door to our apartment, I wouldn't have believed I even walked back.

Food in hand, with a deep breath I headed inside and straight to Allie's room.

I knew I could do this, it wasn't the first time I'd have lied. Thinking about it, a disproportionate amount of my life was built on lies; though I really didn't want to analyse myself like that right now, or maybe ever.

There she was, still fast asleep in her bed. Even just seeing her filled me with guilt, and I didn't even know if she'd care.

As long as there was even a small chance she would care and be angry at me, I needed to keep it a secret.

It wasn't hard to know how she felt, she was easier to read than she thought. Despite not wanting to, she obviously cared about some things. I knew deep down she actually cared about me, and that meant she was going to be devastated by what I had done.

One way to suppress the guilt for now was to double down on my caring; making sure she knew I cared about her. I would accomplish both equally important things, keeping her safe and stopping myself from feeling bad.

More emotional turbulence would only make me feel worse and give me more sensory problems; it was important that I took care of myself too, as much as I didn't want to admit it.

The best thing for everyone was for me to forget about it completely. Even if thinking about the way Clair touched me, and kissed me hard but in a different way than Allie did, and how good she looked made me feel happy.

Why did things I do have to have consequences? And when did I start getting so Allie-like? Complaining about consequences or just plain ignoring them, seemed to be what her entire personality was built on.

I watched her sleep while I processed my feelings, when I remembered about the food. With all the distractions I'd had tonight, there was no chance of it being warm any more. Surely it was still better than nothing though.

"Hey Allie, I've got some food," I told her.

She woke up almost instantly and was surprisingly receptive to eating. I guess there was only so much stubbornness before survival instincts kicked in and made her eat.

Before I started eating, I wanted to make sure she liked what I'd bought her. In her state it was probably more important for her to eat than it was for me. That and caring for her was already erasing some of the guilt.

Tomorrow I could buy her a few more things than I originally planned, then everything would be perfect and even again. Well as even as our relationship ever was...

In the short amount of time it took me to process things, she had already eaten all but one slice of her pizza. Which was honestly quite impressive, even if it did also concern me slightly.

My own messed up eating habits were one thing, but in anyone else they were worrying. Eventually I was going to have to help her with it wasn't I? Whether she liked it or not.

The fact that I had chosen the right thing and gotten her to eat, did make me feel good. Without me she wouldn't have eaten at all.

Hell, if it wasn't for me she might not even be alive after the bathroom incident. She needed me, the proof of that was right there.

It was clear now that taking care of her was the way to absolve myself of anything I did wrong. If I put in enough effort that it outweighed anything bad I did; then logically I was still a good person.

As long as I helped her more than I hurt her, whatever I did was okay.

But for now, I had to be even more perfect and caring than usual. Luckily it was only until I had made up for my mistakes, putting this much effort in with Allie could be a tiring endeavour.

I could only manage to eat one slice. Despite figuring out how to fix things, the guilt was still eating away at me. Eating a small amount was still better than nothing.

After the emotional night I'd had I didn't feel in the mood to eat any more. Everything had tired me out completely.

Struggling to conceal a yawn, I let her know that I was going to bed. Surprisingly, she stopped me.

"Can't you sleep in here tonight?" she asked, holding my arm as I tried to leave.

I needed space from her, but if that's what she wanted what choice did I have?

Doing things I didn't want to do would only prove how much I cared. I took off my jacket, throwing it to the floor while looking at her. Of course she was using all the pillows and blanket, I didn't expect anything else from her.

I left the room for a few minutes to get my own bedding. When I returned something was different and she had an unsettling grin. I could have sworn I took my jacket off closer to the door than the bed?

As I got onto the bed and moved slightly closer to her, I closed my eyes in hopes of getting to sleep.

***

Whenever I got the chance to sleep next to her, I always had one of the easiest nights sleep. Just being near her was nice, seeing her still sleeping beside me made me feel things I couldn't quite describe.

Everything felt still and peaceful. In this moment, it felt like me and her could actually be good for each other; things were going well.

Without even a few seconds to dwell on the nice thoughts, I remembered...

I remembered what happened last night, the irrational decision I made. Well technically Clair made the decision, I just went along with it.

If I knew Allie she wouldn't be the type to enjoy technicalities and loopholes, well unless she was the one using them.

When the pangs of guilt inevitably resurfaced, thankfully I was able to use logic to lessen it somewhat; this was easily solvable. All it would take was being extra nice to her.

In all honesty Allie wasn't exactly the smartest person, and she was as oblivious as they came. There was no chance she was going to find out what happened, unless I wanted her to know.

The most important and pressing issue was easing my own conscience.

At some point I would feel like I'd atoned for everything I had done wrong, even if the majority of the time I questioned if I'd done anything wrong at all.

Society taught us that kissing someone else was wrong, but was it actually? Since when did we ever play by societies rules anyway?

Other than her unassuming somewhat normal cuteness, nothing about us had any hint of normalcy.

It was the breaking of trust which bothered me the most; but even that was for the greater good. Technically I was lying, but it was to protect her.

Intent made a huge difference, lying might be wrong but in this context it was the right thing to do. The sooner I was able to make things even again the better, feeling like I owed her frustrated me.

Having already promised to buy her some cute things because she ate, today posed a perfect opportunity to make things up to her; without her even suspecting a thing. I could just spend more on her than I had originally intended.

If there was one thing my father taught me it was that spending money on someone fixed all the problems.

My memory was still blank on the exact details, but whenever my dad did whatever he did; he'd always buy me gifts, and pretty expensive ones at that.

I wished I could have remembered the exact context, but it did prove my point. I remembered the gifts more than I remembered what actually happened, so as much as I hated it I was going to have to be like him.

Having used logic to stop obsessing over what I did, I finally felt ready to get up. I stumbled my way across the apartment to get the laptop.

When I got back, she was already awake and sitting up. She probably needed to wake up soon anyway, too much sleep was going to be just as bad as too little. From my laptop I saw it was 2:15, which made it all the more acceptable that I'd probably woken her up.

"Can't we go out today?" she asked, which didn't surprise me in the slightest.

Of course she was going to want that, she probably needed her fix of excitement. She needed to be constantly doing something, anything, being stuck here with me must have been hell for her. It was hell for me too.

That didn't matter though, her health was more important.

Her being gone for a few hours, or forever, would have made my life much easier; but the guilt if anything actually happened to her would have been too much for me to deal with. I had already lost one person because I didn't pay enough attention, and I wasn't about to double my tally.

"You still need two, well one and a half days of rest. You know this."

It would have been nice if she listened to me for once, but there'd be more chance of the sun turning into a red giant this very second than that.

"Why can't I go out and do whatever I want without any consequences?" she asked.

It was out of character for her to say that, even if that was her general outlook on everything; she'd never be so blunt about it.

At the best of times she was confusing, but every now and then she'd say something which would completely throw me for a loop. The best thing to do was chalk it up to her messing with me, which she obviously enjoyed doing. Trying to figure out the motives behind anything she did was an almost impossible task.

"Because things you do affect other people? If you go out and get hurt again, how do you think I'd feel?" I asked her.

By uttering that contrived statement, I was being a huge hypocrite.

Luckily she didn't really have much moral high ground in that regard, as long as I was at or above her level it was fine.

"You'd be happy because you hate me," she said, which just didn't have the same emotionality behind it as usual.

She'd scream at me for hating her, not casually drop it as a retort in conversation. Something was going on, the most obvious answer was she was entertaining herself and just didn't have the energy for her usual dramatics.

"I said I'd buy you some cute things didn't I? Because you were good and ate something," I told her, changing the subject.

Sure it might have sounded condescending, but it was the truth. Yesterday I'd promised to get her some stuff and I was living up to it.

"What do you..." I started to ask, before I could finish she'd grabbed the laptop from my hands.

Her browsing style wasn't surprising but it was disorientating. She would scroll quickly up and down, skipping through multiple tabs back and forth, each so quickly that all I had seen for the past 30 minutes was a pink blur.

Seeing her engrossed and focused on something was nice, especially as from the smile on her face she seemed to be enjoying it. She didn't say a word to me the whole time, which was relaxing; a quiet Allie is the most calming of things.

Eventually she broke the silence.

"Can you pay now?" she asked.

In her cart was various cutesy pieces of clothing, unsurprisingly most of them were pink. The specifics of what she was getting didn't interest me very much. Clothes weren't the most exciting of things to me.

She had a different outlook though, her appearance was a major part of her personality.

I had figured out that her intention was probably to give off an adorable harmless vibe. Which admittedly was probably why I let her stick around in the first place; sadly since then I'd learned just how far from the truth her façade was. By now it was obvious she was overcompensating to the nth degree.

After paying, I wondered if this was enough to make up for what I did. Asking her if she wanted anything else was the best option, she'd get more things and I'd make sure I felt like we were even again.

The best part was it would just come across as me caring about her and wanting her to have nice things.

"Is there anything else you want?" I asked.

Without taking a second to answer me, she quickly logged onto another site. There was a stark contrast between the two sites. Instead of clothes, this time she was browsing a site filled with various types of knives.

I just had to ask her didn't I? I just had to ask if she wanted anything else, and now I was in the toughest position.

Her having a knife was a terrible idea, but on the other hand how could I say no? If I didn't live up to my promise, I was going to still feel guilty. It all came down to honour or my life, or maybe even other people's lives, or even her own life.

I couldn't do it, after what she'd done I just couldn't. I couldn't justify buying her a knife.

"Allie this feels like a bad idea," I told her, trying my best to not raise my voice.

"But look how pretty it is," she said, pointing at a picture of a neon pink folding knife.

Sure it was pretty, but if being with Allie had taught me anything; it was that pretty things aren't always the best of ideas.

Tears started forming in her eyes as she turned to look at me.

"I guess if you don't care about me," she cried with tears streaming down her cheeks by this point.

This was completely unfair, everything I had ever done was out of care for her. Saying no to her having something this dangerous was also out of care, but of course she didn't understand.

Anything that went against what she wanted was an affront to her.

I was starting to realize that she didn't want to be cared for, she wanted an enabler. Someone to justify and validate all of her impulses, and I wasn't going to be that.

She had no common sense and would be dead without me, I knew what was good for her better than she did.

"Why do you hate me Pix? What did I do to make you hate me?" she continued to cry.

I wasn't sure if she actually believed that I hated her, or if she was saying it to get what she wanted. Either way this was starting to be too much, and the guilt wasn't making it any easier.

More than anything, I just wanted her to stop crying.

What was the worst that could happen if I bought it for her? I would be the one in the most danger, the chance anyone else would face consequences was pretty low. We didn't exactly talk to other people much.

As long as it only affected me, that made it okay. I couldn't stand that she thought I hated her, especially when the opposite was true.

"You're not taking it out of this apartment," I told her, hoping to hell that just having it was enough.

"You're no fun but fine," she reluctantly agreed.

With the order details filled in, I found myself hovering over the confirm button. Was this the right thing to do?

Out of the corner of my eye I noticed her pouting, out of frustration I clicked it. I would have done pretty much anything to stop her thinking I hated her.

Not even a minute later, her tears had already been replaced with a grin. Her body language had completely changed, which was unsettling.

Without a word she continued staring at me, the silence only adding to my confusion. Clearly I had done something, but what?

Chapter 22

She could have just been happy about getting her way, but that was too simple an explanation for her. That grin usually meant she'd caused some sort of trouble, but I couldn't think of anything.

Trying to figure out Allie was often a pointless task, even if I could read her it could change on a whim or even just to be contrary. The important thing was that she was enjoying herself, which for whatever reason she clearly was.

Eventually she'd let me know what she was doing, luckily I knew a way to speed up this process.

I knew if I refused to engage or give her any attention, eventually she would become frustrated; then it would just be a matter of time before she spilled her plans, or gave up playing and carried them out anyway.

Now she knew she was getting a knife, I didn't even want to think about the fucked up plans she had. This made me regret giving in to her. But it was too late to do anything about it now.

With the laptop closed, I wanted to enjoy being with her. Despite her being the way she is, being with her in these somewhat calmer moments was the best. As I went to put my arm around her, I felt her push me away.

"You think I'm so stupid don't you?" she asked; I did, but now wasn't the time for honesty. She certainly wasn't as smart as me in any case.

"No." I told her, hopefully sounding convincing.

"You think I don't notice anything? You've been acting weird since last night." she said, which caught me completely off guard.

How could she have possibly noticed, I had tried my best to hide it. There was no evidence and I hadn't said a word to her, she had to be messing with me. It was impossible for her to know anything.

"I haven't done anything."

"Really?" she scoffed, clearly she wasn't buying it.

Fuck, she wasn't going to believe me was she? She had it in her mind that I'd done something wrong. I actually had this time but she had no proof.

It was obvious she was going to stubbornly cling to these unfounded claims, but I was just as stubborn.

"I haven't done anything. Maybe you're just tired, maybe you should sleep more." I told her, trying to turn the conversation in a different direction.

"Oh for fucks sake Pixel, you complete ass. You're not exactly subtle you know," she complained.

She was getting back to her old self, which was as comforting as it was terrifying. What did she mean I wasn't subtle though? I hadn't mentioned anything to her, nothing I did should have been suspicious; especially not to someone as oblivious as her.

There was no winning in this situation, nothing I could say was going to convince her. Being alone and saying nothing was the easiest option. Just as I started to leave she yelled.

"Why can't you talk to me? Just run away like usual, whatever Pixel."

The amount of hypocrisy was amazing. She never told me anything.

She was easy to read, but we only ever had actual conversations after a dramatic incident. Whether it be a giant break down, or argument it always took something drastic for her to even talk to me.

Talking about our feelings just wasn't something we did very often, it was only ever after something went wrong. The problem with sharing was there wasn't a way to gauge how she would react, with her it was always best to be cautious. Having to constantly tip-toe around her irritated me to no end.

"Because you overreact to everything. How do I know if one little thing isn't going to send you off in a destructive spiral," I yelled back at her.

As my anger with her rose, I couldn't get past the fact I wasn't allowed to tell her I loved her. If I so much as tried, she would self-destruct.

How could I possibly know how she would react to anything? The safest option was to keep things to myself.

She was happy living in her own world, why should I ruin that? Especially when it would only make my world worse too.

"At least I react at all."

What did she mean by that?

Sure I didn't have huge emotional outbursts like her, well other than anger. How could she possibly think I didn't react to anything, I had yelled at her many times. She had slightly contradicted herself though, I couldn't win this argument but I could call her out on her inconsistencies.

"I thought I wasn't subtle," I told her, it felt pretty good finding a small thing to turn it back around on her.

"I can always tell when something's wrong, but you try and fail to hide your emotions constantly. Last night I knew something was wrong, but you thought so little of me that you couldn't even communicate with me." she said, it was weird when she was like this.

Whenever she acted self righteous, it felt like she was giving a performance. Which made me doubt the sincerity of the things she said.

Even if she didn't believe it, annoyingly she did have a point. It was shocking just how easily she seemed to pick up on it, in an ideal world nobody would have any idea how I felt; or I'd just not have emotions at all, but that sadly was unrealistic.

Somehow she had been able to do what nobody else had or even tried to do, she had figured me out. She saw through my facade just as I did with hers, which left me feeling conflicted.

On one hand, it was sweet that she figured me out and knew me better than anyone else; but on the other hand I felt so exposed and vulnerable.

I had to get better at hiding my feelings.

There was literally nothing I could say, frozen in place I just stared at her.

"You think you're so much smarter and better than me don't you? But I knew something was wrong, then your jacket gave me the answers." she said, in that annoyingly smug tone of hers.

"I'm sorry." I told her, feeling so defeated.

How had I been outsmarted by her of all people. I wasn't particularly sorry, but it was what she wanted to hear.

"Do you think I fucking care if you met another girl and did whatever?"

Actually yes, I thought she would care; but it was clear I was wrong.

But if she didn't care then what was the issue? This girl was the most confusing person I had ever met.

"I just don't understand why you have to hide things from me. I don't share much but I try." she said.

It made sense that she felt bad about being lied to, rather than what actually happened; it came down to trust.

Was she really trying to share more with me? Or was she just using it to make me feel even worse? I always got the impression she wanted me to know as little as possible about her.

"You decided to be a lying asshole, so I decided to use that to have some fun and get some cool stuff. We're both terrible people but I never thought you'd lie to me like that," she continued, it was weirdly comforting that she called herself terrible too; at least we could be terrible together.

The surreality of this moment left me feeling completely crushed. I was supposed to be the smartest, I couldn't get over the fact that she'd completely played me.

Everything was becoming overwhelming again, I needed to be alone.

"If you're going to be by yourself, can I go out?" she asked as I left her room.

I didn't feel like talking to her right now, but that was a terrible idea. With my laptop in hand, I headed to my room locking the front door on the way. Even if I didn't like her right now, I still cared.

Being back in the sanctuary of my own room gave me chance to collect my thoughts.

How could she be like that? Her of all people? What gave her the right to act so self righteous?

After everything she'd done to me and put me through, nothing could justify her treating me like that. If anything I deserved to treat her how she treated me, I deserved to lie and do whatever I wanted.

She changed my life into a weird chaotic mess, I had helped her run away from the terrible things she'd done; but apparently in her world, lying was worse than any of it.

I hated her so much, but as tempting as yelling at her was; I knew that it would only feed into her victim complex.

She already felt the whole world was against her, which may well have been true. But ironically it was her determination to be poor Allie who everyone hated for no reason, that pushed everyone into actually hating her.

In these few weeks I'd known her, I had figured out some of her games and intricacies. At times it seemed as if she enjoyed being hated.

From the little she had told me, over the course of her life she'd been the victim in some awful situations; maybe that was all she knew.

I still hated her, but thinking about her past made me feel sorry for her. Without Allie around my life would have been easier, but there was one annoying thing that made me stay; I loved her.

As much as I wanted to run, and as justified I would be to do so; I just couldn't do it. She didn't have anyone else. Even if she didn't appreciate it, she needed someone to take care of her. It wasn't just a case of her needing it for these three days, she needed someone forever.

Nobody else could care for her like I could, and unfortunately I knew all too well how things could turn out if I wasn't around.

I just had to suck it up, struggling only meant I had to try harder.

Despite how emotionally taxing she was to deal with, there were still positives to being with her. The constant threat of drama and chaos were sometimes enjoyable; one thing I could never say was that being with Allie was boring.

Then there was the sense of purpose and value I got from helping her when nobody else could or wanted to.

Was life before Allie as great as I remembered it? Sitting alone in my apartment, working, and sleeping was all I ever did.

I'd go out occasionally but very rarely; I did all my shopping online, my only communication was for work, it was a lonely existence. One that I wasn't sure I'd be able to go back to, it seemed dull compared to this new life.

And if I were to leave, where would I go? As much as I lambasted her for being a screwed up mess, it wasn't as if I was an amazing person...

Well I was, just not within the lines of normal societal parameters. Nobody else could ever deal with me; I guess not everyone could handle someone this perfect.

Though given the amount of times me and Allie clashed, usually over different world views; it was doubtful if she could really deal with me. She was still doing the best anyone ever had though.

At the moment the disdain I felt toward her outweighed the appreciation. She had been incredibly self righteous, despite me only lying to protect her feelings.

Being this emotional for this long was tiring and if I had learnt anything these past few days; it was the importance of rest. The less time I took to relax, the more overwhelming everything was going to be.

With Allie it was important to not only pick your battles, but to conserve energy for future battles.

Sadly real life wasn't like games I used to play, there was no option to just buy more energy with money.

Before sleeping, and despite my annoyance, I still wanted to check on her.

Slowly and as quietly as possible I entered her room. Her door was still open luckily, otherwise I would have disturbed her for sure. I wasn't ready to talk to her again, but I still cared.

While it was unsurprising that she was asleep, something did surprise me. Under her head was my jacket, I wasn't sure why but it was almost endearing.

Unable to resist her cuteness I leant over and gently kissed her on the forehead, before leaving her to sleep.

There was one way she had more sense than me, and that was knowing when to rest. I could never shake the feeling that there was something productive I could be doing. Whether it was just being around her, or the fact that taking care of her used so much of my energy I wasn't sure; but I had started to notice when I should be resting.

I knew that I needed to sleep, but it bothered me that I could be working right now. Being this tired wasn't helping me focus at all, even just browsing my email was difficult as I was constantly distracted.

As much as I hated the idea, a nap was the most logical thing to do. I could wake up later and work.

A computer with a flat battery wasn't any use to anyone and neither was I. If I was going to be there for Allie, sometimes I was going to have to take care of myself; something which didn't come easy to me.

In bed with my eyes closed, sleep just wouldn't happen. All my emotions were messing with my mind lately, it was as if I was feeling more than I could handle.

I couldn't really comprehend or interpret what exactly these emotions were. There had been so many times I'd been frustrated or even angry at her, but these feelings were different; not only in intensity but there was something strange about them.

My thoughts circled around for what must have been at least a couple of hours. Which only added to my annoyance. Why did everything have to come back when I tried to sleep, maybe it was lack of distractions. Especially with Allie around, I didn't have much time to analyse why I felt the way I did.

What I did feel right now, was intense anger towards her. The more I thought about how much harder she made everything, the more angry I got.

Everything other than those feelings started fading to black. My brain almost shutting down and disconnecting from reality was a confusing experience, but at the same time it helped me to sleep.

So I couldn't really complain, it couldn't have been anything worth worrying about anyway.

With everything being a blur of darkness, I wasn't sure when it happened; but at some point I managed to fall asleep.

Contrary to the common sentiment, sleep didn't make everything feel better. I felt as bad as before getting into bed.

Frustratingly I had somehow managed to sleep all through the night and into the next day, which was clear by the amount of light flooding into my room.

So much for just napping and then working, clearly I had underestimated just how energy consuming dealing with Allie could be.

On the positive side, feeling refreshed with more energy would make it much easier to keep my emotions in check. Hopefully.

Even if she had a point about me hiding my emotions, would it really have been better to let them all out?

If she couldn't even handle the nice things I wanted to say to her, how was she going to handle the not so nice ones? It was best for both of us that I bottled everything up. I just had to be better at hiding it.

Today had to be a day with as little time spent around her as possible, I needed to calm down. With me blacking out again from emotional stress just last night, being exposed to more of it wouldn't have been good at all.

There was actually a chance I could get some work done today, it may not have been the most exciting thing; but honestly I loved it. The more complex and seemingly unfixable the problem, the more fun it was and the more I wanted to prove just how great I was.

Well... as long as it could be fixed with a computer, sadly Allie's brain wasn't as easily reprogrammed.

At least not as quickly; sadly operant conditioning took longer than just changing some coding. Even if it was essentially a similar concept.

Nothing caught my eye while I scanned the job listings. Why was everything just deleting emails or other banal bullshit? It was so unfair that nobody needed anything exciting doing.

After yesterday, I needed to exhibit my smartness. If there was one thing I couldn't stand, it was not being the smartest person in the room. The only way I had value was if I was the best. I had to be the smartest, the most logical, the most perfect.

I needed something difficult to prove to myself, and everyone else that I was in fact all of those things.

I scrolled through pages and pages of listings without anything catching my interest.

Without realizing, I had ended up on the 501st page of listings, with ads from weeks ago. Why was it so difficult to find anything?

Having wasted over two hours I was getting restless, it was so tempting to just be done with everything. The urge to throw my laptop against the wall was hard to ignore.

Remembering what she told me, I closed my eyes and took a few deep breaths.

What would I have done if I had broken it? It was the only thing that gave us any chance of getting out of this mess. I couldn't use my phone any more. It may have just been paranoia but after calling an ambulance using it, I was worried it could have been tracked.

We needed some kind of income, and I really couldn't expect Allie to contribute.

It would have been much easier if she could, especially with all kinds of bills probably coming in the near future.

But she needed to be taken care of and I was the one who had to do it. The idea of her making money in a way that didn't put her in danger just felt improbable. There were things she could do, but I didn't really trust her.

I had to make enough money to get her out of any trouble she would inevitably cause, and enough to stop her from being bored.

It calmed me thinking about how much she needed me.

Not a few seconds after calming down slightly I heard a loud banging. Whatever it was, it sounded like it was coming from the door. With no idea what the hell was going on I rushed to check.

Of course it was Allie stood there furiously banging against the door.

Chapter 23

"Let me out I'm bored," she whined, still hitting the door.

"Allie stop, you'll hurt yourself," I told her.

Like always she didn't listen to a word I said. If anything it made her start hitting it harder and harder, surely she would tire herself out soon. Despite the painful volume of it all, I just had to wait it out.

Just to make sure she didn't hurt herself, I stood there watching. Seeing her do this made me uncomfortable but there wasn't much I could do.

Any attempt to intervene would surely have been met with a fist right to my face, whether accidentally or on purpose.

The moment I saw her place her head against the door, all that went out the window.

Was she really about to hurt herself right in front of me? What was wrong with her? The answer was a lot of things, but this was extreme even for her.

Hurting herself was bad enough, but doing it in front of someone was just malicious. It just screamed of wanting to hurt both of us. Especially when she already had a concussion, I could have been moments away from seeing her die.

With my arms around her, I sat her down on the floor. Without letting go of my grip, I sat beside her. What was I even supposed to do here?

I was already displeased with the way she'd been acting, but this was something else. Even with me holding her, she wouldn't stop struggling.

"Allie please," I pleaded, at this rate she was going to hurt either herself or me, probably both of us.

"But I'm bored," she cried.

Did she really want to hurt herself just because she was bored? Being bored wasn't the best feeling in the world, but it wasn't worth potential death to avoid.

I understood destructive urges though, considering a short while ago I wanted to destroy my laptop.

I wasn't sure anything would calm her down. The only option was to sit holding her, until she either calmed down or ran out of energy.

Eventually she calmed down, or at least stopped flailing.

"Why don't you let me do anything? It's so boring here," she asked, which was all kinds of unfair.

Everything I was doing was to take care of her, why couldn't she understand that?

"I just want to take care of you." I explained.

"I know but I'm just so bored," she continued whining, though the fact that she acknowledged that I was trying to take care of her was nice.

There had to be something we could do. Something that could keep her entertained and allow me to take care of her at the same time.

The one idea I did have was as clichéd as they came. I had never really taken the time to watch movies or TV shows or that sort of thing with someone, and it was becoming increasingly clear that I wouldn't be getting any work done today.

With her basically demanding my attention, watching things together seemed like a nice way for us to have some intimacy. God knows that was something we lacked.

"We could watch things together on the laptop? Go sit near the fire and I'll go get it." I told her.

"Alright" she replied, sounding slightly defeated; which was understandable, she wasn't exactly getting her own way and I wasn't playing into her drama either.

Thankfully her earlier outburst seemed to have tired her out.

She just didn't have the energy to keep up these dramatic scenes, which honestly at times were so contrived; At times she really did act like she was performing to an audience.

Whilst getting the laptop, I figured it would be a good idea to bring a blanket and pillows too. We deserved to be as comfortable as possible whilst spending time together.

In typical Allie fashion, she grabbed the laptop straight from my hands. Before I could even respond, she was loading some sketchy looking website.

I couldn't even begin to image what sort of thing she wanted to show me. Knowing what I knew about her, it would be something excessively violent.

Though to my surprise, what started playing was a cute looking cartoon; though it was probably more correct to call it anime, judging from the Japanese audio and subtitles.

What surprised me even more was when she sat closer to me she put her arm around me.

"This was one of my favourite things when I was younger."

Even though I had no idea what I was watching, the subtitles made it much easier to pay attention. From what I gathered, it was one of those magical girl shows. Even without much context of the premise, the cute animation style made it enjoyable to watch.

What made it even more enjoyable was the fact she was sharing something with me. It must have been the first time outside of a fight either of us had ever really shared anything.

Rather than focusing on the show, I couldn't help but pay more attention to Allie. Even with her full attention being on the screen, I still felt closer to her than ever.

She was clearly enjoying herself, which was honestly all I really wanted; other than being allowed to love her.

From the small details she had shared about her life, she had been through so much and all I wanted was to make her life better. From the smile on her face right now, I was at least helping somewhat.

Suddenly my gaze was interrupted, as she jolted to attention. Somehow paying even more attention to the screen; which was showing what I could only assume was a villain, with pink hair.

Maybe I was jumping to conclusions, but a pink haired character in a formative show seemed like it could be meaningful.

Whoever this was they clearly meant something to her, even if it was just her favourite character. I tried even harder to focus on whatever episode we were on by now, it was a struggle; but her reaction intrigued me.

From watching I saw that whoever she was, she wasn't really evil but just bored. Bored of the order, of the way the world was.

I couldn't really relate, but there was some truth to the sentiment that the way everyone else did things and followed protocol was pointless.

However the character seemed to have more of an emphasis on fun compared to the way I felt; which was that a lot of the rules society placed on us were just impractical.

Surprisingly she paused the stream.

As she turned to look at me, I noticed a grin. This wasn't the usual grin of hers, this was something I had never seen from her before. Even her restlessness was different, normally she would always be moving around; but right now only her hands were moving, almost erratically.

It took a while to figure it out, but I finally understood that it was pure excitement. In moments like these it must have been enjoyable for her to experience everything so intensely.

"Did you see her? Did you?" she almost screamed at me, but again not in her usual way. It was less yelling and more squealing with excitement.

"She's so amazing. I wanted to be her so bad." she continued.

This was so different to the Allie I knew, she seemed to be actually happy or at the very least actually enjoying something; something that didn't involve hurting herself or someone else.

Even though I didn't particularly care about this show; the characters were admittedly a little boring and clichéd. Her excited reaction made me want to know more.

"I'd love to know more about her, if you want to share," I told her, from the instant gleam in her eyes I knew I had done the right thing by asking. It wasn't often I got to talk to her like this.

"Okay so." she said, before she took a deep breath.

"She's Carmine, she's not really bad she's just bored of the world and the way it is. Obviously she has amazing pink hair.

Later on she actually turns nice, there is an even worse villain who wants to destroy everything. She only wants to change things and make it less boring but eventually she manages to have fun in better ways." she continued, amazingly she didn't once take a break whilst dumping a huge amount of information on me.

It wasn't hard to see the impact she had on Allie's life in general. The pink hair, the similar ideals, it all made so much sense. I realized that during her childhood she had probably idealized this character to the point of it becoming an integral part of her identity.

Who knew that such an overused idea like watching a show together, would give such an insight into why she's the person she is.

Happy with telling me about her favourite character, she seemed to be getting restless again. She unpaused the stream and her full attention again shifted to the screen, with my attention being back on thinking about how nice it was to spend time with her.

The episodes began to completely blur into one another, the format of the show really didn't help. The group of characters would be at school, and then some disaster or villain attack would occur and then they'd solve it.

Oh I couldn't forget the same overused transformation sequences, which I was sure they only used to save on animation budget.

My waning attention span became lower and lower, until I couldn't even pay attention to Allie any more.

* * *

I wasn't sure how much time had passed but by now we were both lying beside the laptop instead of sitting up watching it. Allie was fast asleep beside me.

We must have been watching episodes all night, but as much as I enjoyed spending time with her; I needed my own space. It was light outside but I still needed to rest. After closing the laptop, I headed to my room.

She still had my blanket, but being on my own bed alone was all I needed. Even though it was daytime again, I was going to sleep a bit more. Being this drained and tired had the benefit of making sleeping easier, so it wasn't all bad.

***

By the time I was awake again, it was already dark. I knew I was exhausted but not enough to sleep a whole day away. Though I did feel rested and unusually happy.

Even with her attempts at causing drama, these past three days had been some of the best. It couldn't have been further than the way I planned for my life to go, but there was something nice about this. Even her messing with me could be fun, at least in hindsight.

I had never felt like this before, caring for her these past few days changed me. She needed me, and from the way she'd been acting part of her seemed to actually appreciate what I did.

Within me there was a renewed hope that things could actually work out for us, maybe we could actually have a life with at least a sense of normalcy.

Last time I saw her, she was sleeping in front of the fire. Checking on her felt like a good idea, as different as she acted last night; she was still Allie and leaving her alone for extended periods could be disastrous.

In a heap on the floor was the blanket and laptop, which sparked memories of last night again. Relaxing and having fun with her was a new thing, I wanted to do more of it. It really could be the first step toward a nicer relationship.

Before I knew it, I was back in full daydream mode. Thoughts of Allie and me, older and more mature still living here flooded into my mind. Maybe we'd even be able to get a puppy, and I'd be able to call it terrierbyte. Well maybe not that, but something cool like that.

My trip into fantasy world was soon interrupted, as I was shoved out of the way.

For whatever reason, it was Allie charging past me towards the door; looking surprisingly energetic after the way she as last night.

"Feeling better then?" I asked her, slightly confused.

"Well you said three days and it's been three days!" she said, in her usual tone.

That was what I told her, but this dramatic of a change overnight was unexpected. There wasn't a reason to worry though, she was always going to be reckless it was just the way she was.

After all, these past couple of days had give me some proof she actually cared about me. That was the impression I got at least.

"I'm going out to have some fun Pix, wanna come?" she asked excitedly.

The type of fun she was talking about probably involved loud noises, bright lights and a lot of people; something I wasn't quite sure I could handle right now.

"I don't really feel like it." I told her.

"You're so fucking boring, but fine I'll have fun without you." she said, before shoving me again on her way out the door.

An uncomfortable sinking feeling filled my chest, maybe I was wrong. Maybe she was just being nice because I was taking care or her and giving her attention.

Had she just been manipulating me again?

I didn't understand her at all, she had been so vulnerable and caring in her own brash way with me. But now, it felt like we'd gone backwards.

Last night was the closest I had ever felt to her, but less than a day later it felt like she didn't care at all.

I really thought last night was special, it certainly meant a lot to me. Judging from her reaction though, it didn't mean a fucking thing to her.

How could she go from initiating affection and excitedly sharing interests with me that quickly? Maybe there was something good in her, or maybe it was all fake; I had no idea which of those was the truth any more.

Feeling worthless again, I took my laptop, dropped onto my bed and started browsing jobs again. Thankfully there was one thing in this world I was good at, people might not appreciate me but making money could easily fill the void.

There were a few easy jobs that I could power through available tonight, the more distraction I had tonight the better.

CHAPTER 24

I spent the majority of the next couple of hours helping strangers with their inane problems, which improved my mood a little. Making a couple of thousand dollars in a few hours would make anyone feel better surely.

The sound of the door slamming distracted me. By the sound of it, she was back from doing whatever it was she did.

From the clock on my laptop I noticed that it was already 4am; Did I really want to know what she was doing out until this time?

I wasn't sure why I even cared any more, but I still had the urge to check on her.

In the kitchen she was slouched over one of the counters, somehow looking in an even worse state than that night in the bathroom.

Unsurprisingly she smelled of alcohol and cigarettes, I guess that answered the question of what she'd been doing.

She wasn't as out of it as she seemed, she noticed me walking toward her almost instantly.

"Did you miss me? I had lots of fun without you," she barely managed to form words as she spoke, it was shocking that I was able to understand her.

This was an awkward situation, which I wasn't sure how to respond to. I got the impression that drunk Allie wouldn't appreciate me telling her the truth, that having some time alone was enjoyable.

"Of course I missed you," I told her, in the most forced happy voice I could muster. She was so drunk, I hoped she wouldn't notice

"Why are you always like this?" I hate you too." she replied, apparently she wasn't too drunk to notice my admittedly terrible acting. I could have been more convincing, but I didn't really care enough to try.

No matter what I said to her, she was going to take it in whichever way fit with her current mood. Though, if she was going to be like this I might as well tell her what I was really thinking.

"Did you have fun being an impulsive reckless ass tonight? Didn't kill anyone this time did you?" I asked. Perhaps this was too far, but she deserved it for the way she treated me.

If I was more situationally aware, I would have made sure to be further away from her when I said that. Being within arms reach with her ended up being a mistake, as her fist swung behind her; catching me hard in the jaw.

Being hit by her wasn't quite as fun as I remembered it being, but it was what I deserved. The impact of it disorientated me, to the point of blanking out for just a few seconds.

By the time I started to feel grounded again, I felt a grip tightening around my throat. It may have been a mistake to provoke her, but I doubted that it made a difference. No matter what I did she'd find a reason to hit or choke me anyway.

Whether it was the choking or whatever was causing me to disconnect from the world so much recently, everything started to fade out.

With an intense ache in my head, I found myself lying on the living room floor. The faint hint of sunlight shining through the window was the only way I knew any time had passed.

By this point I was getting used to blacking out and falling asleep, though with my last memory being choked... it was probably more correct to call it passing out.

Even though it was morning, I had no intention of being awake right now. I was more confused by myself than I was with Allie, why did I keep putting myself in that situation?

For a few microseconds the rush of adrenaline I got from her hitting or choking me was amazing, but as soon as that faded all I was ever left with was an overwhelming feeling of self hatred.

As I dragged myself to bed, everything hurt. Despite it never helping much before, I hoped sleeping would help me feel better. At the very least it would mean I didn't have to consciously be aware of how bad I felt for a while.

With my eyes closed in the darkness of my room it was still impossible to relax. Even this high up from the street, traffic sounds from below were unbearably loud.

Why was this happening again? The stray glimmers of sunlight from behind the curtains felt as if they were burning my retinas.

Having the cover over my face helped slightly, but even the muffled sounds and hidden light was painful on a sensory level. Of course in the one situation that she could be useful, I couldn't even ask Allie for help.

I must have been lying under the covers for hours, with every slight sound distracting me from sleeping. Pulling on my hair and running my nails down my arm provided temporary distractions from the painful noise, but nothing helped for every long.

At this point even the blanket itself was irritating my skin.

This went on and on and on.

Next thing I knew, it was dark again; I had actually managed to sleep, not that I felt any better for it.

This was different to my other bad moods. Something was going on, but I was too disconnected from my own emotions to process what exactly it was. All I was aware of was that it was night time again.

My futile attempts at figuring out anything were soon interrupted, as she came charging through my door. This was the only safe place I had, and she didn't have the decency to even knock before coming in. Not that I should have expected anything different from her.

Her stomping footsteps and the way she suddenly turned on the light were too much for me to handle. I wanted to yell at her like I usually would, but something stopped me.

All it took was seeing that grin of hers, for images to start filling my mind.

Every time she'd choked me, sexually used me, every punch, every slap all flooded into my mind at once. I knew I deserved it, I even provoked her sometimes. The way I felt this time was different.

Once again pulling the covers over my head, I hoped she would ignore me. Cowering under the covers for a few seconds, the silence gave me hope.

"Pix get up it's already time for us to go out again!" she screeched.

How could I have for one second thought she'd ignore me. She was Allie, of course she'd have to yell at me with her shrill voice. What did she mean again?

I hadn't even been out with her for a couple of days, was she so drunk that she couldn't remember anything?

Maybe then it wasn't her fault that she... yeah it must have all been the alcohol.

"You are coming out with me tonight aren't you Pix?" she yelled again, as she pulled the blanket off me.

Spending time with her was the last thing in the world I wanted right now, I'd rather do anything else than be around her.

It still confused me what caused this sudden change in my feelings, but I needed to find an excuse. Preferably one that would cause her the least amount of anger, if that was even possible.

"I still. Um. need to do some work Allie, this place is expensive y'know," I said, which was technically the truth.

The day that I didn't need to do any more work or anything productive was the day I'd be dead.

Despite it being partially true, she wasn't happy at all with this.

"You're fucking boring, I hope you realize that," she screamed, as if not wanting to go out with her was an insult.

It should have made her feel bad, but nothing was ever her fault; so it was just me being boring.

Her yelling was bad enough, but the way she balled up her fist terrified me. This time though, she just stormed off. Not without slamming all the doors on her way out, in typical Allie style.

As was becoming all too common of a sensation, everything in the whole world was overwhelming. The light she left on was hurting, so was the traffic outside and the distant crashing of waves. All of it infuriated me.

Covering my head with the blanket wasn't doing anything this time, my thoughts intruded on every attempt I made to calm myself. The last hope I had was distracting myself with work, usually it helped me feel valuable.

The loading screen seemed to take forever to pass, and the fans? Were they always this loud? Was the screen always this bright for that matter?

Everything going on around me infuriated me, especially the laptop sitting in front of me. Nothing mattered any more did it? Something was happening and I couldn't even focus enough to figure it out.

Reducing the amount of annoying things in my life could only improve things right? In one sudden movement, I pushed the laptop from the bed; shattering it into at least a dozen pieces.

It didn't make any sense, but I was crying. Once again I hid under the covers, this time it helped slightly. It must have been releasing some of my frustration that helped.

Rest would have been useful, but my brain was having none of it. My mind replayed everything Allie had ever done to me on a loop. Not just these past couple of days, but the entire time we'd been together.

I loved her, but why did I?

As much as I probably deserved it all, karma or something for all the shit I'd done in my life; it was starting to get way less enjoyable.

Provoking her used to be exciting, but now it was terrifying. She wouldn't even talk to me about anything again, apparently it was easier for her to go back to her old self; undoing the little bit of progress we'd made together.

I wasn't even sure if I wanted to be around her long enough for her to snap out of this, if she ever would.

Deep down, I knew I'd never be able to leave her.

As nonsensical as it was, I loved her and cared about her. We'd gotten through phases of her being like this before and hopefully we could do it again.

The alternative of leaving her by herself, while better for me, would undoubtedly throw her into an even worse destructive spiral.

The glimmers of good I had seen sporadically these past three days gave me hope. There had to be something I could do to push through my fear and actually get through to her.

I couldn't give in to these intruding thoughts. I couldn't let the blacking out and whatever was going on with me mentally be for nothing.

It had to be for some greater good, if anything at all is gained from it; then it is all worth it. Hell, she might even let me love her if I do everything I can to help her despite its effect on me.

I had to get over this fear, as much as it terrified me; I knew what I needed to do. I was going to have to have an actual conversation with her. There was good in her somewhere and if I had to force it out of her then so be it.

She was going to do whatever she wanted to me physically, there was nothing I could do about that. It was almost just what I was fated to endure at this point, but I needed it to mean something.

It didn't take much of these deep confusing thoughts for my brain to begin once again almost tuning out of reality, something which at times like these I was quite thankful for.

CHAPTER 25

The next time I had awareness of my surroundings it was light again; at some point my body had given up on consciousness for a while. Well either that or something had taken pity on me and shut my brain down for a couple of hours.

I wasn't sure which of these scenarios comforted me the most, there was a morbid solace in the fact my body might have just given up.

It calmed me to know that if things ever got too persistently overwhelming, there was always a fail-safe, a self destruct mechanism; or in simpler terms, a way out.

Having chosen my own name, I loved it; but never in my life had it felt more fitting. More than ever, I felt completely disconnected from my own humanity.

What was I other than a brain? Which is essentially just a biological computer, and a body which it controlled. It might have been dehumanizing, but not being a person made it easier to cope.

Thinking of myself as just a computer or even just an object meant nothing anyone did to me mattered. Feelings and emotions felt nothing more than bloatware at this point; which frustratingly the system wouldn't let me uninstall.

At least they had now been all but pushed down to being background processes, which while still there could be easily ignored.

My primary designation was to try fixing Allie, or at least bring her back to the level of dependence she had during those three days.

While it was possible that she'd been using me this entire time, there were the times she'd been completely vulnerable. Despite the constant chaos and whether or not I believed the story about her ex, there was something there.

As much as she'd love to believe she was infallible, she wasn't as good at acting as she thought. She might have been using it to pull me deeper into her world, but she did have some amount of trust in me.

Somewhere deep down in that fucked up brain of hers, there was the ability to trust. I was willing to try whatever it took to tap into it.

I could hear the sounds of her moving in the living room, it was strangely early for her to be awake though. The idea that she was awake and possibly about to breach the sanctuary of my room filled me with such dread, that I instinctively hid back under the covers.

The loud stomping of her footsteps already bordered on being too much for me to handle, as they got ever closer to my door I felt the rage building inside me.

Would letting it out have been the worst thing in the world?

She deserved the full extent of my rage, yelling and then some, it would probably help me feel better too.

These past couple of days had killed me emotionally, I felt more empty than ever before. Not that memories before I felt this way were easily accessible. All of which only furthered my feelings of inhumanity.

My processor... brain, only had one available function; Love Allie.exe.

The only thing I could focus on was that I loved her, and that I needed to be there for her. My own wants and needs were tertiary at best now, and as much as it sucked; it was probably what I deserved.

Just as calculated, she came storming into my room again.

Without so much as a few seconds for me to process the situation, she was already yelling demands at me.

"You are coming out tonight right?"

What could have given her the impression that going out with her was something I had any desire to do?

Just the sound of her footsteps was painfully loud, never mind what type of probably illegal place she was planning on taking me.

"Please Pix, you never want to do anything with me any more" she pouted.

Her playing the victim was exactly what I needed to hear, the fear I felt was quickly replaced with anger. Anger was one way that I knew would at least slightly get through to her, as much as expressing any emotion made me hate myself.

"You're really going to blame me for not wanting to do anything with you aren't you?" I yelled back at her.

"You don't want to do anything with me? You really hate me that much?" she cried. I knew her and these were the same old crocodile tears.

Not playing her manipulative games and risking making her think I did actually hate her, made me feel guilty.

But who the hell did she think she was turning this around on me? She was the one treating me awfully. Whether I deserved it or not wasn't the point, the lack of self awareness on her part was staggering.

"I don't like you very much right now, but I'll go out with you if you do one thing." I told her.

She was surprisingly receptive to this idea, which gave me some hope. The smile on her face told me she wasn't expecting what I wanted to be an actual conversation.

"We need to talk right now," I told her.

The look on her face said it all, her almost smug excited look had turned to one of dread.

She must have known this needed to happen, and from the way she didn't leave the room or storm off as she was prone to do; I knew I was right.

Clutching at the tiny glimmer of good in her, I tried to find the right words to say.

I took a few seconds, as I attempted to find the nicest way of telling her. Which she didn't even deserve.

Eventually I gave up trying to be gentle, and exploded at her.

"We had the best couple of days and you have to go ruin everything don't you? Not that you have any idea or even care what you're doing to me or anyone. All you care about is yourself." I yelled.

"Best couple of days? Your idea of the best is me being concussed and having to be taken care of constantly?" she replied.

There was a point in what she said, maybe it wasn't the best situation; but was anything ever the best situation when it came to us? The domestic feeling of it all was what I enjoyed.

"Taking care of you is nice, but it would have been better without you being hurt." I wanted her to acknowledge that I helped her at least.

The way she would always throw it back in my face hurt, I was only trying to help.

"No Pixel, it's boring. What have we ever done together that was fun? Furniture shopping? You making sure I eat and don't do anything you don't approve of? Boring as fuck. I need excitement, I need excitement with people that aren't you. People that I'll never see again."

"So forcing me to have sex or whatever the fuck with you is exciting?"

"You mean like how you force me to let you love me? And how everything you do is because you're trying to wear me down?"

If she couldn't see the difference between forcing love on someone and what was quite literally at the very least sexual assault; then I had no idea what to say to her any more.

"It's not my fault that you're broken or whatever and don't want to have sex with me. What am I supposed to do?"

That hurt, I knew it wasn't exactly normal to not feel sexually attracted to her; someone who would be considered attractive by everyone.

I had looked into some of my experiences though, and whilst I was going back and forth on labelling anything; I could at least use it in this situation.

"Actually it's called being on the asexual spectrum, maybe you'd understand if you weren't such a sex obsessed abusive bitch."

"Well I don't want to love anyone, If I even can... or have anyone love me... and you still force that on me, even though I hurt myself because I couldn't deal with it."

Maybe this was some common ground we could use to help us get to a better place in our relationship. She didn't want love and I didn't want sex, which to anyone else might have sounded like the lack of a relationship altogether; but not only did we not have a normal relationship anyway, we had something better.

Or at least I hoped we could have something better, we had a deep connection unlike anything I'd ever felt; which had to be a good basis for a relationship.

"I think we need to compromise, I'll stop forcing my love on you and you stop..." I trailed off, saying what she did to me out loud once was bad enough.

"I need sex though Pixel," she pouted.

If she ever had the sense to actually talk to me, she might have figured out that I wasn't always against it. I mainly just lacked the drive to initiate or pursue it. The emotional connection it provided was sometimes enjoyable.

"Talk to me about it? I'm not always against it." I told her.

I needed to accept that I might not ever be able to tell her that I loved her. But was it fair of her to control the way I felt about her?

Do we really get to decide how others feel about us?

Every interaction I had with her was influenced by love, how was I supposed to suppress these feelings?

Something that I thought would have been a reasonable request was met with a confused expression.

"Wouldn't asking ruin the moment?" she asked.

As it was Allie, I had no idea if she was genuinely asking or looking for a way to justify what she did.

Either way, reacting to her pleas for validation was only going to derail things; as scary as it was, I needed to be firm with her.

"No it won't, I'll ask you before I do anything romantic and you can at least try the same with me. If you care about me at all then you'll try, please."

Adding the last part was a bit manipulative admittedly, but I knew deep down that she actually cared about me.

"Fine. Whatever. You're such a bitch."

At this point, I was pretty sure that in Allie's world bitch was almost a term of endearment. More importantly, she agreed with my suggestion. I was on the verge of tears, maybe I was finally getting somewhere with her.

"Only if you keep your end of the deal and come out with me tonight," she added.

I really didn't want to; but seeing as she just agreed to do something good, perhaps now wasn't the time to be a hypocrite. I'd have many more opportunities in life to be one of those.

I had essentially promised her, oh the night I probably had in store for me; I couldn't even begin to imagine what it could be.

Without so much as a clue when or where we were going, I decided to take some initiative.

I was quickly learning that the best way to deal with her spontaneity was to be constantly ready for whatever could go wrong. With Allie there was always going to be something, whether or not it was always her fault; there was always an aura of chaos that followed closely behind her.

"Should I start getting ready?" I tentatively asked.

She seemed to be surprised, almost shocked at me asking. I got the feeling that she didn't expect me to go through with my promise, which made me unsure whether to feel insulted or just sorry for her.

The thing with Allie was that clearly she'd been through a lifetime of terrible experiences which made her this way.

Ultimately wasn't everything out of her control? She didn't choose to be this way. But did that mean she had to control everything around her? Not that I could really criticize anyone for a control freak.

Sat on my bed, I was conflicted. Part of me wanted to get this over with, and another part wanted her to forget about me and go out alone again.

Despite my determination earlier, she still scared me. The only experiences of her being drunk had involved me being choked to the point of unconsciousness and whatever my brain repressed for me.

With my eyes closed, I attempted to centre myself before the flood of memories came back. This was soon interrupted however.

"Come on we need to go now," she told me.

I knew what she really meant was that she was ready and thus it was time to go. I was noticing something about her, she had a way of convincing me that what she did was best for both of us. It was usually just whatever was the most fun or dramatic in that moment; nothing she ever impulsively decided was because it was the right thing to do.

While it was never boring being with her, I needed planning. The anxiety from never knowing what was around the next corner was the worst I'd ever felt; and with Allie there were more corners than an apeirogon.

At this point, I had all but given up trying to predict her. That was one game that no amount of logic was going to help me win; especially as she somehow had the insight to know what I thought she would do, and then flip it and go in new unprecedented directions.

There would be more chance of predicting the decay of a single atom, than predicting what Allie would do in a single moment.

Without a chance to respond, she had already dragged me out of my room and then apartment.

There was no use struggling, not only was she deceptively strong; struggling would only get me hurt.

Even with everything going on, I still had the foresight to make sure I had my card and key on me.

One thing she couldn't ever take from me was my logic and intelligence, and with that I could get us out of whatever situation she got us into.

With no idea where she was taking me, I followed... well I was dragged down the cold dark streets of Azura.

This place had a different feel at night, in the day it was bright and cheerful. At night it had an almost shady vibe, as if this was the part that most tourists didn't see.

Which was likely due to the fact she was leading me away from the beach and down darkened alleyways, which didn't help the fear building inside me.

A few minutes further along, there was an unmarked door. Loud but muffled music came from behind it. Outside of which was a large man, who for some reason was wearing sunglasses at night.

"Oh, hi Allie. Oh and you must be Pixel. Go right in." he said, as he opened the door for us.

CHAPTER 26

While it didn't surprise me that people knew her, as she wasn't the type of person who could easily be forgotten.

The fact he knew my name was unsettling, just what had she said about me? Would I really have wanted to know anyway?

It was best to forget about it completely, tonight was about trying to enjoy myself. Well mostly it was keeping my promise to Allie, but I could at least try to have fun. I had always wished I could be more like her.

Perhaps tonight was the opportunity that I needed. If I knew anything about Allie, it's that being with someone like herself would be her dream; everyone else's nightmare, but her dream.

The loudness of the music spilled through the heavy door, so the volume of everything inside shouldn't have surprised me; but it did. Something else that I didn't expect, was how nice the vibrations from the immense bass felt. Increased sensitivity did have its perks, at least when it came to pleasurable sensations like this.

The sound and the amount of people weren't quite as pleasant. Overwhelmed by it all, I was frozen in place having no idea where to go. Whilst I struggled to take in the scene, I had lost Allie in the sea of people.

While having a few moments away from her was nice, being alone here wasn't ideal either. She was difficult to deal with, but at least she was familiar; being surrounded by this many people made me wish for her to come back.

It felt like an eternity before she found me again.

"I thought you were following me," she yelled right into my ear, which still hurt even if it was necessary with the loud music.

In typical Allie fashion, she grabbed my hand and lead me somewhere; this time she lead me through the crowd of people.

Somehow there were even more people over here, the amount of people in one place confused me. Where had she even taken me? Did I really want to know, was the real question.

Once we made it through the blur of people and noise, mostly thanks to Allie not caring who she shoved out of the way; we made it to the bar.

Despite having drank quite a bit in my time, I didn't recognize the names of any of the drinks; It had been quite a while since I stopped drinking, which might have explained it.

From the shape of the bottles it was obvious they were some kind of spirit. Not that I really trusted my perceptions of anything any more, especially not here.

The loudness of the music was already messing with my grip on reality. This place was so removed and distanced from anything I had ever experienced; if someone told me I was dead and this was where you go afterwards, I would have believed them.

Wherever I was it was too new and confusing, and thanks to feeling on the verge of another overload; I couldn't focus enough to use my logic to figure anything out.

Coming here was quickly starting to feel like a bad idea, new places were scary. Routine and relative safety were what I wanted, and I had no sense of that. Squeezing tighter on her hand only got me an eye roll from her.

She was trying to have a good time and I was here ruining it, I needed to try harder. The only way she'd be happy was if I went along with whatever she told me; like usual.

"Drink this," she told me, with a glass shoved right in front of my face.

The last time I drank was years ago; when I let myself be weak and overly dependent on it. If being here was a bad idea, then drinking was a terrible idea. I made a promise to myself....

But what did that matter any more, my self wasn't someone that Allie even liked.

I thought back to all the times I wished to be more like her, the times I admired her carelessness and that was all it took for me to give in.

It didn't taste of anything, but it burned my throat and mouth on the way down. I had no idea what I just drank, but I hoped it was strong enough to help me enjoy the night I was already regretting.

"Allie what the f-" I couldn't even finish my sentence, I was already feeling strange.

"What was that drink?" pushing through the disorientation, I managed to ask.

"Alcohol."

Of course she'd be like this, or perhaps she didn't even know herself. Sometimes her nonchalant attitude made for an exciting game, but in other cases like this; it was grating.

Drinking with her was one thing, but giving me weird drinks without telling me what they were felt like it crossed a line.

Perhaps she could tell I was frustrated and wanted to diffuse the situation, or maybe she was just fucking with me again; but surprisingly she followed up.

"I think it's just grain alcohol Pix, well with a few secret ingredients. Calm down."

That actually explained so much, the lack of taste... the sudden effect it had on me.

But I still had so many questions, what exactly were secret ingredients; being somewhere like this meant it could literally be anything.

The more pressing question however was; why was she giving me almost pure alcohol anyway? It was especially confusing seeing as she was clearly drinking something different.

I couldn't help but think it was my own fault; just being here was overwhelming and it was probably ruining her night. Alcohol seemed as good a solution for making me someone she actually liked, at least for tonight I was willing to try anything.

I just wanted to make her happy, even though I wasn't allowed to; I still loved her.

After she'd finished her drink, surprisingly slower than I expected of her; I was being lead through the crowd again. This time instead of people drinking, we were in the middle of a blur of dancing people.

She stopped, and turned to face me.

From the redness of her face, she was at least slightly drunk; which put me in an awkward situation.

In front of me was Allie who admittedly was incredibly pretty, pressed right up against me leaning in for a kiss.

I wanted affection from her, but I knew she wasn't her usual self.

For a few moments I pretended not to notice her, as I figured out what to do.

If it was anyone else I would have refused, but everything was more complex with Allie.

She had done things to me on multiple occasions that I didn't consent to, which meant no matter what I did I'd still have the moral high ground.

Then there was the fact that any slight rejection had the tendency to send her into a rage or self destruction spiral.

Surely that meant the responsible thing to do was make out with my drunk partner?

If she complained later, there was always the excuse that I was drunk too. With that thought, I made my choice. I pulled her even closer towards me, pressing my lips firmly against hers.

The way she kissed me back just as hard made all my apprehensions to fade away.

The way her tongue and lips felt against mine, coupled with the vibration of the bass and the entire atmosphere was like nothing I had ever experienced.

Alcohol and those "secret ingredients" were playing a big part, but this was the closest to happy I'd ever felt.

Allie was here, we were closer than ever and enjoying ourselves. After we were both breathless from kissing, I held her tightly and swayed softly to the music for a while.

I wasn't sure if I'd ever really felt like me and her were a couple before now. Taking her to the hospital and taking care of her was nice, and made me feel important; but this was different. We were actually enjoying spending time together.

From the look of it, being in her world was exactly what I needed. Was this how she felt all the time? I wanted to feel this way forever, just me and her alone in the blur of a crowd enjoying each other's company. It was almost as if only her and I existed in this moment.

Everything was perfect, the music, the ambience, everything. This was the best things had been in the longest time.

But, as usual it wasn't going to last. Everything was becoming increasingly noticeable, almost as if someone was turning up the volume and brightness.

As the feeling became more intense, I knew what was about to happen.

Letting go of Allie, I pushed my way through the crowd; I desperately needed to be outside in the open air.

Being out on the cold dark street helped somewhat. Why was this happening to me anyway?

How could I go from suddenly having a good time, to everything being overwhelming? The most amazing moment of my life so far, and my brain had to ruin it; it wasn't fair.

There was a chance I was only able to cope because of the alcohol; perhaps it was the answer to helping me cope with everything.

The world outside was almost silent with only the sound of crashing waves in the distance. As I leant against the wall, focusing on the sounds of the sea I started to calm down. There was a slight feeling of guilt within me, but this was her scene; I knew she'd be fine.

I didn't have to worry about her for much longer; in her usual manner she came rushing outside too.

The way she rushed toward me filled me with fear, when she was at her most emotionally charged she was liable to hurt other people; usually me.

But this felt different; it almost felt like she cared about me. Whether she did or not, the fact she was here with me said something. She might have just wanted to make sure I was doing what I agreed to, but she did look concerned.

"Don't leave me like that," she said, almost crying.

"Sorry, everything got too loud in there."

From the expression and redness of her face she was clearly drunk.

"I thought you'd left me, don't do that. I love you Pixel."

Any other time, I would have been overjoyed that I had an opportunity to tell her that I loved her.

I couldn't do it, this wasn't the way I wanted it to happen. There would be no point in saying it now, when she clearly wouldn't even remember. If I was going to get my way, I wanted to make it meaningful and something that she'd remember. Taking advantage of her drunk state, seemed too low even for me.

All I could do in this situation was comfort her, I held her close to me.

"I'm not going anywhere Allie." I reassured her.

She still confused me, the only other times she'd been this vulnerable with me was when she was about to break down. As certain as I was that it was the alcohol, there was a doubt in the back of my mind; with Allie you can never predict what was happening in her head.

Her dangerous moods usually involved silence and distance, which eased my doubts slightly; this was probably just drunk and emotional Allie.

The fact that seconds after her outburst, she was once again trying to kiss me only further proved this.

Getting some air and being outside with her was comforting; something as simple as holding her was the best thing in the world. She didn't seem to be enjoying it quite as much as me, the constant glancing toward the door was a clear sign.

At this point I just wanted to go home, but I had promised her. Leaving early would only give her more reason to be angry with me later; I figured it was best to get the bad out of the way now.

"Do you wanna go back in?" I asked her, forcing the words out even though I really didn't want to.

"Please." she replied.

It was unfair, drunk Allie was so much nicer to me. Why couldn't she be this nice to me all the time? It was much better than the uncaring version I usually had to deal with.

With a sigh, I begrudgingly headed toward the door; even the muffled sound from beyond it gave me twinges of a headache. Holding my head in pain, I reached to push the door open; but she stopped me.

She was acting strange, was she actually taking my feelings into consideration? It must have been obvious how much discomfort I was in.

"I have something that might help."

Before I had a chance to respond, she'd shoved something into my mouth. All I knew was that it tasted really bad; even worse than the alcohol from earlier.

There was no way she just did that? She wouldn't?

This might have been the most fucked up thing she'd ever done to me: Forcing me to have sex with her was one thing, but shoving unknown pill shaped things into my mouth was a new low.

I didn't even have a chance to spit it out before it had dissolved. I managed to spit some of the remnants onto the ground, but it was already too late.

"What the fuck is wrong with you?" I yelled at her, which got no reply. With me by the hand, she just lead me inside through the sea of people again.

I was more angry with her than ever before, how could she do this to me?

More worryingly why did she act like this was a normal thing to do? Had someone done the same to her at some point?

Thinking back, she was acting differently earlier. Had she taken something too? She must have gotten it from somewhere, and she wasn't exactly the type of person to give something to someone else and not have it herself.

All I knew was that she didn't have much common sense. Who would do something like that?

The anger only lasted a few minutes longer, after which I started to feel different. The music wasn't just calming like before, it was exciting and I could feel it everywhere.

Everything I felt was more intense than usual, and not in the overloading way either.

Allie being pressed right against me felt amazing. As I looked down at her, I noticed something; she was unbelievably pretty wasn't she? The pink hair, her cute face; everything was just astoundingly beautiful, how had I never noticed this before.

I couldn't help myself, I pulled her even closer to me. After a short stare into her eyes, I kissed her harder than I ever had before.

Every moment blurred into the next, everything was a blur of colour and physical sensation. It was as if nothing else existed, just me, Allie, and the music.

One concerning thing I did notice however, was everything speeding up.

It.
Was.
All.
So.
Fast.

Everything was so fast. What was happening to me? This wasn't fun any more.

Then...

It stopped, everything stopped, and began to fade away as a veil of darkness overcame everything. A heaviness in my body made it hard to stand. As the last glimmers of light began to die, I felt myself fall onto Allie.

CHAPTER 27

The last memory I had was everything going black; wasn't I somewhere with loud music? I wasn't there now though, from the feel of it I was in a bed.

I had no idea where I was, or how much time had passed. I must have been out of it for a long time.

Once my eyes adjusted to the light, I could see that it was Allie's room. With her pink hair visible from under the covers next to me, we had somehow made it back home.

The majority of last night was a blur, I only had one solid memory.

All I knew was she gave me some sort of pill, well less gave and more forced into my mouth. I should have been more angry at her, but for a short while it made me feel better. It might have been fucked up, but maybe she was trying to help in her own messed up way.

Sitting up in her bed caused her to stir.

"Oh good you're awake, I was worried you'd never wake up." she said.

The lack of concern in her voice bothered me, but at least she cared enough to say something, right?

Her words told me she was glad I woke up, her tone however gave the impression she wasn't that bothered either way.

Even for her this was ridiculous, she actually cared didn't she? She could have at least pretended to be happy that I was breathing.

At this point it was hard to see the line between her aloof uncaring act, and her actually not caring.

The fact she went right back to sleep, made me fear the worst. By the sounds of it, I had been passed out since last night and other than five seconds of concern; she didn't actually care at all.

No matter how she felt about me, being here with her was still nice; but I needed my own space. After last night, taking some time to recharge was probably best for both of us.

Once I got out of her bed it dawned on me, I wasn't wearing any clothes and they were all strewn across her room; which made me fear the worst. What had actually happened last night?

She wouldn't have done anything.... Would she? Though, this was Allie we were talking about.

Even she couldn't be that obtuse surely.

She did care about me at least a bit, I knew; or rather I hoped.

More than ever I needed space, even if I didn't trust my interpretation of what happened; this entire situation was beyond fucked up. Maybe she only drugged me, but that was still crossing a line; or at least I thought so but I wasn't sure. Any line or boundary was non-existent, or at least so far away it was imperceivable.

Whilst I got dressed, I tried to figure out another reason my clothes would be all over the room; but nothing came to mind.

I made my way out of her room as quietly as possible, the idea of being around her was terrifying; especially if she woke back up.

My room was the only place I felt safe, being alone was the only protection I had. But being there wasn't enough, at any moment she could come charging in.

At some point I had to get a lock, it would be helpful for when she was too much to handle.

She'd be banging on a locked door like she was prone to do but at least I would be safe from physical harm. As strong as she was, I had my doubts that she'd be strong enough to plough through a locked door.

Laid on the bed with my eyes closed, I hoped rest would help with this awful mood; even though it rarely had in the past.

I was a little conflicted, last night was mostly fun. Well what I could remember of it anyway, it was the missing memories and whatever happened in her room that was the problem. I wanted more than anything to believe this was just her misguided way of helping me have fun, her intentions mattered.

If her intention was to help me, then there was still hope; but if she really didn't care, what more could I do?

In times like these I hated how logical I was; she was obviously too selfish to care about me.

Never in my whole life had I wished to be wrong so badly. I wanted nothing more than for her to defy logic, I hoped she cared about me despite all the evidence suggesting otherwise.

I'd never wanted to be wrong about anything, but this was different; I wanted to be wrong. I wanted to live in a world where she cared about me. I wanted her to love me; or at least feel like I mattered to her.

Wasn't it better to be with someone who didn't care, than to be alone though? Did she really make everything that bad?

My gaze shifted toward the floor, where I saw the shattered laptop.

Seeing it provoked something deep inside of me. She did make everything worse didn't she? The laptop sitting there in a dozen pieces summed up everything perfectly.

The pieces were all there, but it was beyond the state of repair. She had the ability to take anything good and obliterate it completely.

I was her laptop.

Before her I was alone; but I had my own things. I had my bike, I had my own apartment where I felt comfortable. Azura was scenic but the memories associated with it, in both the recent and distant past, had quickly destroyed my idealization.

Circadia may have had it's own problems, but it had essentially become my home town; and I didn't feel like I belonged here. The recent memories or lack thereof only made me feel even worse about Azura; I couldn't shake the feeling that she'd done something bad, and that more was still to come.

She had completely fucked me over, I worked so hard to create a life for myself. Everything was fine until she showed up out of nowhere.

Why did I have to love her?

What practical purpose did being in love with someone like her have?

If I didn't love her, I could have kept my old life and she'd be someone else's problem. Granted she'd probably be in jail or a mental institute for the murder she committed.

It sounded awful to think but maybe that would be better for everyone.

She had taken so much from me and with my ever loosening grasp on reality; she had clearly started to take the most important thing.

There was one thing that made me special, and she had started to affect that. Somehow I was less logical and intelligent around her.

This realization only infuriated me further, and now the familiar was happening. Everything was becoming too much, the light, the sounds from outside, even the feelings of fabric on my skin.

I had no intention of calming down this time, she deserved every bit of my anger. Everything she'd done since I met her was bad enough.

But last night was the last straw, we had talked about consent just the night before. I thought we were making progress but she threw it all away.

Every sign from last night pointed to her taking advantage of me.

I hoped that it wouldn't come to this, but I couldn't do this any more.

This was it, I had dealt with as much of her bullshit as I could.

This had to end here, before she took even more from me. If I dealt with her reckless self centred personality for much longer there was only one more thing she could take from me; and that was my life.

I loved her, but I didn't love her that much. As long as I was still breathing there was a small glimmer of hope that things could change.

Well in every moment that I wasn't consumed by trying to figure her out, or prepare for how she was going to ruin things next.

She was intent on dragging me to hell with her, but enough was enough. I'd gone down this road as far as I could, I had to take the chance and get off at the next exit.

Telling her wasn't going to be easy; there was the distinct possibility that ending things with her was going to be the hardest thing I would ever have to do.

I knew where this would leave her, without me to keep her impulses slightly controlled; she would be free to do anything.

Knowing her and what she did when I was here, there was a real chance she'd not be in this world much longer if left to her own devices. But at this point, it was her or me.

This was the hardest choice of my life, but I needed to choose self preservation.

I stood behind my closed door, trying to delay the inevitable. Once I left the relative safety of my room, things were going to change. This confusingly erratic chapter of my life would be over.

CHAPTER 28

I knew what my choice would mean for her, but I couldn't let myself focus on that. The important thing was the positives I would gain from this decision, it was my turn to be selfish.

The quicker I got this over with the better, I stormed to her room; without giving myself even a second to change my mind.

I found her still deep asleep, she had no idea I was even there; or what was about to happen.

"Allie." I said in the loudest and most serious tone I could muster.

She awoke quicker than ever, there must have been something in my voice; after all I was almost yelling, and fighting back my tears.

"Pix?" she replied in a confused tone.

"We can't do this any more, I can't do this any more Allie." I continued.

"This?"

"We can't be together any more Allie. It's not healthy. It's not just you, we seem to bring out the absolute worst in each other."

That wasn't even the truth, but I still cared about her.

Telling her that it was all her fault, would only have increased the chances she'd react badly. Not that I expected anything other than complete self destruction.

It was a form of damage control, I hoped that sparing her feelings would stop her from going into full blown suicidal breakdown.

The idea of another person I loved dying was too much to handle. Even if I couldn't be with her, I was going to make a last conscious effort to prevent that.

Her silence was a bad sign; it usually meant that thoughts were bubbling inside her, ready to explode at any moment. Silent Allie was more angry and reckless than usual, she was genuinely terrifying.

"What the fuck do you mean, you're breaking up with me? You? Let me get this right, you're leaving me?" Surprisingly she seemed calm with a grin on her face.

I got the impression she didn't actually believe what was happening.

"I'm sorry." I told her.

"I take you out and let you have fun for once in your boring life, and suddenly you decide you don't want to be with me? What is wrong with you?"

What was wrong with me?

What was wrong with her?

I shouldn't have been surprised that she'd turn it around on me, but this was a new level of obliviousness. We literally talked last night about consent, and she threw it all out of the window. I was quickly realizing that she was all words.

"You do know that drugging someone is bad?" I asked her.

"It's not that bad." she answered, still looking incredibly confused.

This was hopeless, she was too stubborn to admit any wrongdoing.

What hope was there for her ever communicating with me. She clearly didn't respect me, even after everything I'd done for her.

"You can't really believe that? I know somewhere behind that cutesy, feigning ignorance facade you know what you do is wrong. Even if you are that fucked up that it was your way of trying to help, you can't accept that it hurt me." I yelled.

If she couldn't accept that she'd done anything wrong, then we were finished.

This was her one last chance to prove that she cared. Me finally calling her on her shit made her even more stubborn. It might not have been entirely her fault, but that didn't mean it was okay.

Once again she refused to say a word to me. She hadn't even gotten out of bed, still sitting there staring at me blankly; as I slowly made my way out of the door.

"You know it's wrong. You cried about Laura doing it to you, and then you turn around and do the same thing."

I wished I didn't have to go there, but it was my one chance of making her see reason. She still didn't have anything to say to me, though unsettlingly she had that grin on her face. I got the impression she was plotting something, like she had an ace up her sleeve. Well this ace wasn't about to play right into her hand.

We were done here, there was nothing more to say. Looking at her for maybe the last time as I turned to leave, her grin only grew bigger.

"But you love me." she said, as I was all but out the door.

Her saying that gave an insight into how her brain worked. She knew I loved her, but she said it out of pure manipulation.

She never wanted me to love her, but clearly she thought she could use it against me. I was done indulging her, I made sure to slam her door on the way out; even she couldn't be oblivious to that sentiment.

On the way back to my room I heard one of the loudest screams. Even without sensory issues, it would have been excruciating.

It was difficult but I needed to ignore it. She wanted attention and to drag me back in; I had done what I needed to do, all I had to do now was stay strong and stick to it for.... Well forever...

I couldn't stand the thought of being here right now, this was our home. Emphasis on the was, now it was just a place we both happened to live.

There were no distractions here any more, which made it even more unbearable. There had to be things to do in this city, anything that could be a distraction was welcome; anything to stop me from analysing and doubting the decision I had just made.

The wailing and crying made it painful to even be in the same apartment. It was best for both of us that we had our own space right now.

Without so much as a thought, I grabbed my jacket and headed out. Wherever I ended up had to be better than here, the further away I was from Allie the better.

Chapter 29

The early evening gave this place yet another feeling. It was still early enough that tourists filled the streets. The noise was somewhat relaxing, as it helped me lose myself in the blur of crowds for a while. The last thing I wanted was to feel like a person, if I even was one.

Having time alone in the cold busy streets gave me time to gather my thoughts. I had done the right thing, but it still hurt. Despite everything I would miss her. I would never meet anyone like her again, which was probably for the best.

Without giving any attention to where I headed, I took random turns; eventually I found myself by the beach. Which was almost inevitable, almost all roads lead to the beach.

I'd ended up here with her a few times, but I knew it was just a coincidence.

Just like the memories of being here with Allie, it meant nothing.

I didn't have it in me to go onto the sand, even just looking over the barrier was painful. Someday, I hoped that I would be able to enjoy the beach without her; but it was too soon for that. I wished I could enjoy the beach but it was tainted with memories.

The view from where I stood was picturesque; the ocean, surrounded by the glow of the numerous seafront bars. The sight of which gave me an idea.

If there was one useful thing she helped remind me of, it was that alcohol was a cheap and temporary relief from any bad feelings.

The idea of sitting and drinking in a rowdy tourist bar wasn't what I needed; I had to find the most relaxing one.

Obnoxiously bright lights and terribly punned names seemed to be the trend around here. I was operating under the assumption that tourist bars would be too lively for me.

It wasn't the first time tonight that I started to feel hopeless. An overflowing of life was the last thing I needed, especially when I felt dead inside.

A short distance a way, I saw something promising.

It was as tourist focused as anything else around, but the lack of crowd outside gave me hope.

As I approached, the vibe I got from this throwback old fashioned bar was incredible. I wanted to drink somewhere dark and not overly exciting and this place fit the bill perfectly. The most important thing was taking my mind off Allie, I deserved to feel better about myself; especially as this whole mess was her fault.

I sat down at the far end of the bar, away from the few other patrons. I didn't know what I wanted to drink, all I knew was the stronger it was the better.

"What can I get for you?" The bartender asked.

"Something strong and cheap." I told him, without even looking up.

"That bad a day eh, dude?" he said, pouring me a drink of what appeared to be a spirit.

"Sure is." I replied, which was the understatement of a lifetime. Today had gone from bad, to one of the worst days I could remember; not that I had the best memory anyway.

Facts, figures and protocol were easy to remember; emotional memories however tended to get lost somewhere within my hard drive; locked away securely for all eternity. I might have been able to break my way into them, but I didn't really want to even try.

What I couldn't comprehend right now was my reaction to being called "dude". People using gendered terms to refer to me usually felt terrible, but this strangely didn't. It wasn't very often I got read as male, but it felt nice sometimes.

It was quite a difference to the "Miss" which I really hated. I felt comforted by the fact that strangers could see me as something other than my assigned gender.

After a lifetime of being forced to go by female terms, it helped me feel better about myself and my identity.

Sometimes you have to cling to the small victories; which was especially important to remember with all the losses I'd had recently.

I had no idea what I was about to drink, even just the smell burned. What it was didn't matter; what mattered was that it was alcohol. With one motion I poured the entirety of it into my mouth, it didn't really taste like anything.

It tasted better than the drink from that night, though the burning sensation was familiar; which meant it must have been strong.

The ambience was relaxing, it was quiet save for a low volume soundtrack in the background. It was certainly better than wherever the hell she took me last night.

It frustrated me that I related everything back to Allie, she was in the past now. She might have still been in our place, but we weren't together any more.

I was free to do whatever I chose now, the realization of which filled me with both fear and excitement. Deciding what I wanted to do both now and with my life in general, was a daunting task.

Things had literally just changed, I didn't have to decide right now. If I didn't take it day by day, it was quickly going to become overwhelming.

I motioned to the bartender for another drink, tonight was about forgetting everything that happened. For the first time in a while I had the night to myself, and I planned to enjoy it.

Even when she went out alone, I still had to be there for her. I didn't need to care about her any more, I didn't have anything or anyone to care about.

I downed my next drink, then returned to my thoughts.

Having nothing to care about made me feel empty, but at the same time it was freeing. Now I could focus on my own wants and needs, without any distractions I could be anything I wanted.

I knew it would probably lead me to running away and starting fresh again, it sucked; but that way the only person who could hurt me was myself.

There was only twice I'd cared about someone on a deeper level, and both times it had gotten me burned. Both Allie and Cameron made it clear that being alone was better, it wasn't worth the pain and responsibility that came with caring about anyone else.

I blamed myself, but there was only so much I could do to stop someone hell-bent on self destruction.... Or destruction in general.

I consumed my third drink as quickly as the previous two. Everything began to blur, I was drunk and my emotions were creeping up on me. I quickly realized that this may have been a mistake.

There was a real chance I was about to pass out, or go into full sensory overload.

Which meant it was time to go but on the other hand, it might have been fun to pass out in a random bar; I probably deserved whatever came with that. Anything that did happen was surely karma. I'd fucked over all sorts of people for my job.

It comforted me to think that I deserved all the bad that came my way; I suppose it was easier to paint myself as a terrible person than for the world to be bad and scary.

One of the reasons I left Allie was to have my own life; if I threw it all away being reckless like her, it would have all been for nothing. I needed to live and actually have a life for once, which I knew wasn't going to be easy.

Once I left here I had to go back to where she was. I wasn't sure I could handle being that near her, at least not right now.

I paid contactlessly as I left the bar. I dreaded going back to the apartment, I had no idea if it would even be safe for me to do so. When we had petty arguments or I provoked her, the outbursts were scary enough. Just the thought of how bad they could be after I left her terrified me.

I wished it was an overreaction, but there was a real possibility she could actually kill me. She had a track record.

There had to be somewhere to go, somewhere I could delay having to go back; even if it was just for a few minutes.

The perfect idea came to me. I was hungry, and there was a certain pizza place nearby.

I could get something to eat and forget about Allie for a while, maybe even forever. All I had to do was flirt with Clair from the other night, all evidence pointed to the fact that she was into me.

She initiated everything, and honestly? Who wouldn't be into me?

Allie made a huge mistake screwing up with me. It wasn't going to be hard to find someone new.

It was comfortable and familiar to be alone, but it wasn't ideal. Maybe the type of person I usually went for was the problem, there were distinct similarities between Allie and Cameron.

They both placed fun above all else, and neither seemed to care about me in a significant way; except when I was getting them out of messes.

The solution was to find someone nice, and maybe I had already found them.

I only had three drinks but it was enough for the world to feel like it was spinning. I knew it was, but I wasn't supposed to be able to feel it.

Most things around here were relatively close to each other. Anything you needed could be found by essentially following the coastline, and what I needed right now was Clair.

After almost falling over a couple of times, it dawned on me that getting this drunk was a mistake. It was no longer a distraction, and now I just felt drunk as well as emotional.

I somehow managed to find the pizza shop. Through the window I saw someone else working the counter, which revealed a flaw in my plan.

I couldn't help but feel disappointed, how was I ever going to replace Allie if the one person I knew wasn't working tonight. As disappointed as I was, sadly I still needed to eat.

I couldn't manage something as simple as talking to the man working the counter. Without even uttering a word, I pointed at a slice of pizza in the heater and handed him my card. I wanted to be out of here as quickly as possible.

My emotions were getting to me, which caused all too familiar sensations. Every sound was unbearable, the lighting was particularly awful here; bright but also relentlessly buzzing. Without even stopping to say thanks, I grabbed my food and rushed out the door.

A few minutes into the walk home, my thoughts caught up with me.

Why did this all have to happen to me?

Why was the entire world so intent on everything going wrong?

I might have done a few fucked up things to make money, but I helped people; I helped them solve problems that nobody else wanted to help with. Why was I being punished when all I ever did was help people?

My anger, and the thoughts swirling around my mind; made the hazy spacey feelings start coming back.

All I wanted was for the girl who worked there to be working tonight, and maybe to fall in love with me. Apparently that was too much to ask, I should have been used to nothing going my way.

It was just my luck that someone would kiss me, and then when I want to see them again they wouldn't be around. Even though it was probably just her schedule, it was hard to not feel slighted.

Especially as everything seemed to centre around me; Allie chose me, Clair whoever she even was chose me, the lady from my work chose me.

I was constantly at the centre of everything, which came with an immense amount of pressure; which wasn't always the greatest thing.

Thoughts swirled around my head the entire walk back, which surprisingly I managed without much trouble.

Stood in the doorway I felt a surreality about being here; just hours ago it was a comforting place to be, it was physically the same yet it felt so different.

What was once a home, was now just a collection of rooms. The place which was supposed to be our home had never felt like one less.

It was as if this place was frozen in time, everything was the same as when I left.

The moment I crossed the threshold into the apartment, every bad memory of Allie flooded back at once.

Right there was where she choked me until I passed out, the bathroom over there was where she hurt herself, and to the other side of the apartment was her room; the room where she ruined everything.

I had never felt this uneasy, especially not in my own place. Her room was just meters away but I felt so alone; I somehow missed her. There was a lack of excitement without her around, it was safer but at the same time so boring.

Maybe I'd made a mistake? Maybe I didn't deserve anything to go right? Tonight felt like a sign, nothing went right for me. Perhaps Clair wasn't working because nothing was ever supposed to happen between us.

What if the best I could ever hope for was my dysfunctional relationship with Allie? For the past couple of hours, I had tried to convince myself that I was better off alone; but I wasn't sure if I believed it any more.

Was being with her really any worse than being alone forever?

After thinking it over for a few more minutes, it was obvious that this was all I deserved; this was my punishment for being a terrible person.

We had both admitted to being awful people just a few days ago, maybe we deserved each other.

With my eyes closed and with a deep breath, I took a few steps closer to her door and pushed it open.

CHAPTER 30

It took a few moments, but I eventually got the courage to open my eyes. From the quietness, it shouldn't have been surprising that she wasn't here. Part of me would have loved to find her still crying over the break up. It would have felt nice knowing that I mattered to her.

She was probably out enjoying herself and not thinking about me whatsoever. Which wasn't that different to usual was it? When did she ever think about me anyway?

A combination of drunkenness, tiredness and the fact that I missed her, made me lie down on her bed. Even sheets that smelled like her were comforting, which made no sense after everything she did; but I guess that's what love does to you.

I wanted to stay and sleep in her bed, but I wasn't sure how she'd have reacted to finding me there; at best it would cause a dramatic ordeal and at worst she'd extinguish the last glimmer of hope I had.

While it was tempting to find out which; I knew I shouldn't make these type of decisions whilst drunk in my ex-partner's room.

With one of her pillows, I left her room. Knowing how oblivious she was, the chance of her noticing a missing pillow seemed pretty low.

I headed to my room, shutting her door gently on the way.

I needed to sleep even more than I needed Allie, or the girl whose name I couldn't even remember any more. The fun effects of alcohol had long since worn off, I felt like a complete mess both emotionally and physically.

There were always going to be tomorrows and days after that, and while rash decisions were fun in the short term; they often caused bigger problems in the long run, which was obvious from spending any time with Allie.

The moment I closed my eyes with my head on her pillow; I felt myself drifting right off to sleep.

Most of last night was still a blur, but my piercing headache quickly reminded me of the disastrous night; though it wasn't as bad as it could have been, at least I was in my bed alone.

As I started to piece together memories, it struck me that it probably was a good thing she wasn't in last night. Her reactions aside, I wasn't ready to see her; and yet part of me still wished I had.

The last thing we needed was me giving her more opportunity to do something selfish.

Part of me still felt being with her was all I deserved, I knew deep down that I was an awful person. That same thought process gave some comfort however; if I could be a better person, then I would deserve better.

As much as I loved to blame Allie, both of us were to blame for this mess. Our relationship was in the past now; I had to change for myself. The only chance at a better future was to try more than ever,

The fact she wasn't in last night gave the impression she wasn't going to change; which was upsetting.

I still hoped she'd someday come to the same realization that I did; I wasn't in a position to try forcing her to be better any more, I had tried as much as I could. It would have made me feel important to make her change, but she needed to figure this one out on her own.

I couldn't entirely blame her, there was some logic behind her stubbornness. Changing was going to be hard.

Even though it was what I needed, was it worth the effort?

On the flip side, had I ever been happy, or at least happy without it causing harm to anyone?

There were moments with Allie where I thought I was happy, but they were fleeting. It proved that I had the capability to be happy. For once I had to let myself be happy.

Like I realized last night, I had almost endless options. I had nothing, which was both exciting and terrified me at the same time. I could try anything I liked.

I wanted to figure it all out right now, but frustratingly I knew it would take some time.

Everything reminded me of what was, and now couldn't be; all the memories of Allie were making it hard to try moving forward.

The best option was to be away from here, I needed to forget her and focus on my own enjoyment and happiness.

There was still so much of the city I hadn't seen, only the beach and places around it; there had to be more to this place than places tainted with memories of Allie.

Leaving our apartment and exploring by myself, would be a good start both practically and symbolically. Leaving Allie and her memories behind, whilst I expanded my horizons would be the perfect start to a new life.

After adjusting my hair, I was ready to go. It was disgusting, but having no other clothes made it easier to just leave quickly.

I had no plans for the future, or even the rest of the day. The important thing was getting away from here. Baby steps are still steps, but nobody cares about babies.

Downloading an upgrade at a few bytes a second is still upgrading, no matter how slow it is. That was a better metaphor.

With it already being evening, most of the tourists weren't around. It was the quiet time between families going to their accommodation, and the people going out for the night.

For a city the ambience and general feelings were quite relaxing. I'd never taken the time to explore my surroundings. Generally it was busy here, but even with the abundance of tourists there was a real feeling of community.

Which was never more obvious than when I saw strangers interacting. The capability that other people had to be nice was astounding to me.

Seeing strangers helping out tourists was something I didn't understand, trusting anyone felt like a huge risk. But at the same time, helping someone who was probably feeling hopeless in that moment, probably felt amazing.

Imagining the attention and praise made me reconsider my position.

It was a good thing that not everyone was like Allie; some people seemed to actually appreciate help even, from strangers.

The vulnerability that came with asking for help wasn't really appealing; I would much rather be on the giving end of the advice. Putting trust in other people wasn't an enticing concept, and neither was having to do what someone told me was the right thing.

It was better to be needed than the one needing help, needing other people never went well for me.

I found myself once again at the beach, the bars scattered all around here tempted me. Repeating last night and not having to think about anything for a while, was an easy solution to everything happening.

But going down the destructive alcoholic path again wasn't the best idea.

As much as I still admired some of Allie's traits, I knew I should stay well away from her self-destructive habits.

It was more beneficial to channel her uncaring nature into a "nothing matters so I can try anything" mindset.

It took several moments, but I came to a decision.

Repeating patterns and being my same old self wasn't going to change anything; that was basic logic. If anything was to change, I had to be proactive; nothing would change on its own. I had to make things happen.

With my mind made up, I headed down a random street. Along it were various stores, none of which were particularly interesting. That didn't stop me from gazing into every window I passed, hoping for a spark of inspiration to hit me.

There had to be something out here that called to me, something I never considered before.

The old me wasn't a good person, the only logical way to rectify this was to be someone else; everything needed to change.

After an endless line of chain stores and coffee shops, something eventually caught my interest. Beside me was an art supply store; in my old world, logic was the most valuable thing.

Relying on logic for everything wasn't working out like it used to. Something where logic didn't matter, or at least didn't seem to matter as much felt like the answer.

Once inside, I realized that I didn't have a clue about art at all. There were so many things I could try, but the most important question was what would I be good at?

Being different didn't mean I wanted to waste time on something I wouldn't be any good at.

There had to be something that called to me; drawing wasn't particularly appealing, anything involving tools felt like it would be too physical, maybe painting was the answer? It seemed fun.

With a few bottles of paint and a pack of brushes, I headed towards the canvases. As exciting as it might be to paint on the plain walls of my room; I wasn't ready to step that far out of my comfort zone just yet.

The smallest size of canvas they had seemed perfect, especially for a first attempt. A trickle of doubt crept in as I approached the checkout, maybe this wasn't the right thing to do.

At this point my doubts felt ridiculous, what harm was there in painting? I'd survived being with Allie, nothing could go as wrong as that.

The cashier was cute, for a boy at least; though his pink hair only reminded me of Allie. In a vacuum it would be amazing hair, and I felt guilty that I couldn't truly appreciate it.

With my mind back on Allie, I almost completely lost focus of what I was doing.

Something about buying painting supplies; thank god for contactless payment or my lack of focus would have made it even more difficult.

"Thanks." I said, having just enough focus to try being nice to other people for once.

The old me didn't see the point of thanking someone just for doing their job, but being appreciated by the lady I helped out the other night made me feel good; maybe spreading a bit of warmth, like an inefficient cooling system was the way to go.

I hadn't considered that I would have to find my way back home with a large bag. I could have given up at the first inconvenience, but I knew being a new person would take real effort. Nothing good would ever happen if I didn't at least try.

A few blocks towards home, or what used to be home, I felt a slight stomach pain. There was one thing that would never change; my eating habits. I'd tried eating properly so many times, but I always fell back into surviving on caffeine and protein bars. Which I was starting to almost crave.

There was a supermarket on the opposite side of the road. I needed to eat something and I deserved to treat myself to some comfort items. God knows I've had a distinct lack of comfort ever since meeting Allie.

I wanted to be different, but how important was changing my eating habits really? Eating habits weren't based in morals or anything important like that.

I needed to focus on changing my core personality, tertiary things could always be changed down the line.

The store was busier than expected. I wasn't used to being around this many people, but if I was going to take changing seriously I had to learn to be sociable; or at least learn to tolerate other people.

I always stayed inside and avoided everyone; but I didn't want to be like that any more. Throwing myself in the deep end, which at this moment happened to be a crowded store was the easiest way to force a change.

More frustrating than the people, was the store's layout; whoever decided on the order of aisles in here certainly didn't have much logical sense, or maybe they did...

Nonsensically ordered aisles probably manipulated people into spending; forcing people like me to walk around to find just a few things. They probably hoped random sales and offers would catch my eye and I'd spend more than intended; but I wasn't that easy to manipulate.

Though maybe I did need a ten dollar chocolate bar...

After staring for a few seconds, I came to my senses; I couldn't work right now, and I had all but drained my savings.

When this entire mess was sorted out I could treat myself, but until then I had to be careful.

After weaving through the crowd, I finally found what I came for. Caffeine was the reason I was able to do anything, weirdly it seemed to calm me down too.

It had been a long time since I'd had any, which probably hadn't helped the way I'd been feeling. With a six pack of energy drinks in hand, I headed off to find my other craved item; protein bars.

Even though they were food, most stores tended to shelve them with supplement items; which I never really understood.

Unfortunately there wasn't much variety. Strawberry was a decent flavour, but it wasn't my favourite; though this was a trend in my life, I could never get what I really wanted.

Whilst trying to carry the bars, a six pack of energy drinks and the bag of art supplies, I realized that I probably should have grabbed a basket. I barely had the coordination to weave through crowds as it was, never mind with my hands completely full.

Using the self-checkout whenever possible still made sense, even if it was something the old me did. It was quicker and a lot less awkward.

Changing didn't mean discarding logic completely; because then I would essentially be Allie. Nobody wanted to be her, I'm not sure even she wanted to be her; but she stubbornly clung to her old ways even though they were ruining her life. If me leaving wasn't enough of a sign she needed to change, then nothing would be.

The fact she was out last night, stole all the hope I had of her ever changing.

Something finally went my way, I didn't have to deal with the obnoxious "unexpected item in bagging area" error.

Even with my attempts to be better some things never failed to infuriate me; that being one of them.

Things should work the way they were designed to, especially for me. It might have been because I was a terrible person that they didn't; the cognitive dissonance in my thoughts made me uneasy. I was important so I deserved good, but at the same time I was a terrible person who deserved nothing.

At some point I would have to examine some of my thought processes, though the middle of a grocery store probably wasn't the best of places.

As I left I tried to focus on nicer things, like the fact that when I got home I was going to paint something amazing.

I still craved the feeling of perfection, when Allie was around it had fell to the wayside; but it was mostly for her sake. There was no point in being different if I wasn't perfect at it.

I walked back "home" as quickly as possible, trying to resist the now ever present urge to resort to alcohol again. I couldn't let myself be like her, at least not in those ways. I would hate myself even more if I became like her, and that was the only thing keeping me on top of my impulses.

Once our apartment block was in sight, uneasy feelings started to flood over me. There was something about this place, we had made a few nice memories here; but it was always the bad ones that flooded back. It was for the best that she wasn't in last night; I couldn't let myself get sucked back in.

Just being with her had broken me mentally, though admittedly I wasn't the most mentally healthy person before either.

Our relationship wasn't healthy for either of us; I constantly enabled her dramatic and impulsive ways and constantly gave her the attention that she craved.

The feelings only intensified once I made it inside. The living room was the worst of all; this was where she had done so many things.

Whilst my room had a semblance of safety, there was still my shattered laptop which brought back memories. Despite that, this was my space; the only place I had which wasn't filled with memories of her.

The only bad feeling in here was self hatred, rather than the almost flashback and dissociating or whatever the hell was happening to me in every other room.

Once I was on my bed, I quickly opened and downed a can of energy drink and ate one of the protein bars. Why didn't everyone do this? It was way less effort and more practical than actually eating.

Now with annoying biological functions out of the way, it was time to take my first real step in becoming a new and better person; doing something which seemed completely against my character. Art.

CHAPTER 31

I couldn't see much logic in art. From what I gathered, it was an expression of emotions and feelings; both of which were incredibly illogical by nature.

Oh how I wished I wasn't cursed with having emotions. Everything would have been so much easier if I lacked the capacity to care, this whole Allie thing would have never happened. I wouldn't have to undertake this dramatic change just to have a good life.

With the canvas and brushes open, I was almost ready to start. This had to go perfectly, if it didn't I would have to find something else. This was the only thing drastic enough to make a difference, this was my only chance.

The colour pink was still on my mind, it made sense for me to start with that.

Pink was my starting point, the catalyst for me realizing I needed to be better. She gave me the drive to better myself, I should at least be thankful for that. I hoped that someday she would find the same drive to be better.

On some level it would have made me feel good about myself if losing me was enough for her to change. She needed to be better, it was obvious that her chaos came from a place of not liking herself.

At least not consistently, she had such an unstable view of herself; from one minute to the next she could go from acting like she was queen of the world, to smashing her head on the wall of the bathroom. She confused me more than anyone else.

With the brush in hand, I dipped it into the pink paint. Just as I was about to make contact with the canvas, something stopped me; I had no idea what I was doing.

Was not knowing really so bad? Pushing through the unknown headstrong into new things, was a good way to be a new me.

It took a while, but I managed to push through my apprehension; with masterful brushstroke after brushstroke onto the canvas.

I followed up with some black and then purple. It felt freeing to completely cast aside logic even just for a few seconds.

The spontaneity of each individual motion, each one having a lasting effect on my art was exciting. I was already doing amazingly, maybe even perfectly.

Once I stopped and actually took a look at what I'd painted I realized...

I realized that all I had created was a smudged mess of paint that didn't resemble anything.

It could pass as abstract, but realistically it looked like what it was; smudged paint. My perceptions were wrong. Again.

How could I have thought I was amazing at something I was clearly terrible at?

This was impossible to deal with, if anything was going to change I had to be perfect.

The process was enjoyable, but what wasn't was the idea of being flawed. The only thing I ever had was being better than everyone else; even if I changed my entire personality, hobbies, and career, I still had to be the best.

My frustration with the paint began to rise, when once again the all too common signs returned. I knew I was in store for a bad couple of hours.

Why did the world have to be so painful on a sensory level? Couldn't there just be a moment of silence in this universe?

Sound and light or any feeling for that matter was excruciating. Pulling the covers over myself provided a slight relief, very very slight.

Whenever this happened, it messed with my perception of time; had I been under the blanket for a few minutes or had hours passed?

As it was already being dark outside, I had no way of knowing. I couldn't check the laptop, and the phone wasn't safe to use. All I knew was it was night-time, and that I probably needed sleep.

Every noise disturbed me, passing cars, the crashing of waves, sea breezes, all of it. If I stubbornly kept my eyes closed, I had to eventually fall asleep right?

At some point during the night I had managed to fall asleep, this was evident by it being light out.

People may have wanted to deny it, but sometimes sleep did help. I still felt residual frustration that painting hadn't gone perfectly, but with a fresh waking mind I wanted to cling to the enjoyment I got from it in the moment.

If there was anything to take from my time with Allie, it was that fun had value. There was one thing she got right, doing things purely because they were fun; something which I had struggled with my whole life.

It hurt to even think about, but I had to accept I couldn't be perfect right away. I had sort of lucked my way into being good at coding and the skills needed for my last job; they were logic based. Patterns, sequences and rules, those things came naturally to me: art though.

Art was different, there were very few rules and essentially infinite numbers of things I could do.

Well no, not infinite but countless amounts of things to try. I knew it would be hard, but I needed to not be purely ruled by logic; I had to learn to go with what felt right in the moment.

Using logic to make every decision hadn't served me well, I had never truly been happy; so there wasn't much to lose. The thought of being completely illogical scared me, there had to be a middle ground somewhere.

It hurt to admit, but I couldn't change as much as I wanted by myself; I needed help.

There was something I had overlooked, something almost obsolete but something that could help.

Books. Up until the recent past, books contained almost all of humans collective knowledge. That was the answer, though I wasn't surprised my technology obsessed brain had missed the obvious.

There was the added benefit that buying a book didn't come with the same vulnerability of asking an actual human to help, which would have been the worst thing ever.

Just as I was about to leave, I heard footsteps outside the door.

It could only have been one person, but I wasn't ready to see Allie. I still loved her.

Was I strong enough to see her and not be pulled straight back into her chaotic world? I was about to find out just how much of a changed person I was capable of being.

There was no way to predict what was about to happen, instead of retreating to my room I stood frozen in place. Anything could happen when chaos herself was about to walk through the door.

When the door swung open, she looked surprised to see me standing there. An awkward tension filled the room, neither of us wanted to be the first to move or speak.

For a few moments we both stood staring at each other in painful silence. Usually it was noise that hurt, but this silence was excruciating on an emotional level; I never thought I'd find myself hoping for loudness, but here I was.

Eventually she broke the silence,

"Hi Pix." was all she said, as she scurried away into her room carrying something.

As usual she slammed her door loudly behind her, expecting anything different was just disappointment waiting to happen.

There was something different however; where was the drama? Where was the intensity?

She confused me more than ever, but it wasn't my job to care any more. I did care, but indulging her with attention wouldn't have been helpful to anyone.

Now that she was back, there was much more urgency in needing to leave. I would have loved to find out what her new attitude towards me meant, but I doubted that it was worth the risk.

I had no faith in her to actually change; I knew anything she did would be for attention. It was going to take something drastic to give me hope again.

I couldn't live my life desperately hoping that she'd one day be a better person. Nothing good could come from being engrossed by something that could never exist.

I knew that me and her could never have a healthy relationship. I needed to move on, we both did. I had my own life to live and enjoy, I had to take the enjoyment I found in art and run with it. Run far far away from Allie with it.

I left through the door that she forgot to close, slamming it behind me.

I wanted to reciprocate the message that she was sending; or at least the one I assumed it symbolized, shutting me out. Which I hoped was a sign that we were both trying to move forward.

I felt far more comfortable being out on the street than I did being in the same place as her. It wasn't entirely her fault, I played my own part in it all; without my enabling I wasn't sure things would have gotten this bad.

The reason I had to leave wasn't all on her, I had no trust in myself. In the back of my mind I had the temptation to go running back to her, but I couldn't let myself be pulled back into that mess. It wouldn't have been good for either of us.

Nothing caught my eye as I tried to use shop windows to distract myself. There had to be a bookshop somewhere around here. I needed something to take my mind off Allie, all that would come from obsessing over her was more chaos and drama.

Without paying attention to where I was going, I had ended up back at the beach.

All roads in Azura seemed to lead to the ocean.

This area seemed to be the most popular, but it was more likely that I would find what I needed in the less tourist filled parts. Most stores tended to be away from the coast, which made sense financially considering how much our apartment was and that it was quite a walk from the shore.

I decided to go the same way as yesterday, it was the best chance of finding something useful. Various stores caught my eye, but today I was on a mission to find a bookshop.

I could come back anytime and look in the weirdly overpriced vintage stores. It was weird that anyone would pay so much for something old. It didn't make sense, but these stores were everywhere; I had to be missing something.

Not more than a few meters down the road, I noticed a tiny bookshop. The small size made me worry about finding anything, though part of me hoped to find an obscure book; to help me find a unique perspective on art. I figured it would help me gain an edge, making it easier to find my own style; and more importantly become amazing.

Fun was fun, but perfection and being the best was also important if not more so.

The smell of old books overwhelmed me. It had been years since I'd experienced this, probably not since school. It was strange how something as simple as a smell could bring back so many disgusting feelings.

The less time spent thinking about a childhood filled with enforced gender stereotypes the better.

Piles and piles of books surrounded me, shelves crammed to their limits; I was sure any stray movements would get me buried in a literary avalanche. The sheer amount of books made it clear I was going to need help.

That realization scared me, but I needed to face my fears at some point. Me and a middle aged woman working the register were the only ones here; nobody else would see me at my most vulnerable state. The less people who saw me like this the better.

"Do you have any books for new artists?" I asked.

After a few moments of silence, all that followed was a heavy sigh.

It was her job to help people though. Why would anyone work in a bookshop if the idea of helping someone buy books was such an awful concept to them? It wasn't just Allie that confused me, the majority of humanity had the same effect.

"Down there, in that box." she replied, with the most disgruntled of looks on her face.

There was only me in here, I couldn't understand why helping someone was such a pain to her.

None of the books in the box really called out to me. All the titles were condescending, I wanted something that would make me feel good; not something that would treat me like a fucking child.

It took a while to rummage through the whole box but eventually I saw something; Not for the paint-hearted from zero to amazing in just weeks.

Weeks was way longer than I anticipated this taking, but the pun amused me. If there was any reason to buy a book, a pun in the title was as good a reason as any.

Somehow the book was only two dollars, which was amazingly cheap. The lady working the counter seemed to be even more unimpressed that I actually wanted to buy something. With my card in hand, I went to pay; which only earned me a more irritated reaction from her.

"Now I have to start the fricking card machine and for what, just two dollars?"

"There's no rush," I told her, as I forced myself to be nice; which only caused her to roll her eyes at me.

I was starting to get the impression that she didn't want my money, but I needed this book. Moments passed as the card machine just wouldn't work, during which I just stood there awkwardly.

"Just take the book and fucking get out of here, you entitled millennial queer bitch," she hissed out of nowhere. Followed by,

"Expecting everyone to have a working card machine, too good to use cash? What is wrong with people nowadays?" Loud enough for me to hear, but quiet enough to feign subtlety.

I had no idea what her problem was. It wasn't my fault that it wouldn't work. Snapping back at her would have been so easy, but I could read her. Yelling would only play into what she already assumed about me; that I was an entitled mean millennial. Maybe I was, but I wasn't going to give her the satisfaction of being right.

"Aw thanks so much." I told her, with the biggest forced smile on my face. Her reaction was priceless, I could see the rage building as her face went redder and redder.

Just as it looked like she was going to explode with anger, another customer walked in. On my way out I flashed her a victorious smile.

It was becoming more obvious by the day that I had to avoid any highly charged emotional situations. It limited what I could do, but I had no choice if I wanted to avoid overloading.

This was the opportune time to put that into practice, the shop situation had frustrated me to no end. I was on the edge of an overload, I had to calm down. Luckily I was near the beach; it still reminded me of Allie. but it wasn't the worst place to try relaxing. There was a chance I could channel some of my Allie related thoughts into trying to be better.

The sudden drop in temperature and sky turning a dark grey had caused the streets to empty. People, tourists mostly, didn't seem to appreciate the changing weather; I however appreciated the lack of people around.

The sea winds could be frustrating at times, but there was something I enjoyed about it too; I enjoyed the feeling of being pushed as I tried to walk, even though it could be dangerous.

I liked to think it was the feeling of pushing through despite everything trying to push me back; I wasn't quite Allie levels of stubbornness but I was up there.

Upon reaching the beach, I gazed down at the sand, It was practically a sandstorm down there; which wouldn't have calmed me at all.

Leaning over the railing overlooking the beach was calming enough; the sights, the sounds, the fact I was the only person around. Everything about this scene was relaxing, having some space and time by myself was exactly what I needed.

It seemed that nobody else was brave enough, or perhaps foolish enough, to be out in this weather. The only people around were me and a girl at the other end of the promenade, features of whom I couldn't quite make out; both of us leaning over the railings, deep in our own thoughts.

Every so often we would catch each others gaze, before staring back out toward the sea.

I continually shifted between gazing at the beauty of the late afternoon horizon and being drawn to the only other person here. It was amazing how much just being here had calmed me.

It may have just been my imagination, but it seemed like the girl was slowly making her way along the promenade closer and closer to me.

People were always drawn to me, so it wasn't surprising; but who was she? And why was this happening?

CHAPTER 32

With each glance towards whoever she was, it became obvious that she was in fact walking towards me. With each step, a vague sense of familiarity began to grow. There was something different about the hair; the platinum blonde threw me completely.

When she was no more than a meter away, it finally dawned on me who she was.

I couldn't be here with her; Why of all places did she have to be here? It was such a bad idea even being this close to her.

After taking a few seconds to look at her, I turned to leave without saying a word.

As I turned to leave Allie for maybe the last time, I felt her holding onto my sleeve.

"Pixel, wait we need to talk," she stammered, tripping over every one of her words; sounding like she was fighting back tears.

If this had been just a few days ago, I would have agreed so quickly. It was too little too late now, there was nothing she could say to change how I felt.

"I'm sorry Allie." I told her, being unable to even look at her as I turned to leave.

She let go of my sleeve, not being quite as stubborn as I knew she usually would. It upset me that she was showing signs of being better now that it was too late, she could have tried at any point we were together.

I barely managed to get a few steps away from her, when her voice stopped me in my tracks.

"Please Pix, at least talk to me. I get that we can't be together any more, but I really want to try being a better person."

This was different to the way she usually spoke, there was none of her usual fakeness or nonchalant tone; she sounded sincere and desperate.

If she hadn't been out last night, I might have been willing to give her another chance. Her going out only lead me to the conclusion that she was going to stay the same forever. Even with my strange concept of time, she had gotten home at the same time I was leaving this morning; I could only assume where she'd been.

As genuine as she sounded, I still had nothing to say to her. I couldn't trust anything that came out of her mouth, she had manipulated me in the past. Trusting her just wasn't worth the risk.

Just seeing her was enough to make me sad about what could have been between us; but we were both too messed up for anything to ever work out.

"I even changed my hair." she pointed out, as it wasn't completely obvious.

Was changing her hair colour really that meaningful? Some people changed their hair on a whim, maybe it was just her impulses like most things she did. Pink was somewhat of an important part of her identity though....

"Yeah I noticed." I replied, not really wanting to enable or give her anything to use against me.

"Pink hair was a big part of the old me. After watching my favourite show together, it was too much of a reminder that I've probably lost you. It was too painful to keep."

This was something I never expected, the Allie I had always known was so uncaring. She was someone who did whatever she wanted without reason or justification. Painting her this way might have been unfair on my end, she had actually helped me out a few times; but she had also hurt me a lot too.

I wanted to believe that it meant she cared, but there was the issue of last night. If she was going out and doing the same things, just how committed to being different could she be?

"You went out last night, can I really trust you to be different if you're still doing the things we did the other night?" I asked, which made her cry.

I was on the verge of tears too, but it was important that I kept calm; otherwise I'd fall right back where she wanted me.

"I've done nothing to earn your trust I know, but could you trust me just this once? I was out all night, but it was for a good reason. I was meeting someone who said they could set me up with minor acting roles. I thought it'd be a good way to channel my dramatic side."

I was shocked to say the least. I never expected her to try, and it felt nice knowing I was the reason she wanted to change. This situation had me torn, I still loved her but deep down I knew nothing could ever be different with me and her.

The only result I could see in trying again, was a few days of closeness followed by slipping back into our old ways.

"Anyway Pix, I'm sorry for being so self-centred and never thinking of anyone else. I'll always remember the times we had together, even though I ruined most of it."

This felt like the perfect ending to our relationship. We both knew we needed to be better people, not for each other, but for ourselves.

Even though it was the perfect end, I needed to head back before either one of us did something impulsive.

"I'll never forg-" I couldn't even finish my sentence, I found myself distractedly gazing deep into her eyes.

I continued gazing deeply into her eyes, as waves of emotion flooded over me.

I loved her, I'd never really loved anyone like this before. Not even Cameron. People only experience feelings like this once in a lifetime if they're lucky; If anything was worth a risk, it was this.

Leaning forward, our lips met for the first time in days. Oh, how I had missed this feeling. For several moments we gently kissed and everything was right in the world.

"This has to be the last try though, for both of our sakes," I told her, interrupting the kissing.

All she did was nod in agreement.

In any other circumstance this would have been the perfect moment to share declarations of love, but I knew better.

I had tried to force it on her in the past, and I now knew that was unfair of me. It was better to wait until she was ready, even if she never was; I could at least show love and care without needing to say it explicitly.

"You know I fucked up quite a few times too? It wasn't all your fault," I told her.

"I know."

The fact she was being honest with me gave me hope. For a while we gazed out over the ocean together,

"I'm sorry too Allie."

Even though I knew I'd hurt her too, it was still so hard to say.

If there was any chance of this working out, I needed to take responsibility for my own screw ups.

I had to keep the fact that my actions had consequences and could hurt others in the front of my mind; otherwise I would so easily slip back into my old ways.

Whilst we were in the midst of our emotional conversation, the storm had begun to pick up significantly. The wind had made it unbearably cold, being beside the sea was probably only adding to the wind chill. Spending time with her beside the ocean was nice, but it was time we went home.

The turn today had taken was unreal, after convincing myself that we were better off apart; here we were again.

Things felt different this time, we had actually had a conversation; and from it I got the impression that both of us wanted to make a real effort this time.

The past had taught me not to trust her, but I had hope. We could do this, I believed in us.

"I'm freezing, can we go home?" I asked.

Without a word, she nodded at me. Whenever she was silent it made me apprehensive, her silence was usually followed by something bad happening.

Instead of being passive aggressive, this time she genuinely seemed to have no idea what to say. The old Allie would have blurted out anything to fill a silence, this Allie though seemed almost thoughtful.

Walking back home with her beside me felt so right, if not slightly awkward. We had never been like this before, everything had always been so intense; now we were silently and slowly strolling home together.

There was no dragging by the hand, and nobody was walking ahead or behind the other. It felt like we were actually together, walking side by side made us seem equal; something we had always struggled with. It made a change from the usual power play dynamic we were usually involved in.

What struck me more than anything was the way she controlled her impulses. Her hand constantly grazed against mine ever so slightly. I'd spent enough time with her to know she'd usually do whatever she wanted, but she didn't. Even on the promenade she let me initiate the kiss, something she would never usually have done.

I took the hint and held her hand. Nothing felt more right, this was where I belonged; this was how things were supposed to be.

Neither of us spoke the rest of the way back, I was too engrossed in feeling like a couple that I didn't want to ruin it; and I hoped she felt the same way. We had a lot to work on, but this felt like a good basis for progress.

Once our building was in sight, the bad memories came flooding back. Spending time with Allie in the outside world felt different than the prospect of being back inside there with her. She had done so many things to me there, and I had done terrible things too.

Hoping things could be different wouldn't erase the past. I had to acknowledge it, but more importantly I had to be brave.

If anything was ever worth the risk, it was this; it was her. She was the most frustrating person I had ever met, but at the same time nobody else had ever made me want to be better.

I knew this could be my only chance at happiness, I had to give it everything I had.

Inside there was another awkward moment, with both of us unsure what to do. It felt likely that neither of us had thought this far ahead. For me at least, this was the last thing I ever expected to happen.

Whilst standing around trying to figure out the next move, my rumbling stomach reminded me I'd forgotten to eat again. If I let my mood crash because of hunger, it would only make this more difficult.

I broke the awkward silence as I headed into my room. A few moments later I returned with a couple of protein bars and energy drinks in hand.

"I thought you might be hungry." I told her, passing her one of each.

Her only response was to look at me with a confused expression, which wasn't unsurprising; most people find food in bar form weird, well most people I ever knew.

"It's a protein bar, they taste good I swear." I wasn't sure if I believed that myself, they tasted edible at best; though maybe I had just gotten used to them.

Without her usual stubbornness, she shrugged and ate it in one bite. This was quite a change from the reaction to eating just a few nights ago; maybe I was right to trust her this time.

After we both ate and drank, the awkward silence returned. We just stared at each other for moments on end, which filled me with apprehension.

I wasn't quite sure what the protocol for interaction with a partner on the first day back together was.

Now seemed like a good time to put all my "I need to be different" into action, instead of being reactionary I was going to take initiative.

I took a few steps towards her, and hugged her tightly. After a few seconds she reciprocated, which felt even more right than the earlier hand holding.

Neither of us had shown much affection in the past, which made this an important step. The fact we were both comfortable with this, was significant progress in our relationship.

We hugged for what must have been several minutes, enjoying the feeling of being this close to each other again; or honestly for the first real time, at least on an emotional level.

The hugging carried on for what must have been several minutes. I never wanted her to let me go, I wanted to always feel this close to her; we'd never been this close on an emotional level. Just as I was starting to really enjoy it, she pulled away staring at my lips.

I knew what she wanted, and I wanted it too. After waiting for a while it was obvious she was waiting for me to initiate, or at least give my approval.

I gave her a little nod and thankfully she understood. The way she pulled me by the hair into a kiss was even more exciting when it was something I wanted; and there wasn't the guilt that came along with baiting her into it either.

I had really missed the feeling of her lips pressed hard against mine, even if it had been just a couple of days. The soft affectionate kisses were nice, but sometimes I needed more.

After a while, she stopped. With her hand tightly holding mine, she began to lead me towards her room.

"Is this okay?" she whispered, to which I responded with a nod.

After dragging me into her room, she sat down on the bed. Without a moments hesitation I sat beside her. Within seconds of me doing so, we were back to kissing; only this time it was followed up by her hands touching me everywhere. I enjoyed it on a physical level, but another part was uncomfortable.

I was too scared to say anything, but she carried on. Panic started to fill my brain, I knew where this was heading.

As I was verging on full panic mode, she stopped.

"We can stop if you like."

"If that's okay."

"It's fine. I'm sorry I didn't think about what you wanted before."

Her caring about me was the best and most unexpected thing. Lying down on her bed for a second, she joined me.

The way she cared was still surprising, I almost expected her to revert to normal as soon as we got back. I closed my eyes for a few moments in an attempt to calm down. Just as I moved to make room for her, she started to head out the door.

"Um, I'll be back in a minute."

The way she rushed out worried me, I didn't want her taking my no as a rejection.

It wasn't anything personal, sex wasn't something I needed that often. It might have been important or a need to other people, but I didn't experience it like that at all. It was neutral at best, and at other times completely disgusting.

I was worried about where she'd rushed off to. I had to trust her, even if last time it lead to her nearly dying from a self inflicted head injury. If she was serious about changing, me showing a lack of trust in her wouldn't help.

As anxious as it made me, I was going to have to wait for her to come back... Or at least wait longer before rushing out there to make sure she wasn't self destructing.

I had to wait for her to come back, or at least wait longer before going to check on her.

CHAPTER 33

After a few nerve racking minutes, she eventually came back.

"Sorry about that, just needed to calm down."

Her response was better than I expected. I should have trusted her more, considering I'd discovered how helpful having some space was. This entire day had been a roller-coaster of emotions and I was drained.

As she got back onto the bed, she slid her arm underneath my head; which helped me drift off to sleep.

***

It still amazed me how much easier falling asleep was with her beside me. It early evening when I felt myself falling asleep, but daylight was already starting to light up the room.

Today was an important day; The first day of trying to have a better relationship. Last night was fun, but I knew how we both could be. Healthiness for one night was easy, extending it past that was where we always failed.

This had to go well for both our sakes, it was the last chance.

Even her expressions seemed different, from dazed confusion to what seemed like a genuine smile; not the fake overdramacized expressions I was used to.

I could only assume she thought this was a dream; but for better or worse it was real life.

Cuddling closer to her, I wanted nothing more than to enjoy spending time with her. Simple acts of affection always made me feel so much closer to her on an emotional level; I could have stayed here doing this all day.

"What are we doing today? Staying in all day would be boring," she said, in her usual tone which unsettled me as she sounded dangerously close to her old self. I wished she could just enjoy being together like I was doing, though perhaps that was asking too much.

At least she had told me how she felt for a change. The way she needed to always be doing something made me apprehensive; That night gave me an insight into the kind of things she found fun.

Even with all the small changes, I couldn't help but wonder if I'd made the biggest mistake of my life.

"What do you want to do?" I asked. Trying to communicate was better than letting my brain jump to all sorts of nerve-wracking conclusions. She took a few moments to think about it before answering.

"Well it's a tourist city, there must be a reason they come here right?"

She had a point, there had to be a reason beside the beach that people flocked here.

There had to be more to this place than we'd already experienced. I had planned on exploring it more anyway and it had to be more fun with her around.

If there was one guaranteed thing in this world, it was that with Allie around nothing was ever boring.

"We've never been on an actual date have we? If we're trying again it might be a good place to start."

She was right. We lived together, we'd been through a hell of a lot of things together; But the one thing we'd never done was go on a date. Adding some normalcy to our relationship could only be a good thing.

"That sounds great." I told her.

"I think there's a fairground somewhere nearby, I remember seeing the posters!" she squealed right into my ear.

Her being this excited was almost worth the pain, almost. Excited Allie was one of the best things in the world, especially when her face lit up and her hands moved around in joy. What was even better was when she was excited about something that wasn't dangerous.

It was a relief to see her coping with her need for excitement in better ways. She was still the Allie I knew and loved, but a debugged, improved, more stable release; I hoped anyway.

The one downside of going to the fair, was the inevitable loudness and mass of people. I hoped there would be quiet corners, or anywhere quieter for me to take a break when I needed. The way this city was constructed meant there was always a dark alleyway or side street for me to hide down when I needed, so there should be one near the fair.

Before I went anywhere, I needed to eat something. With a stretch and groan, I went to get the last protein bars from my room. Mine didn't even last the trip back, I was that hungry.

Once I was back in the room I threw the other to Allie. I wasn't sure what I expected to happen, but as usual she wasn't paying attention.

She only noticed when it ended up hitting her right in the face. A few days ago this would have been disastrous, but now it was amusing. I tried as hard as possible to stifle my laughter, though I failed miserably.

My laughter and amusement was soon cut short, as I thought back to how I'd treated her in the past. She deserved to be cared for, whether she wanted my love or not. All that mattered was helping her be as happy as possible, I had been too focused on the reciprocation.

Maybe love wasn't all about the reciprocation, maybe wanting the best for someone and caring about them was what love was. It frustrated me that it had taken this long to figure that out.

It still astounded me how oblivious she could be. Not only did she not notice the protein bar flying towards her, she also ignored any pain that must have come from being hit by it. Protein bars weren't exactly the softest of food. It took her a while, but eventually she noticed and began to eat it.

"How do you eat these all the time? They're not that great."

I didn't really want to admit it, but she was right. The main reason I bought them was convenience, especially when I forgot to eat completely. So many times I had been focused on working until the early hours, without eating all day. Cooking or even ordering food was such a chore at times.

"It's because I forget to eat." I explained to her, there wasn't much point lying or being evasive in response to a simple question. There was the added benefit of her being the last person in the world that could take the moral high ground when it came to eating habits.

Any shame that came with being vulnerable, was secondary to the need to actually communicate with Allie now.

Whilst getting ready I was once again reminded how desperately I needed new clothes. I had been wearing the same ones ever since we got here; it was as convenient as it was disgusting.

Even though I bought them, I envied the fact that she had more clothes than I did. My envy quickly faded when I saw how amazing she looked in the pink poofy dress. Pink really was her colour. There was one thing more surprising than how good it looked on her, the fact it had pockets; which I only noticed when she slipped something into one of them.

From my attempts at trying to conform to the gender binary, I knew just how rare it was to get functional pockets.

Hand in hand, we headed out the door together. Everything about today was surreal; we'd never been out this early, let alone to go on a date.

If anything proved we were being different, it was the fact we were awake in the daytime.

The one downside of being out in the day was just how busy it was. The traffic was backed up, and people crowded the pavement. I hadn't quite mastered the skill of being around strangers; being around this many people frustrated me.

Only one person in the world really mattered... Well, Allie did too. As did everyone else here, I guess; but it was hard to remember everyone else mattered not just me.

We were both too stubborn to let go of the other's hand, even when it made manoeuvring our way through the crowd more difficult. I wasn't going to let go of her hand for anything; I had waited so long to have something resembling a healthy relationship with Allie, and nothing was going to take that away from me.

It was quite a walk to the fair, but even with all the people around it didn't take that long. Or it didn't seem to take a long time with my attention almost entirely focused on Allie.

It was some distance to the fair, but even with all the people around the walk didn't take long. My entire attention had been on Allie the whole way here, so in reality I wasn't sure how long the walk took; but it felt quick.

When the Ferris Wheel came into view, I knew we had made it. The idea that Allie was taking me on a date was still strange; I'd never been on one with anyone, and nobody had asked me on one either.

I'd been in a few relationships before, but all it entailed was going to each other's places. Which almost inevitably lead to them wanting to do sexual things, which I usually felt obligated to go along with.

Never in a million years did I think Allie would be the one who took me on my first date. I had always assumed dates were too formal and committed for her.

This train of thoughts stopped me dead in my tracks, as a few tears escaped my eyes.

"What's with the tears?" she asked. I wasn't sure whether to be grateful at her paying attention to me, or hate that she noticed me crying.

Despite her blunt way of asking, it was clear that she cared. There was no way I could tell her what I felt, she would have thought it was ridiculous.

I felt so ashamed, that I couldn't even look at her. I found myself once again wishing I didn't have emotions.

"Talk to me." she said, sounding more serious this time.

I didn't want to open myself up like this, but communication was going to be important. After all the times I'd gotten frustrated at her for not sharing, I couldn't then go and do the same thing; especially not this early into the retry.

"Nobody has ever asked me on a date before, not even Cameron."

"We don't have to do this."

"I want to, It's just all new to me."

"Who's Cameron by the way?" she asked,

It felt like a mistake to mention him; I didn't want to open up this can of worms, at least not so soon after getting back on track.

"He was...." I paused. I wished I could have stopped there, but I had to mention it at some point; and it would have been unfair to leave her wondering.

"My boyfriend when I was a teenager." I continued.

"Oh, I get it. He left and you never saw him again or something? Relatable."

"Yeah."

What she said was a huge oversimplification, but it was essentially the truth. Sometimes it's best to not kill the mood. Sometimes it's best to not mention the traumatising death of your ex-partner; one who had many similarities to your current partner at that.

It was still a struggle letting someone know how I felt, but I had to try. I hoped the way she hugged me would provide me with some positive reinforcement.

I wasn't sure what I expected her reaction to be. She was really trying and I needed to trust her; or it was going to be me that ruined everything this time.

After calming down in her comforting embrace, we continued into the fairgrounds. As clichéd as it was, being here on a date had a nice feel to it. I couldn't help but pick up on the energy of everyone having fun around me.

Paying attention to Allie became increasingly difficult, the amount of people here and the noise was incredibly distracting. There was one thing I could focus on, and that was how good it felt to be holding her hand; especially compared to the way she used to drag me around.

We weaved through the crowds for a while, before we found ourselves by the Ferris Wheel. Even though I had seen it when we entered, it was much bigger than I expected.

"Wanna go on this?" she asked.

"Sure." I said, despite being apprehensive at how high it was.

There was something about being around her that brought out a bravery in me, which I never knew I had.

In hindsight it was a scary thing, but at the same time it opened me up to having more fun.

We waited in the queue for around ten minutes, surprisingly Allie was quiet; she seemed to be in awe of everything going on around her.

When it was finally our turn, the Ferris wheel surprised me for a second time; it was slower and more calming than I anticipated.

The views from this high up were astonishing, and being this close to the ocean only added to them. It would have been more enjoyable without the constant stopping, but I guess other people needed to get on and off.

When we had reached the very top, I glanced over at Allie and our eyes met. The view was only the second most breathtaking thing in this moment; sat opposite me was the girl I loved more than anything in this world. Without a second thought I pulled her towards me.

Knowing what I wanted, she pressed her mouth against mine. It was the most clichéd of moments, but it was perfect.

Time passed so quickly as we shared a kiss and before I knew it we were at the bottom again; being yelled at by the operator to get off. I had missed out on experiencing the views, but memories of that moment with her would last a lifetime.

After I helped her out of the ride, we once again started wandering around the fair. The majority of attractions here were skill games which offered various prizes.

All it took to win was figuring out the right angle to throw something at, essentially it was maths. If there was one thing I was good at, it was those kind of problems. It wasn't just about winning something, I wanted to impress Allie. She already seemed to think more of me than ever, but praise from her always felt good.

"I'll win you one of these," I told her, pointing to the largest pink bunny plush I had ever seen.

To my surprise they had updated the stalls since I'd been here as a child; with most of them now accepting card payment. It made sense, fewer and fewer people seemed to use cash nowadays; and there's some sort of disconnect between paying on a card and thinking of the money people spent.

I guess someone was wrong about card payments being inconvenient. It felt good to be right, but the important thing here was having fun. It was small steps of progress, but I was starting to see the value in enjoying myself. Without letting myself doubt the choice, I paid.

I had three attempts to knock over a stack of bottles with a ball. My first throw fell way short. Obviously the ball wasn't designed to be thrown very far, there did seem to be something off with the weight distribution.

On the second try I threw hard enough to make contact, but the bottles didn't move even a micrometer. I had always heard these things were rigged, but I assumed logic and math would be enough to win out.

The frustration had begun to get to me, which caused me to throw as hard and straight as I could. The ball hit the stack square in the middle.... but still nothing.

I turned to face Allie, expecting her to be disappointed; but instead I found her laughing. I could certainly see the humour in someone getting worked up over a rigged game. As she continued giggling, I couldn't help but laugh too.

My frustration had all but vanished, despite losing I was having fun. Even the owner of the game trying to bait me into another try just made me laugh harder. It was hard letting myself have fun, but moments like this made it work the effort.

"Oi Lass your boyfriend didn't do very well did he. I'm sure he could do better," he yelled, as we turned and walked away from the booth.

I didn't have chance to respond before Allie shouted back at him.

"She's not my..."

"Just leave it. It's fine really." I whispered as I dragged her toward a quieter area; with her looking confused the whole time.

Once we were away from the crowds, I stopped. This wasn't going to be easy but I wanted to explain my recent feelings on gender.

"Sometimes being read as a boy feels right, Allie. It's confusing and makes no sense, but I need to explore it more," I explained, not having a clue what her response would be.

"Well you're the cutest boy I've ever seen then." she replied without a seconds hesitation.

Her reaction surprised me in the best of ways. I wasn't sure what I expected from her, but this was better than I imagined. It was surreal hearing her say those things out loud, but it felt so right. It didn't make much sense considering how vehemently I had been opposed to being gendered in the past; but the important thing was that it made me feel good.

I had never really thought about why, but I had a feeling it came from a place of wanting to be superior; as if I was somehow better than everyone else for being outside of the normal concept of gender. It was hard to not cling onto old familiar feelings; though if there was one thing to take from these past couple of days, it was that stubbornly clinging to things never went well for me.

I had to focus on what felt right in the moment, and in this moment that was being a boy.

Sharing my feelings was still difficult to do, and I was once again starting to feel drained.

"Can we head back soon?" I asked.
"Want to get some real food first?" she asked in return.

I nodded in agreement, she had the right idea. Protein bars weren't the most healthy of things to live on, and she didn't seem too fond of them anyway. They were convenient, but that was about where the positives ended.

There was one problem, around here were multiple restaurants; which was where my pickiness became an issue. Thankfully there was an easy solution, letting her decide.

"Could you choose somewhere to eat?" I asked, wanting to shove the control onto her; which was better than frustrating myself with indecision. She was better at snap decisions than I was, so it made sense logically. It was also a good idea to give her a chance to be impulsive without harming anyone; even though she was different she was still Allie, and Allie liked to be spontaneous.

Without a word, she began to lead me out of our quiet corner. It amazed me how something as simple as walking by the sea with her felt so great. There was no need to talk, the intimacy that came from holding hands was enough.

Several minutes went by as we walked past a few different diners, as she started to seem frustrated. Not long after, we headed into the next place we saw.

For the next several minutes we walked past a few different diners; with her looking more frustrated after each one. This continued for short while, until she headed into the next place we saw. I had never considered the fact that she thought things through; I had always assumed she just acted on a whim. The new thoughtful side of her was a refreshing change.

Sat at the table with her, made me realize just how strange it was that despite going through so much together; We'd never been out like this before.

Finding a table in a restaurant, being at a restaurant in general, all these things were so strange; We'd never done anything like this before. It felt unfamiliar, but in the best way; sitting down to eat together like an actual couple, was new and comforting.

I still couldn't quite believe that me and Allie were on a date though, I guess that just proved how different we were trying to be.

Something that wasn't different was my struggle choosing something to eat. It frustrated me how difficult it felt to make simple meaningless decisions. I flipped back and forth through the pages on the menu before having an idea. Steak was essentially just protein, a natural meaty protein bar; that might not have been entirely true, but it helped make it a safer choice.

With my mind completely focused on choosing my own food, I had no idea if or what Allie had ordered. I vaguely recalled seeing her talk to the waiter, which meant she probably did get something.

There was a comforting silence as we waited for our food; silence had gone from being foreboding to actually peaceful. Not every moment had to be filled with talking, it was nice to take in the moment sometimes.

Even more silence, well lack of talking, followed once our food was brought out. I had no idea what she'd ordered but it looked interesting to say the least. My attention once again shifted back to my own food, letting myself get distracted would only have resulted in me not eating.

It took a while, but eventually I finished. Eating still felt like a waste of time, even if I needed to eat to stay alive.

Not long after taking the last bite, more tiredness soon came over me. I guess that's what I get for eating food high in tryptophan. These past few days, coupled with being completely stuffed on food made me crave a nap.

I wasn't used to being out this long, especially not for three days in a row. Someday I hoped I would get used to it, but until then I both needed and deserved to rest.

After almost dozing off in my seat, I slowly walked over to counter and paid. It wasn't a good idea for me to be out when I was this tired, I needed to get home.

Walking as fast as I could, I didn't have the attention or awareness to pay attention to much on the walk back. I don't even know how long it took us to get back. All I could focus on was getting back and taking a long nap.

Once we were back on the street, I walked as fast as I could; I knew I ran the risk of overloading being this exhausted. All of the surroundings began to blur, but somehow I seemed to know the way home.

It didn't take long before we made it back, or at least it didn't seem like it; I had no recollection of the walk, or how long it took, for all I knew I sleepwalked the entire route home.

CHAPTER 34

Something seemed off as we approached our building. This feeling was only confounded when we reached our floor, there was definitely something amiss. For one the door was slightly ajar; my attention span had been awful recently, but I wouldn't have been that oblivious.

I tried to use logic to explain what was going on, but I couldn't shake the feeling that something was terribly wrong here. The positive was that if someone robbed us, we didn't exactly have anything worth stealing.

I gingerly approached the door, when things started to click into place. The fact there was a boot print on the door, the door still being open, the entire reason we fled here in the first place.

We had both been so encapsulated in the drama of our relationship that we'd forgotten about the biggest of elephants in all rooms that have ever existed.

Chapter 35

Fuck.

Chapter 36

I expected her to be this oblivious, but how could I have forgotten the reason we were here in the first place?

All I could do was grasp her hand even tighter, I had no idea what to do here. It was both for comfort and to stop her from getting closer to our apartment. I couldn't let her take even one more step, it wasn't safe here any more.

This place had just started to feel like a home, and now this.

"Allie we need to get out of here now!" I yelled, it was my turn to forcefully drag her by the hand.

We needed to be as far away from here as possible, I couldn't let her go inside. The best case scenario was that some sort of device would alert people when someone entered. The other scenarios were much much worse than that, there was a real possibility we'd be shot if we went inside.

As I continued to drag her down the street, she started trying to pull away.

"Pixel, what the fuck?" she screamed.

"Someone was in there. We can never go back. What the fuck are we going to do now?" I yelled back.

Her only reaction was a blank stare, as if she was unable to process what I had just told her. It would probably have been my reaction too if I weren't panicking, but now wasn't the time to stand frozen in place. We needed to get out of here, we had to run as far away as possible.

With her still by the hand, we rushed down the main road as I tried to come up with a plan. Overwhelmed with emotion, I couldn't think straight and I couldn't think of anything.

There was nowhere we could go. Anywhere we went would only be temporary, we would be running forever.

As I desperately tried to come up with something, anything, that we could do, we found ourselves once again at the beach. There was a distinct lack of people here, probably caused the overcast and freezing cold weather.

The weather didn't help my energy levels, I was still exhausted. We had to keep running, but I couldn't carry on. I slumped down against one of the beach walls, and a few seconds later she joined me.

This was just my luck. Just when things were starting to look up, this had to happen now.

"What the fuck are we going to do?" I asked her.

"I don't even know what's happening." she replied, sounding genuinely confused. I didn't understand how she could be confused, it was obvious what was going on.

"People found us, and we're probably both wanted for murder." I told her.

All the colour drained from her face. Her shocked expression said it all, we had both been completely oblivious to things happening in the real world. The fact that she killed someone mattered so little to us that we didn't even think about it. I had brought it up to anger her the other day, but other than that it never really crossed my mind since getting here.

I knew we were both screwed up, but I didn't realize the extent of it all; until now. We had both put ourselves, and at times each other, before everything else in the whole world. I had always known we were self-centred but this was a reality shock.

"So what can we do?" she asked, sounding terrified.

That was the problem, I couldn't come up with anything; we were out of options. Either I was missing something or this was it. The best case scenario was we'd be locked up; and with everything I'd done for work, even without this whole thing I was looking at 20 years. There was no way in hell I'd be able to handle that.

As for her, the actual murderer, there was a real chance she'd never be free again.

"There's nothing we can do. I'm so sorry Allie."

Uttering those words broke me completely; I loved her and there was nothing I could do to help. There was pretty compelling photographic evidence out there, which was the reason we ran in the first place. More importantly, it meant I couldn't protect her by taking all the blame.

Which mean there was literally nothing I could do to help her, or even myself, and I hated it.

"Can't we run again?" she asked.

"We'd be safe for what? Another week or so? Plus my money is running out."

"Oh." she said sounding so defeated, which bought tears to my eyes.

We had just turned our relationship around, but now it was going to end again. The only difference was that this time it would be over forever.

Neither of us could find anything to say, we just stared blankly at each other. This lasted for several minutes before I noticed a look on her face that I couldn't quite interpret.

"Would this be better than being locked away forever?" she asked, as she pulled out the knife that I bought her.

One of the conditions was that she didn't take it out with her, but now was not the time to be angry. It was quite lucky that she's been herself and ignored what I told her; It wasn't idea by any means but it was an option.

Considering the other choices, there was something morbidly comforting about the idea of dying here under our own control. God knows we both craved and loved being in control.

This wasn't how I wanted things to go, we were both trying so hard. I believed, I had hope, I really thought there was a chance this time.

But now it was clear that us being better never really mattered; we were screwed way before we realized we needed to change. There was only one option now, the one Allie subtly suggested; but I wasn't ready yet, I had to spend as much time with Allie as I possibly could.

"Can we spend some more time together before we…" I trailed off, I couldn't bring myself to finish that sentence.

Tears began streaming down my face as I pulled her closer to me. I needed her right next to me, from now until the inevitable end.

"This is all my fault Pix. I'm so sorry," she sobbed.

While it was true she set this whole chain of events into motion, the truth was that something like this was going to happen to me at some point anyway.

For work I'd done such shady illegal things, that I lived every day not knowing if I would be arrested, taken to a government facility, or killed at any given moment. I suppose my ego let me feel superior and that those things would never happen to me; but deep down I knew they were a possibility.

I was almost certainly going to meet a bad ending at some point, it was just a matter of when; at least this way I wasn't alone.

In a weird way, I was grateful that Allie had caused all this. The alternative was going through something like this by myself, never knowing what love felt like.

"I fucked over so many people for work, this was going to happen either way." I told her, there was no point lying any more.

Actually there wasn't a point in anything any more, all we could do was enjoy our last living moments together.

I held her tighter, and as she turned to look at me I noticed her eyes. She always had the prettiest eyes, which were somehow always a different shade depending on the light. With her looking the way she does, it's a wonder she ever chose me.

"Why did you pick me anyway?" I asked. It was something I had wondered about, and there was nothing stopping me from asking any more. I had always worried I wouldn't like the answer, but this was my last chance to find out.

"Oh the day I met you." she sighed almost dreamily, before she continued.

"You had the most confident aura I'd ever felt from anyone. It overwhelmed me, I was amazed you even stopped and talked to me."

"I'm still not sure why I did, I guess there was just something about you. I did admire your persistence. It was awkward being followed around, but it made me feel important." I responded.

The loving gazes we exchanged were bittersweet. I knew these were the last moments we'd ever be able to spend together, and that was so painful. There was no choice but to make the most of them, so I pulled her even closer towards me.

Now with her practically sitting in my lap, I kissed her hard. Kissing Allie felt so right, and I needed to experience it a few more times. I had no idea what happened after people die, logic tended to fail when it comes to mortality and death.

However on the off chance there was something more, I wanted to memorize the feeling of her lips and tongue against mine for eternity. The urgency of everything made the feelings even more intense than usual.

It took just a couple of minutes, coupled with heavy touching, for us both to be completely breathless. I caught my breath as I gazed out at the ocean.

Sadly, the tide had risen and was only a few meters away. Our time was quickly running out.

I shot her a look, signalling that it was time. Somehow she always seemed to know what I was thinking, and without a pause she handed the knife to me.

I was frozen in place, stuck staring at the knife for several moments. I had no idea how to do this.

"Do you want me to do it?" she asked.

I wanted to be in control until the end, but I didn't trust myself to do this in the quickest way. For once, I trusted her more than I trusted myself; so with a nod I agreed.

"I'm sorry I ruined your life." she said.

"Honestly, before you it was fucking boring." I told her, which was the truth. The short time we spent together was completely fucked up, but it was always exciting; there was never a dull moment with Allie around.

She slowly moved the knife toward my throat, holding there lightly for a few moments. There was one last thing I needed to say. It was the last chance to tell her how I felt. I knew what I wanted my last words to be, and by the look on her face she wanted to hear those words too.

"Allie, I love you. I don't think I've ever loved anyone else, and even if I did it wasn't anywhere near as much as I love you. I didn't want things to end this way, but at least we're together." I cried out to her.

"I love you too Pix, even if you were a complete bitch sometimes. I am glad you were my bitch though."

That was typical Allie, but I wouldn't have it any other way. I knew that bitch was a term of endearment from her; and I was glad to be her bitch.

I gazed at her for a few moments longer, and then closed my eyes; I was ready. With a deep breath, I once again nodded to her. Less than a second later, I felt an intense pain and blood pouring out of me.

Just for a moment, I opened my eyes, to see her doing the same to herself.

We shared one last loving stare as her eyes began to close, and with my last ounce of strength I pulled her toward me again. Just as everything began to fade to cold darkness, I felt her lips press against mine.

About the author

Lexa Chara Meadows is a Nottingham-based non-binary author, who went from studying Human Sciences to causing drama. Oh and writing it too. She has been writing, admittedly weird fiction, since the age of 8. (Don't ask about the cheese monster that ate the whole city, and her childhood friends.)

Wanting to see more Queer representation, in particular transgender, aromantic and asexual themes, is an important part of why she writes. You can find her, and sometimes her characters @LexaMeadows on twitter.

54 68 61 6e 6b 20 79 6f 75 20 66 6f 72 20 72 65 61 64 69 6e 67

www.ingramcontent.com/pod-product-compliance
Lightning Source LLC
Chambersburg PA
CBHW061558190726
48288CB00007B/2082